A NEW DAY STARTS HERE

MARK ATLEY

A NEW DAY STARTS HERE

TULSA UNDERWORLD BOOK 3

4 Horsemen
Publications, Inc.

DEDICATION:

To all the "Uncle Franks" out there.
This one is for the mothers.

ACKNOWLEDGMENT:

I **WANT TO THANK THE FOLKS (GIRLS) AT 4** Horsemen for taking a chance on me, and I hope to make it very worth their while. I want to thank those of you who follow me on Twitter and offer encouragement, including Martine, Craig, Gareth, J. Todd, Scott, J.B., Stephen, Eric (Beetner—Long live Writer Types), Max, Neil, Alec, and many more I've interacted with over the years.

To my coworkers and family who have put up with me during many story breakdown sessions. A very special thanks to my wife—for putting up with me.

And always, thank you to each and every one who reads this novel. Without you, this would not be possible.

TABLE OF CONTENTS

PROLOGUE:

TANNER BROGDON

TANNER BROGDON CARRIES A SHOTGUN.
He handles it like his riot baton, twisting and readjusting his grip, fighting against the anxious sweat under the black leather gloves. In the reflection of the driver's side window of the dusty yellow pick-up truck, he's a figure in a tan jacket and dark blue coveralls with an evergreen ski mask, revealing an abstract image of a face, eyes and lips protruding from holes in the appropriate places—red, white, and intent.

He closes in on the pick-up truck driver who isn't looking his way. The driver's attention is focused on Tanner's partner, Daniel, standing in front of the truck, dressed the same as Tanner, pointing a long-barrel silver pistol. Daniel touches the tip of the index finger of his free hand to his pursed lips, shushing the man. From their surveillance, they know the driver's name is Earl.

The truck is the only one with a camper shell at the McDonald's parking lot over the highway near Vinita. The camper shell is a sun-washed white, dented and rusted, with

xiii

a cardboard-covered back window. It's early, three o'clock, still dark. Business is slow before the morning highway rush. The parking lot is nearly empty with dormant semi-trucks, like sleeping dragons, and a few cars. Light poles dot the lot like hunched sentinels and cast harsh white glares across the paint and glass of the vehicles.

In blue jeans and a Carhartt jacket, Earl mumbles a half-believing, "What the hell?"

Then Tanner's on him, marching in giant, hurried strides. The shotgun slams into Earl's back, Tanner's weight and momentum behind it. It drums the driver lose from his frozen stupor, causing him to drop his hot cup of coffee, which splashes across his feet. Tanner wedges the guy between his compressed bulk and the truck.

Tanner grimaces like they do in the movies and makes his voice deeper, saying, "Keys? Where are the keys?"

Earl tries to push away from the truck to turn to look at Tanner, but Tanner flicks a wrist and clips the bridge of his nose with the shotgun's barrel.

"Don't you fucking move," Tanner says, shoulder-shoving Earl into the truck. Earl groans. He tries to look without moving his body, but Tanner nudges him again, adding a knee strike to the back of Earl's fat thigh. The blow knocks him off balance. Tanner threatens, "Don't look at me."

Tanner doesn't say, but his actions imply: Don't fight back. Surrender. Know when you're beat.

The element of surprise is a powerful thing; it overwhelms. This type of thing isn't the first time for Tanner; other drivers were like this. They start tough, then come to realize what exactly is going on. Already, Tanner can feel the shivers of fear raking Earl's body, but he can tell Earl isn't the type to roll over without an extra incentive.

Daniel provides that. He stomps forward and pistol-whips Earl in the face. Tanner pushes Earl tighter against the truck to keep him from falling to the pavement. Earl sags, and Tanner lifts.

"Where are the keys?" Daniel doesn't give Earl time to answer and pistol-whips him again, opening a large gash on Earl's head.

Incentive delivered.

Earl stammers an answer, lips quivering, snot and blood running down his face. "My... my pocket."

"Which one?" Tanner asks, constricting Earl's movements.

"You cut me open. What the fuck?" Earl squeezes his eyes shut. "What do you mean, which one? They're in my pocket. Don't fucking hit me anymore. You want them; take them."

"Which one, dumb fuck?" Daniel demands. Eyes searching Earl.

"Left or right?" Tanner adds, increasing the pressure against Earl's back. "Left or right?" Earl's body tenses. Tanner tells him, "Don't move for them; just tell us."

"Jesus," Earl starts but then thinks better of it. "Left pocket," he shouts. "Left pocket."

Daniel slips his hand into Earl's left jeans pocket to fish out the keys.

Earl asks, "Do you know who owns this truck?"

Daniel yanks the keys from Earl's pocket, ripping the man's pants. He shows the keys to Tanner, letting the parking lot lights shine on the metal. Daniel wraps his hand around the keys, making a fist.

"Why do you think we're here?" Tanner says.

Earl spits snot and blood on the ground. "They're going to kill you. Both of you."

Daniel laughs. He can't help himself.

This load belongs to Fat Tommy and Short Philly, and from what Tanner understands, they're running it as contractors for some Siriano adjunct. Old man Siriano is done, going to prison. Oklahoma's quickly becoming a new Wild West.

Daniel says, "If they are going to kill us, they would have done it the first time we did this. They would have taken some precautions."

Tanner adds, "But they didn't."

"Because they don't care about you," Daniel says as if he's offering a revelation of salvation so that a sinner may know the truth. He's pretty convincing. "They're like Walmart; they make money no matter. When they win, they're making money. And when they lose, they're making money. What they aren't doing is paying you enough money to act like a hardass."

Tanner doesn't know much about Daniel. He's seen him around, but he doesn't know his full name and doesn't know how Daniel likes his coffee or what, if anything, he wants on his pancakes. Outside of here, in these moments, they don't talk. They don't interact. All Tanner knows about Daniel is he's old enough to have gone straight for a time, then decide to come back into the life. They don't associate outside of these jobs; this being the third hijacking this month, they don't associate. Daniel doesn't know details about Tanner beyond his first name; he doesn't know that Tanner is a deputy or that Tanner has struggled with opiate addiction. How breaking an ankle in high school football led to Lortabs, how Lortabs led to oxy, and how that eventually led to the German. Not that Tanner can't control the addiction. Most of the time, he can. That's why he works out. But it's always there—an itch begging for attention.

The German is what connects them and their third associate, the deadbeat Jeremy, who Tanner remembers as a dirty, stringy-haired kid from high school a couple of grades back. He's their driver, sitting in his big green boat on the other side of the building, waiting for the truck to roll out.

The German plans and finances these hijackings, using men he has something on. The German knows whose marijuana loads these are, and that's why Tanner and company are hitting them.

Tanner shifts his weight and position and aims a second knee strike, this time at Earl's balls while scraping the shotgun up Earl's spine and knocking the butt against the back of Earl's head.

With the pistol still pointed at Earl, Daniel reaches forward while Tanner lets off Earl some, grabbing his jacket's hood with one hand and dragging him a step back so Daniel can open the driver's side door. Tanner shoves Earl into the single cab pickup and prods him across the seat. Already, Daniel's at the passenger side, the door flung open, grabbing for Earl's arm, yanking him toward the middle of the cab while loading up into the passenger seat himself. Daniel shoves the pistol into Earl's side and tells him to stay still. Daniel reaches across Earl and inserts the keys into the ignition, turning them. Tanner slips in behind the steering wheel. He stores the shotgun barrel down on his left side, protecting it from any brave and stupid move from Earl. Foot on the clutch, Tanner puts the truck in gear as he closes the driver's side door.

The truck with the three men snuggly in the cab slips around the building, heading west toward Tulsa. The opposite of Earl's route out of state. They followed him from the warehouse to here, where he stopped to take a piss and get some coffee.

Jeremy's green Marquis falls behind them as they leave, three car lengths back.

Tanner takes the first country road exit and goes a ways before turning around on the semi-gravel road typical of Oklahoma backcountry. He shifts the lever to park.

Daniel exits the vehicle, jerking the silent, rigid Earl across the passenger seat and out onto the grass embankment.

"Lie there," Daniel says. "Facedown."

Earl grimaces but complies on his hands and knees, looking up at Daniel. He turns face down into the grass.

"Hands over your head," Daniel commands. Earl obeys. "It's just marijuana. It's not your marijuana; don't die over it."

Daniel waits to see if Earl will argue or agree.

When the man doesn't say anything, Daniel tells him, "I don't want to hear about this on the news. We know who you are. We know where you work and who lives with you. I'm not fucking with you. No news. No headlines. Your bosses don't want the attention either. Call this the price of doing business. Count to sixty—slow—and then take your happy ass home."

With that, Daniel climbs back into the cab of the truck. He slams the door. He rolls down the window and pulls his ski mask off his head.

"Remember, sixty—slow." Daniel pauses, staring at Earl in the grass. "Do it out loud, so I know you're counting."

Earl shifts from stunned silence and voices the numbers out loud. He's already at three. "Four ... five ... six."

Daniel says, "Good."

Tanner lifts his mask to his forehead and pops the clutch, letting the truck idle forward. He slips it into gear. By the time Earl should be on thirty—Tanner's been counting at the same cadence in his head—they're back on the highway.

CHAPTER 1:

FRANKFORT CORBIN

OKLAHOMA CATTLE COP FRANKFORT Corbin peers through the binoculars, squinting under the rising sun that washes the brown ground almost white. He is positioned high above the compound on a ridge. The reflection of the light bounces off the hard-packed dirt, nearly blinding Frank as he studies the small figure squatted on the ground below. The figure cradles an old hunting rifle against his shoulder as a crutch and for support, with the stock in the dirt, barrel to the sky, showing no respect to the rifle. The figure smokes a ciga-rette, with fingers of one hand cupped around his chin and lips and couches in the shade of the compound's back fence.

Frank lies prone on a red patterned horse blanket next to his partner Mitchell Lamb. The compound is an illegal marijuana grow. It violates state law by shipping product across state lines. Frank's hat—an off-white felt Stetson—rests on the blanket next to him. His badge, hung on his belt as it has been for thirty-plus years, grinds against his hip.

1

"Looks like he has a rifle," Mitchell says, pointing out the obvious.

Mitchell has smaller binoculars than Frank. Because they hiked into their position, Mitchell chose the smaller, lighter option, but Frank isn't one to cut corners when proficiency and ability are the sacrifices. Frank picked his tried-and-true eyes and hung them around his neck for the predawn walk from the Ford Bronco parked half a mile away.

Mitchell wears a beige button-down work shirt with blue jeans. Frank wears almost the same thing, but his shirt's baby blue.

"I can't see shit with these things." Mitchell lowers the smaller binoculars, adjusts, and raises them again.

"I see the rifle," Frank says, adjusting his binoculars to get a better look, rolling a finger across the middle dial. "How far do you think he is from here?"

"I don't know, but I don't have to know," Mitchell says. "That's why man invented rangefinders."

"I think it's about three hundred yards," Frank says. He spent a large portion of his life judging distances, from hunting men to shooting firearms to tracking and horse riding. "Feels like three hundred—maybe not that far, but close enough."

Mitchell shifts on the blanket.

Frank catches Mitchell lifting a rangefinder to his face from the corner of his eye to measure the distance. Lowering the device, Mitchell says, "About three hundred yards—damnit, I hate when you are right."

All Frank says is, "Yup."

"How do you do that?"

"Do what? Figure my distances?"

"See as clearly as you do at the age you are. I can't see shit without my glasses, and I had to break down and buy bifocals. Bifocals, Frank, bifocals. Bifocals were what I thought old folks like my grandparents wore. Not me."

"You are old."

"Not old like they were old," Mitchell says. "I'm in my fifties. I've seen pictures of my grandfather at sixty, and he looked ninety. Why'd he look so old? Think it's the sun and all? Or do we just have an easy life where they had some hard living? Like just surviving and living sucked it out of their faces?"

"Don't know," Frank says. "Old is how you feel."

"Well, I feel old, unable to read or see without help, tilting my head back and forth. How do you know how far it is? You can't really see it that well, can you?"

Frank can. Sight has never been a problem for him like it has been for others. He's just lucky.

Mitchell says, "How do you do it?"

Frank mashes his lips together, stroking the stray bristles of his gray mustache back in place with his lower lip. "Practice."

Mitchell resettles on the blanket and comments about how he's going to have to take a piss soon and then wonders where the cavalry is and what's taking them so long.

"You shouldn't have drank all that coffee," Frank says.

"You think he's Chinese or Mexican?" Mitchell says, turning his attention to the figure outside the compound's walls. "I bet he's Mexican."

"How can you tell?"

"The hat," Mitchell says. "Wide brim. Mexican."

"He sits like a Chinese man," Frank says. That's how he remembers seeing some Chinese sitting on one of his many trips with Eddie. "Some squat like that when they rest. I tried it. Fell over every time. Don't know how they did it."

"Guess you have to be flexible."

"I am flexible," Frank mumbles.

"Hip flexors, it's all in hip flexors," Mitchell says. "I wouldn't be able to do it. I'm lucky to be able to touch my toes."

Mitchell's younger than Frank by a few years, and Frank's a decade or two into his second career—the first one being a Deputy United States Marshal.

Mitchell broke a hip last year, a combination of age and being thrown from a horse. This morning, after receiving their assignments, Mitchell asked if they would ride in like the old days or hike. Frank told him: "No, we'll take the Bronco." The Bronco is an old beat-up bear of a vehicle, brown with cream trim. Frank said they would park a-ways out and hike in. Mitchell groaned. He's only been back a few months, and while he may be back to full duty, he isn't back to his old self.

Mitchell says, "Like catchers, but those guys aren't squatting for the hell of it; they have a job to do." Then when Frank doesn't respond, which is most of the time Mitchell's talking, Mitchell clears his throat. "So you think he's Chinese? That's your guess?"

"No," Frank says.

"No, what do you mean no? You said he sat like the Chinese. All these growers are either Chinese from California like we've decided to build a railroad and shipped all these fine young men to our great state, or they are Mexicans fleeing from the bullshit on the border, which really means they're searching for more money. They make more working at one of these hothouses in the middle of nowhere for sweatshop labor wages than most would do down where they're from doing the same thing."

"Not all of these people are from Mexico."

"Well, shoot, Frank, I know that. You've got Mexicans, you've got Hondurans, you've got Guatemalans. Had some genuine," squealing the last part of the word stressing the syllables like he's saying swine, "Colombians. I asked the guy at the last one, the Colombian; I said, 'You, Pablo.' Guy just looked at me. Blinked a few times. I said, 'You know, the guy from Medallion. Esco-bar.' All he says is that's not how you say it."

Frank sighs. Not because of Mitchell's insistent talking but because life used to be simple. He had Eddie. He had Kelly. But the one rule of life, something Eddie said to him before she died, is things change.

And Oklahoma's changed a lot in the last few years.

Frank guesses he's just tired. Tired of this new Wild West. Tired of being stuck between this new green rush with the medical marijuana combined with the state's lax drug laws and the Indians' assertations on the land, post-McGirt.

It feels like he's stepped back in time a hundred years.

It used to be that all Frank cared about was finding the bad guy. It didn't matter where he was. Then, when he left the Marshals and joined Oklahoma's fledgling bastard version of the Texas Rangers, finding the rustler didn't matter if he was in Kansas, Texas, or Oklahoma. The Agriculture Agents, the Cattle Cops, became a hodge-podge combination of law enforcement, gaining some freedom to work in the three states and coordinate between all the different agencies: feds, Indians, State Police, municipalities, and the County Sheriffs.

Mitchell says, "Frank, you have to pick one. Mexican or Chinese. It's no fun if you don't play the game. We've been here all morning; play the game."

Frank doesn't play. He says, "He's just a man, no different, regardless of where he's from or skin color. He's a man."

"Frank," Mitchell says quietly.

"Yup?"

"That's sexist … assuming that man identifies as a man," Mitchell says, trying to make a joke.

"Well, if he were wearing a dress, something that indicated he wanted to be a woman, I'd say he was a woman. I'd have no problem with that."

Frank hasn't always been flexible about the changing times. He used to be pretty rigid, black and white. But then Frank loosened up. Eddie helped him with that. He figured if he could love her and it was supposedly taboo at the time, even though he didn't really see it as a problem, then people could do what they wanted as long as they weren't hurting others.

It wears on him when wrong seems right, and he's finding himself a dinosaur of another age. Hence, he feels tired. Changing's a complicated, exhausting process, and he feels like a dying breed.

Mitchell says, "I don't care. What do I care if a man wants to be a woman or a man? Except it makes it hard to know the bad guys from the good guys when you can't find a way to describe how a person looks. Knowing John Smith, a white male with blue eyes and brown hair, keeps you from arresting John Smith, a black male with brown eyes and hair, or John Smith, an Asian male with black hair and hazel eyes…"

Mitchell goes on, but Frank stops listening to Mitchell's tirade. It isn't anything Mitchell hasn't said before as he's railed against and tried to process the changing times.

"He's not wearing a dress," Frank says as if Mitchell hadn't rambled for a few minutes. "He's wearing clothes that make him look like a man, so he's a man."

"Frank?" Mitchell says again.

"Yes?"

Mitchell waits a beat and then says, "You're no fun, you know."

Frank knows and grumbles in agreement.

The man in the shade is blissfully smoking his cigarette … or is it a cigarillo? It's hard to tell from here. Frank only sees the smoke billowing to the clouds and the orange-red glow from the tip.

The compound is one of many that have materialized in the vast Oklahoma country. Some recent law changes and a liberated gentry ushered in a new gold rush, or in Oklahoma's case and history, a land rush but green this time. Like dandelions on the sidewalk, legal and illegal grows have popped up in every town and county.

The compound is down in a depression with a good-sized pond to the west. It consists of two large structures, five greenhouses with clouded curved plastic tops, and a scattering of smaller buildings. The compound has ten-foot corrugated tin walls, making it look like an old western frontier fort.

To the east, Frank spots the conga line of vehicles closing in on the open main gate—a handful of SUVs and a few cars, which contain lawmen, except Frank knows not all cops are men. The vehicles look like some modern-day posse riding down outlaws, barreling toward the compound.

From here, the scene looks like a line of ants descending on a discarded sandwich.

The procession appears silent, but Frank's spent his fair share of time as part of that law enforcement alphabet soup posse to know the engines under the hoods of those vehicles are growling something fierce as they race to close the distance before eventual discovery. From this distance, Frank hears nothing but the soft kiss of the wind biting at his earlobes intermixed with the faint rumble of the vehicles, muted as they are, making their cinematic approach nearly silent.

Noticing the arriving cavalry, Mitchell says, "Game time."

Frank sets his binoculars to the side and shimmies his rifle into place, a Henry Big Boy Carbine with a 6-to-1 scope. Nothing too fancy. Something Frank finds dependable and easy to maintain. Something he was able to carry into position from their Bronco. They hiked in on foot and settled in place before the sun broke the horizon. Their job: watch the target and report any significant movements. They've been here most of the morning, taking shifts watching the compound, sipping coffee from Frank's rugged thermos, and pissing while discussing current events.

Frank and his partner are stationed near a back road that leads down toward the compound. A handful of vehicles hover over the ridge to their west, awaiting the frontal group's approach before they sneak, or rush, down this road, depending on how first contact goes.

If it goes bad, Frank has his rifle and the overwatch job while the vehicles withdraw.

Frank works the rifle up from between him and Mitchell, who takes up Frank's discarded binoculars, and settles the rifle tight against his shoulder. Frank focuses the scope on one of the larger houses: the barracks for the illegals working the fields according to the surveillance.

During the operational briefing conducted at four this morning, Raley Freeman told Frank, Mitchell, and the others that surveillance consisted of a generator repairman and an undercover OSBI agent (Raley) visiting the compound under the guise of fixing the generator. The fellow in charge of this illegal growing operation had recently purchased it in New Orleans at an auction for a now-defunct hospital.

"The fellow didn't know he couldn't work on the generator himself," Raley explained. "Or, in this case, farm it out to a hired hand, which resulted in a dead body. Took a crispy Mexican to figure that one out. So the fellow called the generator manufacturer and requested the company send someone out to service the thing."

Frank knew the next part because, after stumbling across the compound tracking backwoods cattle rustlers turned meth cooks who worked as roustabouts in the area, Frank asked OSBI Agent Raley Freeman for coffee to ask him about the compound. Raley never passed up coffee while working and told Frank the compound was a marijuana grow that OSBI has been looking at for a while. He also told him about the walls and the type of generator, which Frank knew was a common brand out here, away from power grids and civilization, as he likes

to put it. OSBI couldn't figure out how to get eyes inside the compound.

Frank said, "Why don't you bypass the company and just get with their tech when he gets to town? Ask him to tag along or take some cameras in, and no one would be the wiser."

Since there was a wire up and running, it didn't take OSBI long to figure out when the repairman was scheduled to arrive. They approached the technician and pitched their idea. The tech told them not to ask the bosses; they'd say no. He taught the state cop Raley and two others how to act like an assistant and picked the best of the three students, joking about how those boys should be glad they're cops because they'd never make it in a field like his. Frank oversaw the ruse since it was Frank's idea.

A shout rings out down below.

Frank shifts his view from the line of vehicles to a small figure at the front gate who's yelling out the alarm. The shout of alarm won't matter.

"Took them long enough," Mitchell says.

Frank says, "That fellow is not a very good lookout."

"You'd think the guy at the gate would have seen them sooner. Good thing they're almost on him."

Mitchell radios in his observations, telling those arriving in the vehicles about the shouts of alarm. The vehicles over the western ridge begin their downward approach.

Frank listens to the faraway shouts. "What do you think he's saying?"

"*Policia*," Mitchell guesses, repeating the word a few times. "*Policia*... I don't know; how am I supposed to know? I don't know what 'police' is in Chinese."

That's when the shooting starts. The man at the front gate who shouted the initial alarm shoulders an AK47 rifle and fires twice at the approaching line of vehicles, striking the windshield of the front SUV. Then the man disappears into the compound.

The radio crackles. The voices are alarmed and distressed, but Frank can't focus on that right now.

Mitchell's voice trembles as he says, "Frank," to get Frank's attention in the way partners communicate vast amounts of information to each other in seconds. Frank sees it but wishes he didn't. The figure who was sitting in the shade smoking clambers to his feet. He spots the second group coming from the west and shoulders his rifle.

With one squeeze of the trigger of the Henry and a quick half-thought prayer, Frank drops the man before he can fire.

CHAPTER 2:

JERILYN KISSEE

JERILYN KISSEE DOESN'T KNOW WHAT TO make of the deputy standing next to her laying out his pitch. The mirrored aviators he picked up at the gas station down the street hide the deputy's eyes, and she doesn't know what to think of the idea the deputy's going on about.

"All's I'm sayin' is," he says, "there's a way to make this work. You want him gone, right?"

She does, but she doesn't know how foolproof this idea of his is, and he hasn't fully convinced her of anything yet, not his qualifications, not his ability, not nothing, but he's tried his darn hardest, laying it on thick, smiling. Cooing almost, like he's telling her it will be okay, trying to convince her this is a good idea.

He dresses nicely. She has to admit he looks alright dressed in street clothes, a checkered button-up shirt— some type of faux flannel for men who want to pretend to live in the country—and blue jeans that look either new or rarely worn accented with shitkickers beat to hell. It's nice,

13

but it's not a great look considering it's just as much a uniform for him as his actual uniform. Still, it's alright even if
it's weird when all she's ever seen of the man has been his
deputy uniform. His hair is cut short on top with the side-
walls skimmed low and a day's worth, or so, of facial hair
showing he doesn't shave when he's not working. Maybe
Jerilyn can do that with Wayne—not shave her legs when
she's not working and ask him what's it matter because
she's not squeezing into booty shorts today to wait tables,
no one will care.

Even with his eyes hidden behind the sunglasses, Jerilyn
can tell the deputy keeps glancing all over the place, doing
that cop look, aware all the time, hyper-vigilant, worried
about someone seeing him with her doing this clandestine
meeting at the park. He texted from a number that's either
a burner phone or one of those internet numbers. She's not
sure who would be watching him. It doesn't seem like the
sheriff's all too worried about internal affairs when they
broke a man's neck, threw him in a cell to die, and had
a geriatric cop shoot to kill someone, confusing his gun
with his taser.

The park's a no-smoking area, but she's outside the
boundaries, standing on the parking barrier to put her
small frame even with Brogdon. She's far away from the
playground where her two girls are playing. She takes a drag
from the cigarette to buy time to think things over without
showing she's thinking things over because women don't
think, not around these parts, and not where she's from—
not women like her. Yeah, right.

As the nicotine hits her lungs and she feels the smooth
comfort of the smoke—not caring what it is doing to her
lungs after watching her granddaddy die from cancer—she

keeps her eyes on her little ones. She watches Kasey on the swing set, little legs hanging down from the seat, squatty and fat, just old enough to stay upright, seated, and enjoy the ride, her mess of hair blowing in the wind. She still remembers when Kasey was so frightened of the swing she couldn't push the thing without the girl wailing. Katherine's behind her pushing—Katie to her friends but Katherine to Jerilyn. She's nearly ten going on twenty and old enough to know what's going on, clued into the world around her, far sooner than most of her peers. Her listening's a little rough at times, but she's a good kid, ready to please, and loves making mac and cheese, their Tuesday and Thursday staple. Jerilyn will have to be careful what she says around Katherine about Deputy Brogdon.

Jerilyn thinks over the pitch, unsure if she wants to buy in, although the offer does sound attractive. She'd have *her* kids, only hers, with Wayne gone and out of the picture. That's the gist of what the deputy's saying. He could make it happen. They wouldn't have to break any laws; in fact, the whole thing hinges on no one on this side breaking laws, not real ones, but it seems funny, him coming to her this way.

She says, "How many times have you done this?"

And there it is, that bashful look. Cheeks flushed red, lips cresting into a slight smile, a bullshitter's smile. Her daddy had one. Wayne has one. Brogdon's no different. He may cut his hair, shave his beard, and dress better, but he's the same man; only a badge separates him from them. But his answer sounds real enough. "Few times, a few times," he says. "It's gone different ways each time."

"And how's that?"

"Well, it's easier in situations like this," he says, "with people like yours. I suppose the more I do it, the better I'm gettin'."

The richer too, but Jerilyn holds that back.

"There was one fellow who wouldn't just stay away," he says. "This was the first time. I push him; he'd push back. Basically, your number one fear when trying something like this. Most difficult. Maybe that's why he was my first."

Deputy Brogdon laughs as if he's making a joke, showing that he's juvenile even though he's ten years older than she is.

"He stalked her. That's what got me in it the first time around. I didn't take no money, not for her. She was sweet. Beautiful even. Not after him, though. She's something different now. And, I'm not saying I was tempted into doing anything—un-gentleman-like—but I thought about it. Not saying I haven't done that sort of thing either."

Jerilyn expects him to wink, and maybe he does behind the sunglasses.

"I mean, if they call, what's the harm? But I knew a fellow got written up for just getting a girl's number in the jail lobby when he was working the front desk. She was there visitin' someone, dropped her number right in his lap, so to say, more like slipped it into his pocket; he told me about it later, after everything. She called him a cutie and told him to call her later. He liked her. She was a beauty; he showed me her Facebook later. The problem was when she was arrested a week later for all sorts of stuff—drugs, bringing shit into the jail—and she's yelling his name over and over."

Jerilyn sighs, frustrated with his rambling, and says, "So you didn't charge her is what you're saying."

Not saying, but thinking, *but you are charging me.* Then thinking, *it better not be by the minute or the word.* Jerilyn wouldn't be able to afford it.

She smokes the cigarette as a form of biting her tongue.

He shakes his head. "No, I didn't charge her." Back on track now, he continues, "That's right, no siree... I mean, ma'am."

Jerilyn snorts smoke out of her nose and drops the arm with the cigarette down to her side, holding it there, supporting the arm with the other crossed over her midsection, hand on the elbow. The wind tugs at her sundress. The weather's nice, but she's wearing a light cotton hoodie zipped to the base of her neck to keep the nine o'clock morning chill off her skin and Deputy Brogdon's eyes from peeking down her cleavage. The way he looks at her makes her feel naked.

He should read her body language; it's as bright as a neon sign. Brogdon says, "I didn't charge her because he was a vicious son of a bitch. It was righteous what happened to him. He beat her to within an inch of her life." He holds up his fingers width apart to make his point. "Stalked her for a while. Sneaking in, moving things around, making her feel like she was crazy. Course, she didn't help matters. Got hysterical a time or two. Threw one helluva fit once. She loved him, don't you all? But he was abusive. Beat her. But she was afraid to leave is what I'm saying, you know?"

She knows. Knows the feeling. Too frightened to stay, too scared to leave. It's a bad place to be. It's worse than just getting a divorce and more complicated. It's not as easy to explain to others. Not when they say, just get a divorce. Why don't you leave? It's all patronizing. It's not that easy. Sure, for these people—the ones who never had to struggle—it might be easy for them. It's not for Jerilyn. She could take off, start a new life. The thought of it causes her anxiety, and she does wonder about it. Could she really do it? She thinks yes, but it's one of those nutcuttin' moments; that's how Wayne would describe it. You never know until you know.

"So this goes on, and I'm watching it happen," Deputy Brogdon continues. "Oh, say my first year out on my own. I was too wet behind the ears to take it seriously or understand what was happening. At first, I believed he snuck in and replaced all her plates and dishes with paper products, crazy-sounding stuff like that. Who would report that to the police if it wasn't true? But then I got to thinking she was making it up. That she was crazy. Paranoid. Then you get to thinking, 'Alright, sure, some of this is happening.' He probably is calling and hanging up, following her around, that type of stuff, but no way would someone do some of the weirdo bullshit he's doing; he's driving her crazy, you know?"

Again, Jerilyn's all too familiar. Wayne always had a way of knowing when she was with Michael. She doesn't know how, but he knew.

When they first met, Deputy Brogdon had told her, "Check your car; they can put a GPS tracker in it—the size of a credit card or smaller: an AirTag. Slip it right in the area around the spare tire and you'd never know. I've seen magnetic ones, too, seen them stuck to the underside." But he didn't explain how he knew. He said it like he'd done it, like he had experience.

Mainly, she saw that he doesn't like Wayne's type of man because he is this type of man. Not all cops are that way. Jerilyn knows this. Some are just jocks, wanting to be in it for the same reason they wanted to win high school football games. Some genuinely believe they're helping. Some just do it because it's something to do. Some do it because they were bullies or have been bullied, and now it's time to get back at the world and confirm their view of it. Then, some are like Brogdon. Predators hunt predators while enjoying prey.

"He did this for about a year, and then this girl's dad calls one day. He says he hasn't heard from her for a day. A day. That's nothing. I don't call my mom for a few weeks sometimes; life gets busy. I text from time to time. I'm not heartless, but to not call for a day, that's nothing. We go out to the house. Everything seems fine. Nothing kicked in. No windows disturbed. Come to find out later; he made a copy of the house key. By this time, she's moved three times and changed the locks twice, but still, he made a copy."

"What happened to her?" Jerilyn asks, but really, she means what happened to the guy. That's what this is. A job interview, and he's giving his resume, trying to impress her, which should be a red flag, but Jerilyn really wants Wayne gone just as much as this deputy wants money.

"Dad calls a second time. He says he's over at the house, and we need to get over there. Those weren't his exact words, but I'll save you what he said. When we get there, she's naked and on the floor, head bashed in with a frying pan. It's bent nearly in half and tossed over to the side, in the sink. It was cast iron, if that tells you anything about the beating. The worst part is her dad thinks she's dead. We think she's dead. She looks dead. See, the blood's congealed all around her, and she's stuck to the floor, like a movie-theater-floor type of sticky. And when we pull her up from the floor, it sounds like wet Velcro, an awful sucking noise. I still hear it sometimes. Makes me cringe. Worse. No one knows she's alive until one of the others there starts taking pictures of the 'crime scene,'" putting quotes around it while leading up to the big reveal, "and she gasps like a zombie coming back to life."

"Like in the movies or whatever when they get all quiet and still?" Jerilyn adds to show she's paying attention.

"And then they take this huge breath of air." He demonstrates, making an awful, strangled squealing sound, which sounds like her granddaddy when he was living with them when she was younger, and he'd stop breathing in his sleep while sitting in the recliner in the living room. Gasped for breath. "Yeah, just like that." He grabs at his chest. "I jumped two feet in the air. 'Course, we get her help, and she's good now, but then I was pissed. We all were."

"You find him?"

"In a hotel."

"You kill him?" Jerilyn asks.

The deputy looks away for a long time at Kasey, his face softening like he doesn't like thinking about it. There's a difference between a killer and a man who killed; that's what her granddaddy always said. He's the latter. He doesn't have the coldness. "Wasn't the plan. Don't feel bad about it, but..."

He trails off as if there's more to the story. And with killing a man, there probably is.

"But he didn't cooperate?" she offers.

"Something like that," the deputy says, still looking away. "He shot me. I shot him. It is what it is."

"But you don't want to do that with someone else?"

"No," he says, coming around again. "But being in the hospital is expensive. I had plenty of time to think things through. I thought, 'There are others like her, right?' I mean, there's you. There's dozens of you. Most deaths around here, and I'm guessing nationwide, have a domestic component. What if they paid, not much but a little, and I put some pressure on these assholes? Get them put in jail. Keep them there. Do them dirty."

Now she says it. "And get paid?"

"Well, that too," Brogdon says. "As I said, the hospital's expensive. Have to pay for things somehow."

"Sheriff wasn't willing to flip the bill?" Jerilyn asks.

She's naïve, but she's heard of workman's comp.

"He did, he did," Brogdon says, "but there are other expenses. Rent, bills, those types of things. If I'm laid up, I'm losing money."

"How much?" she asks, cutting to it.

"Five thousand," Brogdon says without a pause.

"That's a lot of money for me." She rubs her arms and stares at the girls.

"It's enough to make it worth my while," he says, "to take the risk, but low enough for someone like you to pay."

"Where do I scrounge up five thousand?" she asks, annoyed at the condescension. Brogdon was like that the first time they met, and now he wears it like a paternal smock. "Wouldn't that cause alarms? Get people to take notice if I'm taking money out of the bank, that much, and he ends up dead?"

"Woah," Deputy Brogdon exclaims. "Hold your horses. No one's killing no one. Not even talking about that. What I got in mind—"

Now she's playing with him. "But with your story—"

"I tell you that to tell you my..."

He removes the sunglasses so she can look at his eyes. If she didn't see this as a sales pitch, she could almost believe it's genuine: the watery redness, the sincere lip quiver, the thoughtful pause. Please... She's been beaten and terrorized, growing up with complicated men.

"...Tell you my motivation about why I'm doing what I'm doing. I mean, yeah, I could lose my job over this, but what I figure is, if I'm careful about who I make this proposal to, and I'm selective, following a certain set of rules, then it's for the better. A win-win type of thing."

"So you won't kill him?"

"God, no," Deputy Brogdon says. "Scare him, maybe. The idea is to get him sent to prison so you can file for full custody; that's what you want, right? Get him out of the picture for a few years so you can get out of here, start a new life. Now, don't overestimate the criminal justice system; with what I've seen, you have maybe a year or two at the most of freedom, so you'll have to make the most of it."

"So I'm still going to have to pay for a lawyer?" she asks. "Pay for filing all that paperwork to ask the state to keep what's rightfully mine. It'd be easier if you killed him."

And then there it is again, that look—the grin. The dark eyes Jerilyn can see this time. He slips the sunglasses back on and looks away from her.

"Might be," he says, almost humming it to himself.

"But that'd cost extra is what you're saying," she says.

"I'm not saying nothing about anything like that," he says, but the way he says it, the tone combined with the smile—that's precisely what he's saying.

"Five thousand may be doable," she says, doing the mental calisthenics and figuring out how she could make it work. She could get it all from one place, but that'd be no good. She has to spread it around. She could sell damn near everything she owns, and she might be able to get half that. Then she could borrow some from her momma. The salon's doing really well. Maybe she could work there in the evening, clean up, etc. Jerilyn's never been one for cutting hair. She's not good at it. The kids can sit at the back table, eat dinner, and watch cartoons while she sweeps, mops, and wipes everything down. Yeah, that could work. And then there's Jeremy. Her brother's always trying to offload a pound of marijuana to some college kids or high school kids. They don't know any better. They pay higher prices. Jeremy loves doing it. He always talks about how pretty she is and how they'd fight one another to buy from Jerilyn if she were willing to let them slip a hand up her shorts. Jeremy could give it all to her without her selling nothing, but then he'd want to know what the five grand was for, and then he'd be involved, and that wouldn't help anyone.

"I'm glad to hear that," Brogdon says like the car guy did when she asked about taking some money off the sticker price of the one she wanted, telling him she was interested. "I'm glad. I was worried about you, to be honest."

"Oh, yeah," she says. "Why's that?"

"First time I met you, you were beat to hell, you remember?"

"I wasn't..." Jerilyn pauses to think about it. Was she? Wayne's done it so often, not that she didn't give him cause plenty of times. She gives just as good as she gets sometimes, but she didn't think Wayne had gotten to her when she met the deputy.

"Yeah, you called about him following you around," Brogdon says, "following you to your boyfriend." He giggles. "You were so embarrassed to mention that like someone's going to judge you for it. You looked tired, and when I asked you if he'd hit you recently, you lied to me. Told me no, but that look. That look said yes. I know that look."

Damn Wayne for doing this to her, making her second guess herself. She wasn't beat to hell, not physically, at least. He's just a smug bastard that thinks he's right: further proof her read on him is correct.

She throws the cigarette down on the concrete barrier and stomps her foot on it. "How's this work?"

"Well, you pay me, and then we work on filing reports over the next few weeks," Brogdon says. "The idea is that we start a paper trail to work up to stalking. I know he's doing it now. You know he's doing it now. It's about gettin' others to know it. You have the protective order?"

She nods.

"Good, then this won't take long. You file those reports, and then *you* file some of those protective order violations. He'll do those no matter what, so we don't have to fabricate too much. Basically, we're going to stack the deck against him."

The cliché grates on her nerves, but she nods and says, "Okay."

"Okay, you're on board?" he asks, voice searching her. "Or okay, you understand?"

"I understand," she says, teeth clenched.

"Okay," he says.

Now she wants to do it to him, give it right back. "Okay."

He pauses and scratches the back of his head. "So where are we at? Okay, okay? Or Okay? Or what?"

"Okay," she says. "Let's do it. It will take a few days to get the money, but I want to get started now."

"Wait, wait," he says, pushing his hands out. "Just hold on. You got to pay first."

Jerilyn turns to face him. "No, you're going to start it right away. He's behind on child support, something like twenty-eight thousand. He comes and goes as he pleases. He's found me any time I try to run away. I can't run away. I live with him to keep him happy. But I'm tired of it. Anytime the law comes around, somehow he finds out."

Brogdon considers his options. He doesn't like it, but he's not in a position to negotiate. She said she'd pay him. He said it would take some time. If she doesn't have all the money in two weeks, it won't matter. "Alright, I'll get started."

Jerilyn glances at her girls.

"How about a peck on the cheek for good luck?"

She anticipated this and was prepared. She plucks the cigarette from behind her ear and digs the lighter from her hoodie pocket. She sticks the cigarette in her mouth and lights it almost simultaneously. "No, I'm good. I'll get you half next week and the other half after."

His head tilts to the side as she steps off the parking barrier and away from him and the parking lot, smoking her cigarette and walking back to her girls. She thought she would feel a sense of relief or dread, but instead, she feels nothing. Maybe when she pays... Perhaps that's when she'll feel something. When she nears Kasey and Katherine, Kasey giggles at seeing mommy, and Katherine turns towards her, swiping her brown hair out of her face, making Jerilyn genuinely smile. Her girls—hers alone—that's a nice thought.

The feeling fades but not the frozen muscles. When Brogdon first started, he told her to consider it an investment in her future. Remembering those words now, she reluctantly admits he's right; that's a good way of describing his proposal.

She lifts Kasey away from the swing; her little arms grab at her but not really. She's showing she wants mommy. Jerilyn tucks her to the side on a hip as Katherine comes over and gives her a big hug.

"Who was that?" her little girl asks.

Jerilyn looks back over her shoulder at the deputy who's now in his Jeep, fettling with the ignition. "No one, baby," she says. "Just someone who thinks he's right, but you know what?"

"What?"

"You're right," Jerilyn says, "Both of you are the rightest thing in the world, and if I'm doing something for you, then I'm doing something right."

CHAPTER 3:

JEREMY HALL

THE BASEBALL BAT SLAMS INTO JEREMY'S stomach, stealing his breath. It drives the oxygen out of him and makes him spew hot wheezing air through cracked lips.

Red-eyed and struggling to remember to breathe, Jeremy doubles over and drops to his knees. He places a hand against the pavement to steady himself and groans.

"What the fuck?" he manages to say, hand on his mid-section, teeth clenched.

The pain is nearly unbearable, and the suddenness of the sharp blow to the stomach came as a complete surprise. Someone yelled out, "Hold up," which caused Jeremy Hall to turn just in time to take the blow to the stomach. He was about to unlock his car door, an older Grand Marquis parked behind City Cleaners, all square, and forest green. The morning pre-dawn condensation covers the windows and beads on the dark green paint.

Jeremy didn't see the blow coming, but he knows what to say. "It's just five hundred bucks. I'll get it to you."

Short Philly, who's not all that short and the one holding the bat, laughs. He acts like he's going to hit Jeremy again. Jeremy holds up a hand, ripping his floral print shirt, cuffs rolled back, trying to stave off the next barrage of blows. For a brief moment, Jeremy worries that Short Philly won't hold back and that he'll slam through Jeremy's arm, so he whimpers, which is a mistake. It shows weakness and only makes Short Philly laugh harder.

Playing with Jeremy, Short Philly practice-swings a few more times, smiling with every speedy mock swing for the fun of it. Each time, the swing, the fake, gets more extreme. The bat swings through quicker and stops later. All Jeremy can do the whole time is squeeze his eyes shut tight and pray Short Philly doesn't lose control, swing too hard or fast, and let the barrel strike through and true.

But the taller of the two men, Tommy Schafer, comes out of the darkness and stops Short Philly by placing a staying hand on Short Philly's broad shoulder.

"The fuck is," Tommy starts, mocking Jeremy and repeating his words back to him.

They are nothing but two-bit, low-rung criminals, bigger than Jeremy admittedly but still low-rung. They're country bumkins compared to the German.

"You owe me money. Owe us money." Tommy turns to Short Philly. "What the hell's wrong with you? You don't have to break him. He just owes money. We talked about this."

"You said you wanted me to hurt him," Short Philly whines, his nasty voice indicative of his Pennsylvania upbringing. He shuffles side to side on the balls of his feet. He likes violence. "Teach him a lesson."

Short Philly didn't get his name because of his size, although he somewhat fits the moniker because he's the shorter of the two. Jeremy would say stout is a better word. He's Italian, dark-headed, ill-tempered, impatient, and built for winter. Real name: Tommy Sciotto from Philadelphia, which to the Oklahoman ear sounds like Shorto. If Jeremy knows one thing about Short Philly—beyond the fact the guy's a coronary waiting to happen because he can't keep his temper in check and he's permanently red-faced, hence the Short moniker—is that Short Philly likes to dress in expensive clothes and is always eating food, never getting up from the table until he's stuffed.

Short Philly's a black bear, short for a bear but still a bear, which means steer clear.

Right now, staring up at him, with him all red-faced, short of breath, and cheeks puffing in and out, Jeremy imagines Short Philly as what he is, a walking, talking tomato. Albeit a tomato that is pointing the tip of the bat at him as he says, "I'm hurting him. This is me hurting him. That's what you wanted. That's what you said you wanted."

"Hurt, yes." Disappointment shows on Tommy's stone-chiseled face. "Not kill. Not maim. He'll do me no good with broken limbs. Broken people tend to be broke, which means what little measly money he's scrounged selling his bullshit ditch weed will go to fixing what's broken and not in my pocket. I'd rather the money go in my pocket. Hospitals already make enough money as it is."

Tommy pulls on both pant pockets exaggeratedly. He tugs the fabric away like people do who've lost weight and show off their new waistband by wearing their old pants, posing for the picture, smiling at the camera, and hamming it up.

Short Philly nods along. "But what about his ribs? You didn't say nothing about his ribs. He don't need those intact, does he?"

Tommy rubs his chin with one bony hand while the other bony hand slips into his pocket. He considers the argument, rocking on his heels. He's thinking it over.

If Short Philly isn't short as his name suggests, Fat Tommy isn't all that fat. In fact, Tommy's a beanpole and is called Fat Tommy because he only carries cash. When he pulls out his roll, which he always keeps in his left pant pocket, it's three inches thick and held together with rubber bands. The bills in it aren't small. He's a man of locally distilled wealth with the brains of the tall man-short man duo. Jeremy knows this. That doesn't mean Tommy is any less frightening.

Tommy is only fractionally taller than Short Philly, which is a point of curious observation for Jeremy, and something he'd been thinking about all night while sitting at their poker table playing the game. He was thinking that he could fucking make a sitcom with these two. They're a calamity of errors, two country rednecks who think they can be someone now that the laws have changed, trying to make some moola shipping marijuana out of state.

Tommy Schafer inherited a moderately successful trucking company from his old man, Schafer Logistics. For every three legitimate loads his company runs throughout the Midwest, he runs one illegitimate load back east, which is where Short Philly and his people come in.

With the baseball bat dangling over his head, Jeremy doesn't think the sitcom would be all that funny. It'd be more like an anti-sitcom, with all the anti-pasta jokes they made all fucking night—Tommy ribbing Short Philly for saying he wanted a salad, and when he asked what kind, they got into a heated who's-on-first type of conversation about a Caprese salad. Jeremy mentally agreed with Tommy that it ain't a salad. The bickering got annoying after a while.

No, if there were a sitcom, the show would include shady dealings by people who claim to be legitimate, which is funny because Tommy's family has never been one hundred percent legitimate. They started as rumrunners, moved on to bootlegging, and now do a bit of everything under the guise of pillars of the community.

If Jeremy were directing, which is what he wants to do with his life—direct movies, TV, porn videos, whatever— he'd build the show around the concept of irony. Partly because of their names, a guy named Short Philly who ain't short and a guy named Fat Tommy who ain't fat, the gold is there to be mined. These guys could have been something like contributing members of society, but they're lazy, dumb fucks who only pretend to be contributing members of society. Jeremy would do it like HBO's *Barry* but without the acting class nonsense and Bill Hader... Hell, Bill Hader's from here; if he wants to be a part of something like that, then why the hell not? He'd play Tommy Schafer because he'd be a goddamn dead ringer for the guy. They both have that same look.

Thinking about it, if Jeremy actually tried to get his life together, he'd run circles around these two. He tried. He failed. Now he's back at home, saving money, working for the German, and planning his future. When he's not selling, he's writing. He likes writing. First, it was writing scripts, but the formatting pisses him off. He sold some when he lived in Vegas, but nothing that ever amounted to anything. He's thinking about books, maybe going back to scripts… but that fucking format. Now it's whatever he feels like. He sees potential in writing something about here, Tulsa, Oklahoma, and guys like these two shitheads. Call the show Tommy and Tommy. A fucking sitcom.

Why does he need to go to LA or New York when he has diamonds that just need some polishing, and by that he means dramatic flourishes, right here?

Jeremy sat at the table—winning for an hour, losing for six—and played with the idea of them in a show, wondering what the angle would be. The shtick. You got these two guys. One guy blusters while the other one stands around like a wooden log. So yeah, it would have to be irony. That's how he would do it. Bill Hader could handle that. So could Tim Blake Nelson—if he could gain some weight, he'd be a good Short Philly. Or maybe that kid from Richard Jewel—the one who played the title character—he has some Gandolfini vibes swirling underneath the surface. You'd need that for Short Philly, always fucking angry.

When Jeremy starts thinking about directing, framing a shot, scenes, acting, and especially making money off his writing, these thoughts question why he hasn't gotten his life together.

Is it the weed? It's probably the weed. That's what his mother would say. He hears her saying, "You smoke too much of that stuff," in his head. "Have you ever thought about quitting, cutting back? How do you make any money smoking as much as you do?"

Short answer—Jeremy smiles now thinking about it—he doesn't.

Short Philly snaps at him, "What the fuck are you smiling about?"

Jeremy ignores him, thinking the weed isn't the problem. It's the lack of motivation. Like, where the fuck is he going to go? The world's in the shitter. Living at home isn't that bad. He makes close to a G a week pushing product for the German, which is comfortable, and that's just putting in minimal effort. He runs food for Grubhub from time to time, and he gambles. Imagine if he actually applied himself like his mother wants. He could be something.

But he knows if he had real motivation, he wouldn't be gambling with someone else's money, risking it the way he does. He's only trying to put the extra to good use, growing it like the Bible—this being the Bible Belt; now the rust belt—says he needs to do. The landowner would praise him, not beat him with a baseball bat.

The German isn't Tommy or Short Philly, and Jeremy was only trying to earn and make everyone happy.

All night as he lost and lost and lost in the damn humid air of the back end of Tommy's dry cleaners, these thoughts distracted him. Jeremy figures that is why he lost the way he did and might explain why Tommy looks the way he does, like dried-out beef jerky, darkened rawhide, tanned leather, worn and beaten. With his thinning hair. Thin frame. Thin lips. He has drawn cheeks with dark circles under bloodhound eyes.

Tommy finishes thinking about Short Philly wanting to turn Jeremy's ribs into pulp and turns toward Jeremy. "I don't think he does need intact ribs—good idea."

"Fuck you," is all Jeremy can muster before Short Philly hits him again. The first blow brings him back to his knees. The third sends him flopping to the ground.

Jeremy's arms shoot up to his head to protect the skull because that's instinct. Sharp bent elbows cover the upper part of his trunk. All those years of playing sports, half-ass boxing, hearing his coach say, "Protect the head, you fucking dumbass," come rushing back. Jeremy's a fucking dumbass for getting in this pickle with these two fucking guys.

As Short Philly beats Jeremy with the bat, the first blows are hard, but then he, not being the peak physical specimen of his fucking heritage, loses steam until Jeremy thinks that this isn't so bad and he can handle this.

Tommy taps Short Philly on the shoulder. "That's enough."

"Haven't I been good for you?" Jeremy wheezes, unfurling his body, hesitant at first, fearing another round of blows, but judging by the panting, the guy's worked himself into an exhausted lather. "Every time I play at your place, I lose; I bring you the money. What's so different about today? Why all this?"

"You know what," Short Philly says between deep breaths. "You didn't pay."

Jeremy rolls to his side, eyeing Short Philly, confident he's swung himself out. It's like when he watches out-of-shape heavyweight boxers going at it in the ring; by the twelfth round, neither guy can lift their arms. Might as well be hugging the other guy. Short Philly's movements are slow and sluggish. It must be all the guy can do to hold on to the bat.

"Give me a goddamn hour," Jeremy says. "What time is it? Five in the morning? I can get some cash at five in the morning."

Short Philly turns toward Tommy. "He's got a point." He sounds like he feels terrible about Jeremy's predicament and is confused about why Tommy's treating Jeremy this way. Jeremy knows Short Philly enough to know it's sarcasm. "He's always paid us before."

Jeremy chooses to ignore the sarcasm. "Give me a few more hours, and I'll get you the money."

He refuses to plead with these guys. He won't beg, but he sounds like he's begging.

Tommy asks, "You're going to do, what, borrow from your mommy?"

That's what Jeremy has in mind, but he lies. "Nooo."

Short Philly senses his hesitation. "You were—you stupid little shit." He runs a stubby hand across his forehead, wicking away sweat.

"It's hard work beating someone," Jeremy taunts him. "Especially when you look like an expensive wrapped hoagie."

Short Philly's bulk under his dark blue shiny shirt, almost metallic, constricts and bulges as he points the bat again, threatening to pound Jeremy with it. He takes a two-handed golf swing stance, but Jeremy swipes it away, knocking it from his face.

"I'm going to break you," Short Philly threatens like he'd enjoy nothing else.

"No, you're not," Tommy says.

Short Philly glances over at Tommy. "The fuck I am. That little shit is going to pay for his disrespect."

"You wear shirts that look like they're coated in foil. If you don't like it, do something about it. Lose weight.

Buy different clothes. Something." Tommy shrugs like he's telling a friend the hard truth. "But you look like you're shoved into your clothes the same way clowns test their numbers gettin' into cars."

Short Philly stares daggers at Tommy but lets the insult go.

Tommy turns his attention back to Jeremy. He says, "I need the money, Jere."

"I don't have it, not right now, but I can get it."

"You can't borrow money from your mother," Tommy says. "I mean, you can, but what's that going to say about you?"

"I'll get it from my sister. She'll cover me."

"You can't borrow from her either. And I know you can't borrow from the German."

Jeremy doesn't say anything.

"That's whose money you were playing with, wasn't it? The German's?"

Jeremy tries to read Tommy's face, but he can't get a lock on what the man's thinking. Tommy doesn't seem upset. Not about the five hundred dollars. So the baseball bat was to teach a lesson, and the lesson's been taught. Although Short Philly wouldn't mind tenderizing him some more, just because he's angry.

Something else is going on here.

Jeremy says, "I don't know what you're talking about."

Tommy, sounding understanding, patient even, says, "You know exactly what I'm talking about, just as I know you were going to ask your ma' if you could borrow my money."

"If it's her money." Jeremy sits up, still on the ground on his ass, feet sprawled out in front of him, arms on the pavement, looking up at the two fuckers, "what the fuck do you care if she lends me some to cover your fucking measly five-hundred-dollar deficit?"

"You lost a lot of money," Short Philly says. Like Jeremy needs reminding. "Whose money were you playing with?"

Jeremy looks at Tommy and then back at Short Philly. "I don't know what you're talking about."

It's a lie. He knows what they mean.

"Whose money were you playing with?" Tommy repeats, slower, louder, more explicit, like Jeremy's one of the many immigrants flooding the area.

"I don't know what you're fucking talking about," Jeremy lies again, frowning, trying to play like he wasn't playing with the German's money.

Tommy sighs. "Why do you have to make this difficult?"

"You hit me with a fucking ball bat," Jeremy says. "I say that's a reason to make it difficult."

"And you owe me money," Tommy says.

"Us," Short Philly corrects, digging the end of the bat into the ground and leaning on it, "owe us money."

"You owe us money."

"Then why come at me like this?" Jeremy says. "You've never come at me like this before."

"Your mind don't understand what's happening here?" Short Philly asks.

"You should have expected something like this," Tommy says, that patient, fatherly tone coming through again. "There's only so many games you can play with someone else's money before you lose, and people want to be paid."

"The cards are like that," Short Philly says. "Sometimes, they come up roses, and then sometimes they come up with a Deadman's hand." He acts like he's going to hit Jeremy again.

Jeremy doesn't move.

Tommy says, "Today isn't your day."

"But five hundred is nothing," Jeremy pleads, sensing a foreboding urgency descending on the parking lot. He won't die on his butt. He struggles up to his feet, leaning against his car. A sharp pain rips at his insides. He left the keys on the pavement, but it's too much effort to get down and pick them up. Too painful. He stays bent over with his hands on his knees, talking up to the two men. "Besides, you guys know I'm good for it. It isn't like this is the first time I'm behind. Give me some time. I'll get the money."

"How?" Short Philly barks.

"I just have to move some product."

"Whose product?" Tommy asks.

Jeremy feels like Tommy's toying with the idea. "Yours?"

"Mine?"

Jeremy's mind's working fast now. "Yeah, you all are moving shit all over the place, right? How much do you skim off the back of the truck? I could sell it for you, turn ... what, five pounds? Turn it into a couple of thousand in a few days?"

"That would make us competitors of the German," Tommy says. "We don't want to compete with the German."

"You wouldn't be competing; it would be..." Jeremy tries to think of the word, but nothing comes to him. "Shit."

"Shit is right," Short Philly says.

"We don't skim," Tommy says. "I do have ethics. My word is my bond. If I promise to get you a truckload from point A to point B, I get you a truckload from point A to point B. Same weight at the beginning as the end. No funny business. What would it say of me if my customers couldn't trust me?"

Jeremy doesn't have a good answer, so he continues to hang his head and prop half his body up with his hands on his knees.

Short Philly says, "Why do you think I'm here, jerk off?"

Without thinking, Jeremy spouts off. "Because you two are butt buddies?"

Before Jeremy can blink, Short Philly drops the bat and charges him like a bull. His hands wrap around Jeremy's shirt, and the inertia pins Jeremy's back against his car door, breaking the side mirror that hangs bent and broken from the side of the car.

"Listen here, you little shit," Short Philly growls, just inches from Jeremy's face. "One more word from you like that, and I'm going to take you out to the country—"

"And do what? Reenact *Deliverance*?"

William Goldman was Jeremy's favorite screenwriter.

The comment causes Short Philly to freeze for a moment, and then he growls, "No, I'm going to kill you, you stupid piece of shit. You worthless momma's boy. I'm going to shove my—"

"Your cock?" Jeremy says again, about to break into a grin. "Why are you talking about giving me your cock?"

"No, not my dick..." Short Philly lifts Jeremy off the ground, wedging him against the car, "...my gun. I'm going to put my gun in your mouth and—"

"Shoot your load in my face?" Jeremy says, fucking with him. He has nothing to lose.

Short Philly tilts his head to the side, eyes intent on carrying out his threat. Jeremy's heard the rumors. His heard how Tommy's competitors disappeared or lost heart. Short Philly grumbles, "Yeah, something like that."

"Let him go," Tommy says, stepping forward. "Put him down."

Short Philly holds Jeremy for a moment longer and lowers him to the ground. As Jeremy's feet touch the ground, a sense of relief flushes into his limbs, a warmness, unless he has pissed his pants. Then Short Philly throws his ham-sized fist into Jeremy's face, sending him reeling to the side. Jeremy puts all his weight on the already broken mirror that drops to the ground and shatters. Jeremy stumbles. He uses the hood of his car to stop his momentum.

Tommy says, "Your debt isn't five hundred."

"Sure it is," Jeremy says. "That's all I owe you."

"No, it isn't," Tommy says. He reaches into his back pocket and pulls out the envelope Jeremy brought into the dry cleaners at the beginning of the night. He recognizes the business name stenciled on the face—Whispers—his mother's hair place. "Here's the ten grand you walked in with, plus the five you used for the buy-in."

"Fifteen," Short Philly says. "Where the fuck does a shithead like you get fifteen grand?"

Jeremy says, "I've been saving."

"Like fuck you have," Short Philly says.

"Look, Jere," Tommy says, still calm, still understanding, "we know who you work for, and we know you do a good job for that man. He leaves you alone for the most part and provides you protection when you need it, but we also know the odds of you walking in there with fifteen grand of your own money are pretty slim—I mean, you still live at home with your mommy."

Short Philly shoves Jeremy on the shoulder, knocking him back against the car. His hand is wet with sweat. "It's the German's, isn't it?"

Short Philly shoves his hand into Jeremy's right pocket, ripping the pocket. His fat fist yanks out the last bit of Jeremy's money, the remaining five hundred dollars he pocketed from the thousand he borrowed from Tommy as a stake when Jeremy thought he could win back what he'd lost.

Jeremy doesn't say anything. The money did belong to them. If they want it, they can have it. He adjusts his stance, rolling the sore shoulder forward.

"That's why you're not dead," Tommy says. "Philly here doesn't like when people borrow against the house and can't make the payment. That's what you did. I'm not going to take money that belongs to the German." Tommy stretches his hand out so that the envelope hangs in the space between them. "Take the money."

Jeremy doesn't take the envelope. He considers putting up a fight or arguing.

Tommy says again, "Take the money."

"Do what's smart for you, kid," Short Philly says, calm now, fixing his collar. He wipes sweat from his forehead.

Jeremy studies them both and accepts the envelope. "What's this mean?"

"Means," Tommy says, "you owe me fifteen-five."

CHAPTER 4:

WAYNE KISSEE

THE POOL CUE FEELS RIGHT IN WAYNE'S hands as he selects it from the wall where he had let it rest. It feels almost as good as the beer did, which now sits on the high top next to the billiard table, sweating. The beer in his hand felt smooth, cold, and comforting. When he drank it, it felt even better. It always does.

Wayne walks around the table, studying how he wants to make the break. He rolls his head, stretching his neck. First, his head goes back, chin up, and then down before shifting from right to left and back again, loosening the tightness in his shoulders. The guy staring daggers at him isn't helping him concentrate. He needs to concentrate. He's lost too much money as it is, and the guy looks like he can handle himself if it comes to that.

Usually, it does come to that—backroom bar brawls. Bet on pool games. Lose them. Pay money or don't. The guys he plays against, win or lose, know the other way of collecting payment is in bruises and blood. If you can't

45

pay, you take it out back and settle the debt; you take the beating and move on. Lately, Wayne's taken too much punishment. He prefers to hand it out, and when he can concentrate, he does alright in delivering it.

Wayne leans the cue against the table as he collects his long hair, gathering it back and securing it behind his ears. He strokes his long mustache, satisfied with how he wants to make his break. He picks up the chalk to ready the cue.

Jeremy likes to tell people Wayne just stepped off the set of *Dazed and Confused*, teasing Wayne about the way he looks, which seems fitting because Wayne likes the seventies rock and roll rodeo look Wooderson wore in the movie. But he didn't grow up during the seventies, and he's not colored like Wooderson. Currently, Wayne's wearing a tight red flannel button-up, sleeves rolled up to display his lean muscled arms. Wayne likes this shirt; it shows off his sharp shoulders. Below the large, buckled belt, he wears blue, deep ocean blue jeans, which match his eyes, with cowboy boots. He never goes anywhere without the boots. The dirtier, the more beat up they are, the better.

"You going to take a shot or just chalk that thing to death?" the guy, who goes by Daniel, says. "Doesn't matter how long you rub the tip; it still won't cum in your hands. I know how you like it."

"Shut up," Wayne says as he props himself up on the edge of the table, slots the cue in his fingers, and lines up his shot. Push. Pull. Push. Pull. He slides the cue through his fingers as he readies himself, trying to block out Daniel's jabs.

Daniel, circling behind Wayne, says, "If you fuck this up, I'm going to clean you out." Trying to intimidate him. It isn't working.

"Not today," Wayne says, talking over his shoulder, keeping his eyes on the spot on the cue ball. "But shut up so I can make the shot."

"Make the shot? You're eighty bucks down, and we're going double or nothing. That's one-sixty. That's good money. How many others you play today? You were here when I got here. You got a bottomless pit in those tight-ass cowboy jeans?"

"Are you going to talk or let me try to win my money back?"

"I'm just looking out for you."

"You don't know me."

"I know a loser when I see one, and that's you." Daniel doesn't touch Wayne, but that's how his words feel. Like he's poking him. Like when Jerilyn used to poke him in the shoulder as she berated him, calling him names, telling him in very declarative sentences You. Are. A. Looser. Even now, he can hear her going on, getting at him.

Daniel sounds a lot like her, an ungrateful bitch.

Wayne continues to focus on the spot on the ball and thrusts the cue a few times, getting a feel for it between his fingers while he says through clenched jaws, "I'm not a loser."

Sort of like how he tells Jerilyn he's not a loser when she starts in on him. "I'm not a loser," he would say. She'd yell, "Then why the fuck do you not have a job." He'd say, "I have a job. I drive." And she would yell, "Once a month, you drive your rig; otherwise, it sits out there nearly broken down. What do you do with the rest of your time?" Wayne wouldn't have an answer. So Jerilyn would finish the little skit, seeing they played it out every morning for breakfast. "You're a goddamn loser. That's what you are. A loser."

The balls break in a loud crack, but nothing goes in. A few do teeter right on the edges of the pockets.

"Shit," Wayne says, hanging his head.

The break sure makes him feel like a loser, but not the kind Jerilyn accused him of being.

"I would say I feel bad for what I'm about to do, but I don't know you." Daniel bends at the waist and sets up the next shot—a cherry-picking shot, right there, easy. No talent needed, but it's enough to start a streak. That's how the last game went: Wayne missed a shot, and Daniel cleaned up.

Watching the guy start his streak—first knocking in a yellow striped ball, then one with green—Wayne doesn't care what the numbers are because the only number he cares about is balls left on the table, and that's quickly dwindling.

Wayne picks up the beer and takes a swig.

He just got paid, but now he's five hundred down. This one-sixty-plus will be a good chunk of what's left of what he walked out of the office with. His cash roll is now crumpled pocket lint.

When Daniel finishes off with the last ball, Wayne throws the cue onto the table and goes to the bar.

"Where you going?" Daniel yells, talking to Wayne's back.

Wayne refuses to turn around. "To get a drink."

Daniel says something like, "Pay me."

Wayne blocks him out, and it doesn't hurt that the loud bar, crowded for happy hour with people wearing different versions of what's considered business casual, which Wayne never understood as a thing, helps blot out Daniel's half-assed bellows.

How does someone know what business casual means? Wayne's business is different than other people's business, reminding him of something his father always told him. Your business is your business, not no one else's.

Wayne half turns and, over his shoulder, tells Daniel, "I'm getting a drink first." Issuing it to the man like a challenge. He's unconcerned if Daniel can hear him or not.

When Wayne half turns, he finds Daniel trailing him like a shark, six paces back, closing the distance. He says, "You owe me money."

Daniel reaches out and places a hand on Wayne's shoulder. Probably to slow him down, maybe to stop him, but mostly to make a point and get Wayne's attention. Wayne shakes him off, ducking out from under the hand.

Wayne says, "I'll get you the money, but I'm going to go get a drink. You want one? Or you want to bust my balls?"

Daniel lets him go. He stands there as impotent as an alcoholic accountant, wearing his dad-shoes and cutoff jeans under the pretender black leather motorcycle vest with some saying on the back of it about Christ, which just means Daniel's not as tough as he's bluffing.

Wayne slides up to the bar. The bartender has seen him coming and is waiting for him.

The bartender is Shelia. She's wearing a plaid skirt and black T-shirt, both tiny and hugging her body in different ways. She's not bad looking, better undressed. The soft lighting of the bar improves her looks. It doesn't show the dark spots under her eyes or the battered skin from the year she decided to fuck life and do meth. She's clean now, but the effects haven't faded, aging her more than they should. She's not his typical type. Wayne's grandfather would ask him what the fuck he was doing hanging around with someone like her? Wayne's never been one for those types of insults. There's a lot in this world to hate; good pussy's good pussy, doesn't matter your skin color, and Wayne loves pussy.

"You lose?" she asks, popping the cap off a beer bottle, the cheapest thing in a glass bottle they serve.

Wayne drinks cheap. Liquor's already taxed enough as it is. If he were at home, maybe he'd drink something better than this piss water. At home, he drinks Kentucky Deluxe to get the buzz going. Switches between that and some cheap ass vodka. Doesn't matter what brand. They all are kind of the same after a while. Lately, he's cut the hundred-proof vodka with something sugary, and he can tell the effects on his love handles. He's developing some. He's decided to stick to the whiskey, straight, warm, and a lot of it when he wants to get drunk. He's not looking to get drunk tonight. Just make some money playing pool.

Shelia passes Wayne the cheap beer bottle. "Yeah," he says.

She picks up another bottle and pops the cap off. "You're not drunk yet."

With losing, he's considering trying to get that way.

"Have to have money to get that way," Wayne says. He looks at the bottle in his hands and studies the label, frowning like a kid reading the back of a cereal box. "Won't get that way off this shit, that's for sure."

His comment makes her smile. She toasts him, holding the neck of her bottle out. He clinks the neck of his bottle against hers, and they both take a drink.

Shelia says, "They came around again today looking for you."

Wayne's eyes pop up to her. "Who?"

She smiles as she says it. "Brogdon. He's hot for you."

"He's hot for my wife."

"He's hot for you," Shelia says again.

Wayne takes another swig from the beer. "Great, I already have to drive extra careful around town as it is."

Wayne doesn't have a license. He lost it on his last DUI, driving home to Jerilyn's from Shelia's. That was a bitch to explain. Jerilyn asking him, "Who were you with?" and Wayne lying, not able to tell her the truth but still telling her the truth, "I wasn't with no one. I was coming back from the bar," giving Jerilyn the name of Shelia's bar, essentially saying, "I'm coming back from Shelia's."

That type of nuanced thinking, or hair trimming as Jerilyn calls it, helps him sleep at night, not that he wouldn't sleep at night, just helps him sleep in her bed and not on the couch.

"Don't you need a license to work?" Shelia asks, bringing Wayne back to the moment.

"Fat Tommy Schafer doesn't care if I have a license or not. Short Philly slipped me a knock-off CDL, which I keep in the truck. It's for a Wayne Kissee, just not this Wayne Kissee." Wayne points a thumb at himself. "But the particulars are close enough. So it doesn't matter that the state took my actual license. If I'm out of state, driving, no one seems to care any more than a courtesy check.

"Before I got the knock-off CDL, one cop pulled me over in some podunk town and checked my license. He returned to the window saying, 'Sir, you know your license is suspended?' To which I, playing the part beautifully, acted surprised. 'It is? Wild.' The cop bought into what I was selling. Said, 'You're running a hotshot, right? You said something about it being for the power transmission industry?' That's what I tell everyone. I'm running electrical and mechanical parts for the power transmission industry, and by the time I finish the sentence, they've all lost interest. Their eyes glaze over. Kinda like yours are doing now. Even saying it makes me bored.

"Anyways, I told that cop, 'That's correct,' and said, 'There must be some misunderstanding. I'm sorry... you know how it is. I thought I got all my fines paid.' The cop, not wanting to arrest a hardworking man for something as small as a suspended license, especially when all my paperwork checked out, said, 'Drive slower,' and let me go."

Shelia listens patiently with her arms crossed. "I don't think Deputy Brogdon's going to let you go."

"He just wants to fuck everyone." Wayne finishes his beer. "I mean, what did I ever do to that guy? I can't drive down the street without him looking to stop me. Hell, he's just looking for me. Looking to fuck with me."

"Are you behind again?"

Wayne asks, "Am I behind? I'm always fucking behind."

"How much?"

"Twenty-eight," Wayne says. He can't bring himself to say grand. He's down twenty-eight grand.

"Jesus. Why so much?"

"All of it, child support," he says. "How the fuck do I have to pay child support when I still live with the bitch? Like, what the fuck? I'm living with you. Why do I gotta pay?" Wayne sinks into the seat. "I thought we patched things up."

Some sorrow enters Shelia's tone. "I thought so too." She grows quiet for a second and then doesn't like the silence. She adds, "So what's going on?"

"It's all because of that fuckhead, that deputy, or because I didn't make good choices. I'll let you pick whichever you want."

Sheila doesn't say anything.

"He just wants to fuck Jerilyn," Wayne says. "He has ever since he caught us fucking at the park that one time… Oh, the stupid little grinning fuck doesn't think I remember him from that, but I sure fucking do."

Wayne motions for another beer. Shelia hands Wayne hers. Wayne doesn't miss the eye she's giving him, half hurt, half angry, all of it possessive. He loves the attention but decides to let it go for now. Give him a few more beers, and he might take her out to the parking lot, show her how it's done on the hood of his car, for good old time's sake. But he has to wait until it's dark.

People tend to frown on public fornication—that's how Deputy Do-Dah's partner put it when they found him and Jerilyn in the park.

"Jerilyn doesn't remember," Wayne says. "She thinks the first time she met him was when he came out to the house after she got out of line, but that little fucking elf was grinning ear to ear the night he saw Jerilyn naked with my cock inside of her, making her moan like I'm giving it to her good." Wayne pauses, feeling the need to add, "I was giving it to her good."

Shelia smiles. "Wayne, it's me. I know you."

Wayne nods and licks his lips. "Yes, you do," he says, tipping the beer bottle toward her. "I'll tell you one thing; Jerilyn don't want other people knowing about her. If she ain't one thing, she's a fucking slut when she wants to be. Taking it good. She likes to have it hard and rough: hands on her neck and that sort of thing. Slapped."

He sips the beer.

Shelia says, "I don't need to know that."

That's because Wayne knows Shelia likes it rough, too. She's the type to scratch down his back, so when he's with her, he has to be careful, telling her the whole time, "Don't leave any marks, don't leave any marks, don't leave any marks." And nearly every time, she leaves something. Having to remind her kills the mood sometimes; sometimes, it doesn't.

Wayne says, "That fucker was there that night shining a flashlight in my face. With his light in my face, he thought I couldn't see him ogling her, but I could. I said, 'You like what you're staring at?' The horny bastard couldn't even answer, just stood there stock still, staring, like the fucking pussycat got his tongue, and I guess in a way it did. I said, 'You can have a turn if you want, she don't mind,' fucking with him. Jerilyn didn't like that too much. She swatted at me, her perky fucking perfect tits bouncing because the pervert wouldn't let us get dressed. He stared, eyes saying he loved the show. Her pink nipples erect and pointed at him. Probably better than anything he's ever had the opportunity to have. He strikes me as the kind who likes mopeds and strip clubs."

"What?"

"Fat chicks and girls he has to pay to get undressed," Wayne says, mildly annoyed he has to explain it. He goes on. "I stood there with my cock swinging in the breeze, showing him I wasn't worried about nothing, hands on my hips. Showing he didn't make me lose my erection or nothing. He could watch for all I cared. Finally, his partner speaks for him and says, 'Get dressed.' They let us go, too."

"You think he wants your ex-wife?"

"Wife," Wayne corrects. It's stupid, but he can't let it go. It's a pet peeve of his. "She's still my wife."

"The courts might have something else to say about it."

"I don't care what they think. She's mine."

Shelia nods. "So how old is your oldest, now?"

"Eight," he says. Then counts on his fingers. "Fuck, no, she's ten."

"When's the last time you were home?"

Wayne rolls his eyes and jokes. "How can I go home if there's a PO out?" he says. "That PO's no longer good, but Jerilyn keeps threatening to file another one. She knows better, but she won't let the money thing go, saying it's out of her control. And you want to know how it's so high? 'Cause when we first separated, I didn't care about nothing. I thought. Fuck you, bitch. Fuck your PO. You won't let me see my kids. Then fine. Fuck you. I'm not paying."

"How'd that work for you?"

"Like a revolving fucking door."

"What do you mean?"

"That Brogdon comes hunting for me every time a warrant gets issued, and one gets issued nearly every damn time I get in front of the judge."

"What are you telling the judge?" Shelia asks it like it's his fault.

"The first couple of times," he says, "I said what I said. Fuck your PO; if you won't let me see my kiddos, then I'm not paying. And the judge would just look at me like she pitied me, which I found the worst, by the way, and she'd say that's not how it's done. 'Do you understand what Child Support is?' And I'd say 'Yeah.' And she'd say, 'Do you? Because it's not going to your ex-wife, it's for your kids. You care about them, yes? Or should I terminate rights and cut you loose?' Which always gets my attention, and I'd say 'No, don't do that.' Then she would say 'Then you need to pay.'"

"How many times did you do this before it got through to you?"

Wayne shuffles in the seat, uncomfortable with being honest and ashamed of his hardheadedness. "Six."

"How many times were you arrested?"

"Ten. Brogdon did eight of those."

"But you're working on paying now?"

Wayne glances over his shoulder. Daniel's gone. Probably to the bathroom. "Yeah, yeah, two hundred a month."

"Are you making your payments?"

Wayne sighs and dips his shoulders. "I was. Did it for almost a year. Until we got back together. But last month, I was on a run... Did a hot shot to New York, then back to Philly, and then a hot run all the way out to LA. Ran for Tommy, then picked up some classic cars for the guys in Philly to run to LA, picked up some body parts to make the run home, not that any of these people feel like they should pay me for my time ... and I hear Jerilyn's getting on my case again about not paying. She bitched at me on the phone, telling me she doesn't have enough money to cover rent. I'm like, yes, you do. I just paid you your allowance. I told her you got a job. You want to be queen bitch, then pay the bills with your precious money. I'll take care of whatever else I need to when I get back."

Wayne got back today. It's because of that conversation he's here and not at home, well, that and Shelia. He wouldn't mind going a round or two with Shelia because he knows for damn sure he's not getting any from Jerilyn when he gets home. Not with how that last conversation went. He threatened her, again, and this time, even he believed he'd kill her if she said the wrong thing to him when he got back to the house. It's been too long since he got any. That's what the doctor needs to order: sex. When he's on the road, he's working; he has to stay focused. No sex. When he's home, well, with who he works for and how hard he works, it's stressful, and there's no better way for Wayne to deal with stress.

His favorite—current—stress reliever is Lori Hawkins, Jerilyn's best friend. She has magic hands, and she makes him feel things he's never felt before. He doesn't get angry with her like he does Jerilyn, like he has with the others. He wants to impress her. Maybe it's because she fights back just as hard as she takes it. He likes that, but it also reminds him of how sometimes, when he was on the playground, if he got punched in return, then there was this sort of friendship, a bond, that would form. Wayne doesn't have that with Shelia. They're friends, but the river isn't all that deep. He'll go see Lori tomorrow. Lori doesn't want Jerilyn knowing she's seeing Wayne—so it has to be after Lori gets off work.

The thought of seeing Lori behind Jerilyn's back makes Wayne smile now. He finishes off the bottle and hands it to Shelia.

She picks up another bottle and sets it in front of him, but she doesn't remove the cap. "All that work's got to be good money... right?"

"It is," he says. "It is. I do okay. Put some away. Pay for the trailer and have an apartment. Nice box truck. It's expensive being in business for yourself. I'm trying my best."

"And the gambling?"

"The gambling is so I have some money," Wayne says, which, for the most part, is true. Playing pool isn't like Jeremy playing cards. More skill. Less chance.

Wayne is about to say something more when Shelia suddenly grimaces, a strange flaring of the nostrils and wide eyes, sucking air in quickly through her open mouth. Canting his head to the side, Wayne barely has a moment to look up at her and wonder what the fuck is making her face do that scrunchy surprised thing when the pool cue breaks across his back.

CHAPTER 5

KEVIN ALEXANDER

SHELIA MOODY RELAYS THE EVENTS OF the previous evening to Kevin Alexander, her boss, telling him all about it. "Shards of wood flew off Wayne's back in nearly every direction. It was crazy."

The house lights are up, making the place brighter than ever when it's in use. Kevin's dressed in baggy clothes to hide his true stature, standing on one side of the bar, opposite Shelia with a clipboard in his hands, doing inventory. He checks off different boxes. He wears a flat bill hat low over his eyes to block out the lights. From under the brim, he flicks his eyes up to the broken glass pile neatly mounded near one end of the bar. He asks Shelia why he has to pay for a new glass shelf and close to twenty new liquor bottles—then wonders why she swept up but didn't throw all the glass out. It makes him question how well she swept the area. Not that he's going to go barefoot behind the bar, but he doesn't want little glass pieces in the treads of his shoes.

Shelia tells him she wanted to make sure he saw the damage. "You know, so you could see what happened."

"Looking at empty space where the shelf should be would have been enough for me to comprehend, much less, see the damage," he says.

This is just laziness, and he still doesn't understand how it happened.

Kevin says, "We've talked about this. I don't like violence here at the bar. Don't like the police in the bar either. One begets the other."

Shelia, smoking a cigarette, suckling the filter, says nothing.

Kevin says, "Still, I'm mature enough to understand I don't always get what I want. I'll have to accept the police were here. I'll have to accept there was a fight over billiards, which I still don't like—I've told you to stop allowing pick-up games for money—but still, I'll accept it because otherwise I'll stress out, and I don't like stressing out."

Kevin doesn't do stress when he can help it. He's built his whole life avoiding it—the key was avoiding a regular job and living the life he's chosen. Not living a life anyone else has chosen for him. His father wanted him to be straight, to work in the lumber mill, or whatever the fuck his father did when he left the house. He'd always come back looking like he spent six days underground digging coal, dark-eyed, pale, shell-shocked. Kevin didn't want that. So the first time he fucked a boy, he did it at home in the living room and made sure he left evidence behind for his old man to figure out what was happening. Let him come home shell-shocked to find that. Why would he want to grow up to look like that, a bored working stiff, beholden to some clock? Don't people understand the lessons they learn on vacation, on island time? Why people in New York City are fucktards, yet people down south are all friendly and hospitable? It's time. Beholden to time. He didn't want to be a slave to a clock or societal norms.

Shelia listens to him, doing that bored eye thing where she jams two hands under her chin and stares at him, blinking every few seconds like someone who has to remember to blink. A cigarette hangs out the side of her mouth.

"Shelia," Kevin says.

"Kevin," she says back.

Kevin takes a deep breath. He wants to slam the clipboard and break it in half, kick the glass pile, and break a few more shelves. "Hand me a cigarette."

Shelia, using just her index finger and thumb, picks up the box of cigarettes like its dirty underwear. It might as well be because she keeps the box shoved into the top of her bra when she's working. She tips the box to the side, letting two of the crumbled, sweat-dampened tobacco sticks fall out onto the bar top. She plucks one of the cigarettes from the bar and holds it up, but right before Kevin can grab it from her, she pulls her hand back.

"Are you serving?" she asks.

"Don't Lucy me," Kevin says, "Hand the fucking thing over."

"No one's Lucying you. I'm just asking, do you want to hand me that bottle?"

"What bottle?"

"The opened one."

Kevin looks over his shoulder and scans the opened and "unopened" bottles. Some of the unopened ones have sat on the top shelves for years. They're not real. They were opened, used, and put back there. He refilled them, sealed them, and made them look new. Sat them back up there to give the appearance ... because appearances are important; if he's learned anything in life, that's a sure fact ... to give the appearance of more, heavier priced alcohol than there is. It is an old trick he learned coming up, like cutting some of the bottles with water and then overpouring the six ounces, so the guy watching feels like he's getting his money's worth, but he's getting less.

"Kind of like decaf," his mentor in the bar game explained to Kevin when he first started at this bar. It was a drop bar for old man Siriano before he went to jail. The mentor said, "If you want to sling drinks, fine, sling drinks. We can make some money doing just that. But if you want to put on a show, then you're going to put on a show. It's like Vegas, all glitz and glam so people don't know when you're conning them out of everything they have. Treat the bar like Indians treat a buffalo; use the whole thing— nothing goes to waste. Nothing is free. It's all got a price."

Kevin was just a dumb kid back then, and Neil, his mentor, was being nice, hiring Kevin to work at the bar.

When Kevin met Neil, Kevin had just broken into the bar to steal money from the cash register. He was wrist deep into the cash drawer when Neil, a toad-looking man with white hair, round glasses, and a hand-knit tan cardigan—from his daughter up north—put the muzzle of a shotgun, an authentic old relic of duck hunting past, on him and said, "What the fuck do you think you're doing?"

Kevin, having grown proficient in his short years at breaking into homes, taking things, and sometimes confronting homeowners, learned early on to fight aggression with coolness. "I'm stealing," is all he said.

"I fucking see that," Neil said.

Kevin said, "Then why the fuck are you asking?"

Neil lowered the shotgun and smiled. "There's not much in there."

"There's enough."

"Not enough to lose your life over it."

Kevin realized that even if the old guy calmed down, and backed off, it didn't mean he wasn't willing to carry out his threat.

Kevin removed his hand from the "cookie jar."

"You got a name, kid?" Neil asked.

Kevin told him he was Kevin Alexander.

"Neil Smith."

Kevin made a face.

"Look, not everyone gets a cool name," Neil said. "I get Smith, one of the most common names around, and you know what... I'm fucking a-ok about it, so wipe that smirk off your fucking face and come out from behind the bar so I can get back to sleep."

Kevin looked toward the only other door besides the front door, which was the door at the back end of the elongated space. "You sleep back there?"

Neil said, "No, I sleep on the cot you stepped over, but I was back there taking a piss."

Kevin remembered the cot but didn't think anything of it. He thought it was something you put boxes on or something.

"Here's what we're going to do," Neil said. "You're going to sit there all night. I'm going to go to bed." Neil rounded the bar and retrieved a liquor bottle from the shelf, sat it down on the bar near Kevin. "Pisser's in the back like I said. But what you're going to do is you're going to sit there the rest of the night." He checked his watch. "Which is about three more hours. I'm going to lay down. You're going to do nothing. Sure, you could shoot me. Sure, you could leave. But if you leave, I will go to the people who own this joint, and I will tell them Kevin Alexander robbed me, and then I will let them figure out what they want to do with you. If you shoot me, same thing happens, except they have to work at figuring out who you are. Good thing we got cameras. Otherwise, I'm going to get some shut-eye, and if you're still here in the morning, then maybe I'll offer you a job. You look strong. You look like you might be able to handle yourself. You'll be my barback—start there, and I'll see how you do."

Smoking the cigarette now, Kevin thinks that for having started as a freelance burglar, he's done pretty well in life. But this latent ambition, which has propelled him from a nobody earner to a somebody taker, Iris King's confidant, which was something Neil warned him against, telling him, "You don't want to play with the big dogs. It's alright having a thing and doing it well." It has added a crinkle of stress to his otherwise mostly stress-free world.

What he can't accept is how a fight on that side of the bar, looking now toward Shelia, imagining the man sitting at the bar top drinking the beer bottle as he watched in his surveillance—the same surveillance he told the police didn't exist—how that man sitting there getting hit with a pool cue could break the shelf, and the twenty bottles of liquor, shitty liquor, but it still costs money. Turning to retrieve a bottle of whiskey, Kevin asks, "Yeah, but how did the shelf break?"

Shelia, who sits on one of the stools on the other side of the bar, smoking the other sweaty cigarette perched limply in her off-hand, says, "Not that one."

Kevin sets the bottle down. Goes for a second one.

"Not that one either."

"You want to come back here and get it."

Sheila says, "I'll have to put my shoes on; I don't want to step on glass."

Kevin gives in, selects one of the opened, nearly empty top-shelf liquors, and sets it on the bar. "That work for you?"

"It's not whiskey," Shelia says.

"You got that right—it's free," Kevin says. He pours clear vodka into a glass, remembering when he played this game with Renaldo. This was days before he put a bullet in the guy's head. That vodka was the same brand as this vodka.

Kevin stares at the glass and sloshes the liquid around some, playing with it.

"You going to drink it?"

Kevin pauses his examination and looks past the glass at Shelia. "You going to tell me how my fucking shelf got broken?"

Shelia says, "The pool cue broke when he hit Wayne with it."

"When who hit Wayne with it?"

"When Daniel... Daniel Cooley, you remember him? He used to run with a biker gang until he had them twins, and his girl, Nessa, left him for a bit. He calmed down some."

"I thought he wasn't coming here no more?"

"He wasn't, but then Nessa came back into his life. She's at home with the kids, or so he says."

"Okay, so let me see if I understand. Daniel hits Wayne with a pool cue on the back—"

"You've seen the video. Why are you making me go through all this?"

"Because cameras only show you so much. There's in-frame and off-frame, and what I can't see is off-frame. I need to be able to see everything, and I learned a long time ago that it does me no good to make decisions or jump to conclusions without looking at all sides of the issue."

Something Iris King has a problem doing. She is too much the card player, reacting to what she has and playing against the other person instead of finding out what they have, too, and then using it against them.

Neil taught Kevin a lot about life. Rumor had it, Neil chose Smith, not because it was his given name but because it was his "new" name when Neil left a life behind back east. Rumor also had it Neil and Russell Siriano, the old man, used to be pretty close, like really fucking close, and that Neil's bar—now Kevin's bar—brought in nearly a quarter of Siriano's money. Siriano didn't just put anyone in charge of the main drop bar—he put Neil in charge of the main drop bar, and when Neil, who still comes around, retired, Siriano saw fit to put Kevin in charge of the bar.

Which, in Kevin's mind, lends him a sort of usable lineage.

"The pool cue broke into two pieces, one that bounced off the bar and then collided with that lower-level shelf," Shelia says, pointing to Kevin's left. "It broke glass and knocked bottles over. The other stayed in Daniel Cooley's hands."

Kevin sets the clipboard down and places both hands on the bar top, extending his arms through the elbows, and locking them. He hangs his head out in frustration—stress. Kevin says, "That shelf alone will cost nearly a thousand dollars, not to mention the liquor I got to replace."

Shelia doesn't seem to have heard him, or she ignores him. She says, "So he was just holding this big brown jagged stump, about as thick as my wrist. His face was a mask of anger and all red."

Kevin doesn't care about the fight. He cares about his bar. "How am I supposed to pay for that, a thousand dollars?"

Shelia shakes her head and continues with her story. "Shit, Daniel, I thought, knowing Wayne and knowing how Wayne's going to react..."

Sheila goes on, but Kevin stops listening and shuts his eyes. He tries to center himself. Take himself out of the moment, as his therapist once suggested. After he ended things with Gene, his ex-boyfriend, he thought about going to therapy. Well, he did more than think about it. He went to a handful of appointments, but after a while, he just got tired of all the talking. The therapist asked, "Why do you break into houses? Why do you feel the need to shit on people's rugs?" He told her because he had to, like a kleptomaniac stealing. He liked the power, the feeling it brought. The shitting was his calling card. He told the therapist that he considered it something like a business card left in the bowl at the restaurant. It was something to say he'd been there. She told him he shouldn't do that, and he told her to go fuck herself.

Shelia says, "So now, Daniel's seething, like breathing heavily, in and out, face all red, rage. He yells out to Wayne, 'You owe me money, you mother fucking scumbag.' But Wayne, he's just sitting there processing, you know?"

Kevin removes his ball cap and sits it next to the clipboard. "I thought we talked about the pool betting thing," he says. "I told you not to allow that anymore. It causes too many problems. Bands don't like when there are problems. They won't come play here."

Not saying he won't have an opportunity to pull burglaries if he can't distract people with a concert. Checking bags and coats and things when they walk in, lifting their keys, going to their house, or sending a crew, and robbing them blind—the trick being they had to make it look like an amateur—and then returning to the club and putting everything back just like Kevin found it. It's an excellent little side money-making operation, but it's weeks' worth of work to cover all the cost of the damage from the latest bar brawl.

And with what's happening to Iris King's newfound empire, he doesn't, and she doesn't need the headache of all this nonsense. She has enough problems as it is. Vultures are closing in on every side, trying to pick off the bones of the once-great Siriano organization, which is now a shadow of itself since the old man is back in prison, in protective custody, or wherever he is after the kidnapping escapade. When his boy died, Iris seized control.

All of that was her plan. Kevin helped. It was her plan and end game all along, which means Kevin's now her trusted advisor and can't get tied up in these little disputes; he has an empire to steward. He earned it. He started this power gambit by helping her kill her beloved Renaldo Luna, then placing Wilson Notaro, Siriano's bastard, in charge. Just in time for Wilson to catch a bullet while trying to take down the competition.

Again, Iris's plan. What is not Iris's plan is all these little startups causing problems, fighting against her while she tries to keep control. Kevin made her believe the German was moving in from the west. It's funny, thinking about it now; Franklin gave him that name because of his middle name and the one time he made his childhood friend try sauerkraut. Franklin said, "You all eat this every week?" To which Kevin responded, "Every Sunday for dinner." Then Franklin tried some, made a disgusted face, and laughed while letting the fermented cabbage fall from his mouth. "Yo, Kevin Germaine—Kevin the German."

Then there are the people that are Iris's real competitors, like the Russos, coming in from the east. Tommy Schafer. Short Philly. Others. All rushing to fill a void Siriano's absence created.

Kevin started the German persona just to fuck with Iris, but then the rules changed, and he built a nice fiefdom for himself within her domain, under her nose.

The bitch.

But the more Kevin's climbed the ladder, the more stress he's accumulated. He feels he can handle it if he's working for and with the right people. Also, the more he's climbed the ladder, the shorter and closer the rungs are, and now Kevin's wondering if he played his cards right, figuratively speaking—Iris loves poker, and it all started over a poker game—could Kevin have something more?

Could the German take over?

Could he settle the disputes plaguing her recently? The issues with the cousins down south. The issues with Flavia and Omar pressing in on the side while maintaining a brittle truce.

Everyone seems to tolerate Kevin, and they all fear the mysterious German. He's built the connections. He's trusted... He knows enough about the old days to speak to the old dogs, but he's new enough, smart enough, to show people that this is his thing—he's devoted, invested, a part of something. Something he believes in. Something that, with Neil's help and maybe a few others, he could turn into something better than a shadow of itself. Maybe he could turn it into real power.

Maybe he could go to Flavia?

Tell her what?

Tell her he's taking over, put it to her like she doesn't have a choice. Tell her he'll kill her if she doesn't fall in line? He could do that. He could and would kill to take it all. Iris thinks she can kill, but she hasn't ever pulled the trigger. Kevin did. He killed Renaldo and didn't feel a thing. Kevin saw how Iris dealt with death when her husband died. It distracted her. She played it off well enough, but when the other side started making moves that weren't on the board, she was knocked off-kilter when things didn't go as planned. Kevin could take advantage of that. He could be someone.

Fuck that; he is someone. He's the German. He's Neil's protégé. He's Siriano's trusted advisor, who was already setting up deals behind Renaldo's back before all this started. Wilson trusted him and made him his personal steward. Iris trusts him.

That's her mistake.

How would he do it? How would he take her out?

Shelia takes a drag of the cigarette. "You told me not to let people play for money, but what's a little betting on friendly games here and there?"

"Here and there..." Kevin says, motioning to his side and the aftermath of destruction. The broken pool table, the toppled chairs, the smashed jukebox. Wayne Kissee slammed Daniel Cooley's face into it, breaking the front. "...Is what leads to this. We've talked about it."

"No, you've talked about it," she says, pulling the words out.

"And I've told you not to let Wayne Kissee in here either. Why was he here?"

Shelia's face says she's thinking his question over. "He came to see me."

"Does he give you a cut of his winnings?" Kevin asks, facing her. "I mean, I can get it if he's giving you a percentage or something for allowing him to play his little games. But then you have to pass on a piece to me."

"I don't have to give you anything," Shelia says, defensive, with her hackles up.

"Okay, well, what happened after the fight started?" Kevin asks.

Shelia looks to the side, thinking back on it. She says, "Brogdon stepped in."

"The deputy?"

"Yeah, that guy, the pretty frat boy..." Shelia's voice trails off for a moment as she sips the vodka. "...He's weird."

"He's on the payroll," Kevin says. Good, he can handle any fallout from the bar. "He knows what to do."

"I wouldn't trust him."

"I don't. What'd Deputy Brogdon say?"

Shelia says, "Brogdon told Wayne, 'I got a call you were here.' But I don't know who would've called him. I thought that was weird. Like, Brogdon's here, you'd think he was here for the fight, but it just started."

"So he was looking for Wayne?"

"Seems like it."

"What happened after that?"

"Wayne told Brogdon to fuck off, to which Brogdon said, 'Wrong answer.' He told Wayne to try again. Wayne said, 'I don't have nothing to do with you. Fuck off. I'm not doing nothing.' Except he was; he had Daniel's, or what's left of Daniel's, hair in his hand, lifting Daniel's face from the jukebox. Wayne was caught in the act. Brogdon smiled and said, 'You missed another payment.' I guess he was talking about child support."

Kevin sips his vodka. "What do you mean?"

"Before the fight started, Wayne was telling me he was behind in payments, like twenty-eight thousand," Shelia says.

"Jesus," Kevin says, mind working.

Desperate men are his type.

"...and you know what, come to think of it, I heard his wife—ex-wife—whatever the fuck she is, was getting mighty cozy with Brogdon and looking to make some money, but to hear Wayne tell it that's all she cares about, money. She's always on him about money. She was when they were together, too... always telling him he couldn't go out because of the money. Telling him to get a job because of the money. Telling him money didn't grow on trees. No, it comes out of my daddy's back pocket cuz he's the only man in town crazy enough to hire Jerilyn; everyone else wants nothing to do with her. 'Course, that's on account of Wayne."

Kevin asks, "So Brogdon arrested him?"

Shelia nods. "Wayne said, 'Man, I was working. I'm trying,' but then Brogdon said, 'A warrant's a warrant.'

Wayne looked confused at that point. He dropped Daniel's head. And now that I'm thinking about it... yeah, that's weird because Brogdon had said something about having a call, not being here for a warrant."

"He could have got a call that Wayne was in the bar."

"Yeah, I guess he could've."

"The bar he wasn't supposed to be in no more."

"I guess that's possible," Shelia says. She imitates Brogdon's voice like she's trying the scenario out, "I got a call." Then she switches back to her normal voice. "I don't know, seems ... doesn't matter. Wayne said, 'You don't got no compassion? When's the last time you had to deal with me for anything other than this chicken fat bullshit? When? A year, more, I'm not stealing no more. I'm staying away from those hotels. I haven't even touched another car that ain't mine. I've been good.'"

Kevin says, "But he didn't pay his child support."

Shelia says, "He missed one payment. One! That's what he said. He asked, 'Have you ever missed a payment on something?' He told Brogdon he was working. He was out of the state. Wayne's been good the last few months."

Kevin stubs out his cigarette on the bar top, throws the butt on the floor, finishes off the vodka, and pours some more. He's celebrating. He knows the answer to the question he's about to ask, but he wants to double-check. He lifts the cigarette out of Shelia's mouth, sticks it in his, and breathes in. He releases some smoke. "Who's he working for, again?"

"Tommy Schafer," Shelia says. "But he spends most of his free time when he's not trying to get in my pants hanging out with his wife's brother, Jeremy. You know Jeremy?"

Kevin knows Jeremy. He knows him very well. Jeremy's one of his best producers, even if he's gotten cross with Fat Tommy and Short Philly. Jeremy's done an excellent job of building the mystique of the German and done well to keep Kevin's name out of people's mouths beyond whispers, which is what Kevin wanted.

Shelia says, "He made it to one of those world poker championship shows or something. He's back in town. I think he used to know that Iris woman way back in the day when she first got started. Wayne says he sells marijuana for the German, but I didn't think Jeremy did anything, much less was connected. And that's a silly nickname. Anyways, my daddy says Jeremy still lives at home, or that's what Jerilyn tells him."

Kevin returns to the idea forming in his mind. "How much money did Wayne lose?"

"What do you mean?"

"Betting, how much money did he lose, playing Daniel? Some of that could have gone to his child support?"

"Wayne said one-sixty," Shelia says. "He dropped the bills on Daniel's knocked-out face before Brogdon arrested him. But knowing Wayne the way I do—hell knowing that whole white-trash clan—they all are always hurting for money."

Kevin sees the opening now and feels like a shark entering the fray, smelling blood in the water. "So what you're saying, Wayne needs money."

CHAPTER 6

GABRIELLA LUNA

GABRIELLA LUNA STANDS IN FRONT OF the white marble slab, staring at Alejandro Danois's name etched into the stone when the woman approaches from the direction of the large, wooden double doors of the cemetery's Rose Chapel.

The walls are lined with names and dates. Death days. Birthdays. Couples. Single names. All enshrined and engraved into creamy marble slabs, uniform at first glance. Upon closer inspection, the slabs have differing veins, forming various designs running through each piece, unique for each set of names. They're evenly spaced and adorned with cast iron light fixtures that give the chapel its only light beyond the sunlight coming in through the two sizeable half-circle stained glass windows placed at opposite ends. The windows depict a garden of roses and Jesus. Beyond the two women, the names, and the dead, the space contains ten rows of pews, empty for the moment, and a podium used for the few memorial services held here. The wood of the pews matches the dark wood paneling of the ceiling above the marble. Streaming through the windows, the sun casts intersecting shadows across the floor. Gabriella wears a simple black dress and a black jean jacket. She dabs her face with a white handkerchief that she clutches in both hands. Her small, black purse is wrapped around her arm.

"Gabriella," the woman says as she approaches. Her tone is nice enough, but it assumes friendship; she isn't even an acquaintance. Gabriella only agreed to meet with the woman because she promised information about her son.

The woman is dressed in nice clothes, expensive. She doesn't try to accentuate her natural beauty nor hide it. She wears a simple blue button-up, a man's shirt, and blue jeans, which at one time were considered mom jeans and seem to be back in style. Gabriella remembers they first were in style when her mother wore them. The woman's hair is dark, and her face is younger than Gabriella's, with full lips and sharp cheekbones. She wears black and white Converse with white cross lacing. The cuffs of her jeans are rolled up to reveal slender ankles. She walks with confidence. Each stride says she controls this space.

Gabriella examines her for a moment. How the woman is dressed tells Gabriella everything she needs to know about her. She reminds her of a younger version of herself; not that she's old in her early fifties, but she is old enough to have an adult son and old enough to have lived a little.

"Excuse me," she says, turning toward the woman. She stuffs the handkerchief into her purse.

The woman lifts both arms and motions to the space, walking toward her. "You are Gabriella Luna, correct?"

Gabriella nods. "You asked to meet me," she says. She checks her watch. "I will be late if this meeting takes any amount of time. The least you could do is be on time."

Settling ten paces away from Gabriella, the woman forces a smile. The smile is false. The woman wrinkles the crowfeet forming at the corners of her eyes in her attempt to sell the smile, but Gabriella can tell the difference. "I'm sorry, it couldn't be helped."

Gabriella reads the woman as talented at hiding her emotions, but there are things women see that men do not, and no man would read this woman's face as anything but pleasant. Gabriella knows better. This woman's face has an undercurrent of determination. It tells Gabriella the woman wants something just as much as she wants to give Gabriella something.

Gabriella says, "I have to be going soon. I shouldn't be here, and I need to get to work—"

"You work in an office building, don't you?"

It's the woman's clumsy attempt at showing knowledge. Gabriella is a cleaner. It isn't embarrassing. She's lived in the same home for nearly three decades.

Gabriella nods. "I have to be there by six. It's five o'clock now, and I want to pick up some coffee before I go to work."

The woman asks in disbelief, "You don't still clean, do you?"

"I do," Gabriella says, with pride in her voice. "I may be in charge, but that doesn't mean I'm above getting in there and doing work myself."

The confident woman tilts her head to the side. "But you own the building, right?" As if she's asking why Gabriella still works as hard as she does.

Gabriella smiles out of politeness. "I own my life just as much as I own the building."

The woman says nothing, so Gabriella adds:

"I prize my work ethic," she says. "It's a lesson I learned a long time ago. I love working, and I love being in charge. But that doesn't mean I will ask my employees to do anything I am unwilling to do, and there's no use in sitting behind a desk, managing when I can be upstairs, helping. There is a schedule to keep, and I pride myself on years of perfection. I've never fallen behind, even when I was sick, even when my mother cleaned the building before me. My parents built this cleaning business. The building ... it means something to me just as it means something to my family; in a way, it's my home. This is how I came to own this office building. I could change my hours and work normal hours, but I still keep my cleaning hours because years and years of habit are hard to break."

Besides, she prefers the multi-story office building empty or as near to empty as it ever is. She disdains the hustle and bustle of a typical working day. Not that she's ever had what the middle-class worker ants would consider regular working hours. The weekends are heaven. Sometimes when the building is silent, not even the air thrumming in the background, she walks through the halls, touching the walls with trailing fingertips, amazed that this is all hers. This is her space. Her building. Her life. When she does this, her mind flutters to the past, and she marvels at all she's accomplished.

The woman says nothing. She steps forward.

Gabriella tells her, "Like you... yes... I see a part of myself in your face, the way you are looking at me now. I started on the bottom, as low as anyone could ever be, getting pregnant at a young age and having to drop out of school to care for my child, to care for Renaldo. Although I never dreamed this would be my life, I wanted better, and my mother wanted better, but this is my life, for better or worse, because of my decisions and mistakes.

"I am a daughter of not even first-generation immigrants; I would be the first generation. My son, who I've not heard from in months, and why I agreed to meet with you, would be considered the second generation. My mother loved this and was proud Renaldo wouldn't know what life was like in Mexico, only what the United States had to offer. I still remember when my parents brought me to the United States. I was eight years old and clutched a brown rag doll. It was my only tether to our past life. My grandmother made it. Everything else was left behind. My parents wanted it that way. They sacrificed so much. They strived for a better life, for me, for my siblings, and eventually for my son. They achieved their dream."

The woman settles in next to Gabriella in front of Alejandro's slab.

"Alejandro made everything possible for you," she says like she knows the story.

Gabriella corrects her. "My mistakes and my successes are my own."

The woman shrugs. "And what of the doll?"

"I keep it somewhere at home."

"Where?"

"Stuffed into the bottom of a box." Like most of Gabriella's feelings. "I keep it as a reminder of where I come from."

Staring at Alejandro's name, the woman pauses and asks, "Did you love him?"

Gabriella raises an eyebrow. "That's a bit of a personal question, isn't it?"

The woman's dark eyes study Alejandro's name intently. She reaches out, and her fingertips trace the letters, slowly moving up and down the engraving. The woman muses. "I suppose it is, but I feel a connection to you. I thought I could ask you this."

"A connection to me. Why?"

The woman retracts her hand from the marble, her fingers falling away. "Alejandro, of course." The woman turns to face Gabriella. Now that she is closer, with the light across her face, Gabriella sees the frown lines, the gray creeping into the roots of her dark hair. Gabriella had dark hair once. She dyes it. Maybe this woman does as well. Maybe she should now. The woman asks, "Do you know who I am?"

"Of course, I do. I've seen you before, but your name escaped me before I got your phone call."

The phone call simply started with a demand: "You want to know what happened to your son; meet me." The woman did not ask and did not put it to her as a question. It was a demand that promised information. Information Gabriella desperately seeks and craves. It hinted the information comes at a price. Even before Alejandro's death, her contact with Renaldo was scattered and uneven. After Alejandro's death, she thought Renaldo would come to the funeral, but he didn't. She thought she would hear from him, but she didn't. And now, she wonders what happened to him. Regarding the woman's name, she wouldn't have been able to put a name to the voice, but the woman gave her name and asked where they could meet privately. The word was stressed, so Gabriella named the first place that came to her mind. Rose Chapel, four-thirty on Friday.

That's how they ended up here. None of that explains who this woman is and why she wanted to meet Gabriella to tell her about her son. The woman was thirty minutes late. Gabriella visits Alejandro every Friday afternoon when there aren't any memorials. She spends thirty minutes speaking with Alejandro about her son, and then she leaves to go to work. If this woman could provide information about Renaldo…Reni…

The woman thought the location was perfect, nearly purring the word, and told her four-thirty was doable. Gabriella agreed to meet her and hung up the phone.

Gabriella misses her son. It makes her heart hurt.

"Flavia Sanchez," Gabriella says. "I remember seeing you around Alejandro's diner… I suppose now that he's dead, you are in charge?"

"Of the diner?" Flavia says, turning toward Gabriella. "Sure, my husband and I run it."

"And of the neighborhood?"

Flavia licks her lips. She's considering her response carefully. "What was Alejandro's is now mine, I guess you could say … and my husband's."

Gabriella nods again, but the pause tells her what was Alejandro's is now Flavia's. She is in charge, not her husband.

Gabriella says, "That's not what I heard. I thought … what was his name?"

"What did you hear?"

"I can't remember the name, but the boy with the bowl cut … what was his name? I thought he was in charge."

The woman acts like she doesn't understand and asks the question again, "What did you hear?"

Gabriella knows the woman understands. She can see it. Anxiety racks her nerves too much to play games. Gabriella shakes her head once.

"You want me to connect pieces and come up with your preselected answer," she says, "but I won't do that. I won't play your game. All I want is to know what happened to Renaldo: where he is, if he's still alive, and why hasn't he called. But I won't play games."

"You didn't answer my question," Flavia says, pushing, her tone sharper. This is a declaration, not an observation. "Did you love him?"

"Do you want me to concede that you are in control," Gabriella says. "Do you want me to say I pledge my allegiance to you as I had pledged it to Alejandro? Do you want me to say I've heard the rumors about my boy and that you don't have anything to worry about from me? Fine, you have the power. Is that what you wanted? You have power. You have nothing to worry about from me."

"I have Alejandro's power," Flavia says, nodding.

"Good for you," Gabriella says. "You can have it."

The woman steps around Gabriella. She pauses to admire the stained glass window. "But still, I must know, did you love him?"

"Why is this question, this personal question, so important to you?"

"I need to know."

"Why?"

The woman turns toward her, her face softening as she reveals a truth about herself, a pain. "Because I did. I loved Alejandro. He was like a father to me. He was more than that, more than that to both my husband and me ... but he was ... I considered him my father. I thought maybe we were both connected because of how we felt about the man."

"You loved him?"

"Yes," Flavia says, touching her heart, "very much. Maybe not like you. Although I think if I had allowed him to taste my body, he would have done so, every man has a weakness. Alejandro respected Omar too much, my husband. I only wonder if you loved him because when I was at the memorial, and I saw you—"

"I shouldn't have gone," Gabriella says and faces away. The tears threaten to overtake her and moisten her cheeks again. "But to answer your question—although you don't deserve to know—yes, I loved Alejandro. How could I not? Sure, he took advantage of a young girl. I was what? Fifteen when we met, sixteen when I had Renaldo. I loved him, but he did not love me. I knew that then. I know it now, but he was so handsome, so strong. This neighborhood was his— he was powerful. He was Alejandro. He wanted better for the people living in his area of the city. He knew what it was like for people to look down upon the brown-skinned Mexicans flooding into East Tulsa, black, white; it didn't matter. All they saw were us, his people, changing this slice of the city—with its shiny new mall—from what it was, a suburban escape from the encroaching north, to what it is now, a multi-cultured, lower-class, rundown slum on its way to becoming what North Tulsa is now. That mall, the place where we met—the pizza place in the mall that he owned—is now defunct, nearly abandoned, with only a few surviving businesses, which were never meant to live in a shopping mall and a church inhabiting the forgotten husk. I think it broke Alejandro. I think that was his last great hope of working with the others. So whether or not

I loved him doesn't matter. He didn't love me, and all of that is in the past."

Flavia listens, arms at her side. When Gabriella is done, she says, "He was a complicated man."

"He let his hate blind him," she says. "That mall, his neighborhood, they're linked. When the mall fell to ruin, so did his aspirations, his hope for unity. He just didn't know it yet. He refused to admit that others were moving into the area, taking advantage of his people. Siriano, the cartels, the gangs, the violence, the drugs—he thought the mall didn't work; maybe he could work with them in these other ventures. He thought he could control them by giving them what they wanted … but do you want to know what he did? He fed poison to his own neighborhood. He worked with the evil men infecting my home country and made them feel special like they were in control. He helped them start the genocide that's happening where I was born, blinding them into believing they were gods… that they have the power over life and death. They are nothing." She spits on the floor. "They are evil. Devils … destroying what was a great country, a great people."

"If it was so great, why did your parents come here?"

"You don't understand what was there for my parents after Clinton, after NAFTA? Nothing. My father drove a truck that crossed borders delivering goods, produce, and carpets. These men, who had been slowly migrating north, slowly morphing from local dons into something … more nefarious … let money corrupt their souls. They come to my father and tell him he will transport their goods across borders, regardless of the law—they weren't asking. They told him he would bring home whatever packages their partners on this side of the line gave him. My father, he was a good man. He didn't want to do this. Why do they ask this of him? He was a nobody. A truck driver with a family. But that's why they asked him. He had something to lose, something they could take. His family. These people were not good. They didn't care about him. They didn't care that if he was caught, the authorities wouldn't care either. Wouldn't care if he was threatened into carrying out this task. He faced prison if caught; death to everything he loved if he refused, so he did the only thing he could do. He left. Started over, and snuck off in the middle of the night. Fled. He'll never admit that to anyone, but that's what happened. It's not because he wanted to but because there was hope on this side of the Rio Grande. Hope for life for his family. For my siblings. For me. And then for Renaldo ... but for Alejandro, he couldn't accept this truth. He thought ... he couldn't accept that by working with those ... savages who now control the South... he thought he could control everyone."

As if Flavia is trying to defend Alejandro and partly admitting Gabriella is right, she says in a small voice, "He tried to control a lot of things."

Gabriella's nostrils flare. "And how did that work out for him?" She points to the marble slab. "Should you ask him or me? Because I know the answer. He's dead."

Her anger finally breaks through.

Her anger at this woman's tardiness.

Her anger at her love-hate relationship with Alejandro: how she still loves the man, even in death and how she misses his counsel but couldn't stand his politics.

Her anger from not knowing what happened to Renaldo, where he is.

Her anger from hearing the things people have said Renaldo did: how he killed Alejandro, but how could they accuse her boy of doing this? It doesn't change the fact that's what she heard.

Her anger at Alejandro's wife: how she wouldn't even look at Gabriella when she paid her respects.

And her anger with his daughter, an adult, not much younger than Renaldo: how his daughter spit at her feet and told her how dare she, how dare a whore, the mother of his killer, ever show her face at such an affair, at church, and how she chastised her, told her she should burst into flames for what her son had done—murdering her father— and threatened to call the police. She promised whatever support her father had given Gabriella was done. Anything that could be taken back would be returned to Alejandro's family. She told her how she went to Pablo Jimenez, the man Alejandro left in charge, and he'd already promised this. Did Flavia see any of this? Gabriella doubts it.

Flavia asks, "Would you like to know how he died?"

Gabriella snaps her eyes at the woman. "I know how he died. I heard the rumors."

She doesn't mention what his daughter told her. She doesn't mention how she was treated, doesn't mention how losing Alejandro was like losing part of herself, and doesn't say he may not have loved her when she first met him. Still, when she reintroduced herself into his life and told him the truth about Renaldo, Alejandro welcomed her. He did everything he could to make life comfortable for her, even helping her buy her building—his building but in her name, and she managed it—did it all for the son he never knew but hoped to know.

"Then you know Renaldo killed him," Flavia says.

"That's why I shouldn't have gone to his service," Gabriella says, barely accepting the truth of her own words.

She doesn't understand how it could have happened. She's heard what they said. She's heard what the police told her when they questioned her about her son's whereabouts, but what could she say? Nothing. She didn't know where he was. No, she hadn't heard from him. No, he hasn't told her anything. She doesn't know where he would go. She doesn't know why he hasn't contacted her. Yes, she will call if she hears from him. The last statement was a lie but one of necessity.

Gabriella can't believe what she heard. She can't believe Renaldo would kill his father—even if Alejandro made her promise never to reveal this truth to Renaldo. Even if Renaldo never knew—he treated Alejandro as a father and saw him for something more than his employer.

She says, "Renaldo would have never done such a thing. He loved Alejandro. Why would he kill him?"

"I've read the police reports," Flavia says, reaching for Gabriella's hands, and for some reason, Gabriella allows the woman to take her hands, which are cold and lifeless. Flavia's voice is as emotionless as her hands as she tells Gabriella the truth. "Renaldo killed Alejandro. His bodyguard Pablo was a witness. He gave a statement to the police. "

Gabriella yanks her hands back and turns away. "Where is this, Pablo? Let him tell that to my face. I don't believe it."

Yet, she does believe it.

Flavia's eyes fall away as she tells Gabriella that Pablo is dead. She says, "You know how hurt Alejandro was when Renaldo left to work for Siriano. You know it hurt him."

"But he controlled things, his emotions," Gabriella says, throwing the woman's words back at her.

"He controlled his emotions to a point," Flavia corrects. "For what it matters, it took me a long time to learn the truth. At the time, before what happened happened," her eyes shifting to Alejandro's engraved name, "I told Alejandro not to take the course of action he intended. He wanted to kill Renaldo for working with Siriano, for being arrogant, for asking for help, and for showing disrespect. He tried to kill Renaldo. Had Pablo do it. He failed."

Gabriella searches the woman's face to see if what she is saying is true. "Why would Alejandro want to kill his own son?"

Flavia's eyes widen. "Son?"

Gabriella's brows furrow. "You didn't know?" But then she thinks about how secrets work. "But how could you... It doesn't matter now. You said you know what happened to Renaldo. Where is he? Why are you here?"

"I know what happened," Flavia says, "I don't know where he is, but a mother should know what happened to her son."

Gabriella examines the woman's features. "I do want to know, but that doesn't tell me what you want, why you are coming to me now. Why you are here."

"I want what you want."

"I doubt that."

"You want to know what happened to Renaldo?"

"I do."

"I know what happened to him."

"How?"

"I was told."

"You believe who told you?"

Flavia says, "I have no reason to doubt the information."

"And why do you want to tell me this?"

"I have my reasons," Flavia says, "but mainly because no one's child should ever go missing."

Gabriella thinks about the woman's words. "My son isn't missing, is he?"

"In a manner of speaking, he is," Flavia says. Her face absorbs the seriousness of the space ... and the death. "He is dead. I know this. I know how he died and who did it."

Gabriella squeezes her eyes shut and allows the truth to wash over her.

"I knew, but now I know."

"That's why I wanted to meet with you. I wanted to tell you what happened."

Gabriella opens her eyes. The anger fills her from within like water rushing into a breached tunnel. "I should be asking you why you are coming to me now, make you tell me, be persistent like you were about my affection for Alejandro, but it doesn't matter. Someone finally knows something about Renaldo, and I want to know what you know."

Flavia takes a deep breath. "Three people were responsible for your son's death. One of these persons is already dead. I saw it happen."

"Who lives?" Gabriella growls, "I don't care about who is already dead."

"The man who killed your son is Kevin Alexander," Flavia says, "and the woman responsible for Alejandro and Renaldo's deaths is named Iris King."

"I know this name," Gabriella says. "Iris King. I saw the news about the woman's husband, the DEA agent killed in a drug deal."

She doesn't mention she knew the woman's name before she saw it in the news. She knew it because she teased Renaldo about being in love with a married woman during her last conversation with him. She asked him what he was going to do with a married woman. Then threw the question at him when he balked: "What will you do for a married woman?"

What did she do for a married man?

A lot of things she wishes she could take back.

"What is it you want?" Gabriella asks.

"I want you to know the truth," Flavia says, "and..."

Flavia throws a look over her shoulder. A man appears near the double doors. Maybe he was standing there the whole time, maybe not. The bald man emerges from the shadows. He's wearing glasses and carrying a case. Flavia pauses long enough for the man to cross the space and hand the case to her.

Flavia accepts the case and dismisses the man.

Gabriella recognizes the type of case; she's seen the triangle-shaped leather case in some of the offices she cleans.

Flavia unzips the case and shows her the gun inside, a revolver. "I want you to have justice."

CHAPTER 7:

FRANKFORT CORBIN

RUSSELL SIRIANO SHUFFLES INTO THE small gray room, with its gray floor, gray walls, and gray chairs, and moves to sit on the other side of the round gray table, opposite Frankfort Corbin who is already seated. Frank, in addition to the simple cream work shirt and blue jeans, wears his faded white Stetson with a smart turn to the brim: a sorta trademark of his. The color and wear of the Stetson fit the motif of the room.

The old gangster limps from the door to the table with a slouch and plops into the molded plastic chair. Siriano wears red scrubs with orange cloth shoes with white soles. The red fabric is the sign of a federal prisoner.

To Frank, Siriano's posture looks defeated, body sunken in, eyes hollow, skin a grayish pallor. It reminds Frank of one of those chameleons he once saw on one of his many trips to Central America with Eddie. Those critters could blend into their environment, turn green, tan, and gray...

97

Eddie.

God, he misses Eddie.

Thinking of her now makes his heart hurt.

In a way, if it weren't for her, he wouldn't be here. Kelly, her daughter and his adopted daughter, asked him to come. She said Siriano begged. Frank didn't think Siriano begged for anything, but losing his son changed him. He lost something: his vitality, stamina, the will to fight.

Kelly told Frank she wouldn't go, blamed regulations, but she reminded Frank he didn't have to follow any regulations. He was his own man, a free man with multiple jurisdictions attached to his name. And besides, the marijuana grow from the other day had been one of Siriano's. Kelly teased Frank, Wouldn't he like to know how Siriano's name ended up on a farm in the middle of nowhere when he was locked up?

Of course, looking at her, hearing her tease him the way she does, Kelly's a lot like her mother, obstinate, hardheaded, and influential. She wears a necklace around her neck that Frank bought for her mother a long time ago, about a year after he moved in next door, and they started taking up with each other.

It was taking the trash out, checking the mail—Frank, a trained investigator, working for the Marshal's office then, realized that every time he went out to the mailbox or took his trash to the curb, so did the pretty lady next door with the one daughter, who looked good in barrettes.

Even since then, Kelly's been in his life, always for the better, and Frank loves her all the more for it. He misses her mother but is thankful for his relationship with Kelly.

He has no right to have a woman like her in his life.

But Eddie... Every thought, every time, takes him to morning time where he wakes up, looks over at the clock, and moves to call her, just to hear her voice ask him why he's still in bed when the sun being up should tell him what time it was, hearing her say, "It's time to get up."

All Frank said to Kelly was he couldn't believe it. It wasn't hard to believe that Siriano asked Kelly to come to the jail, but it was that Siriano begged. Even from what little Frank knows of the man, he knows Siriano doesn't beg.

Stroking the edges of his mustache now, Frank thinks that the way Siriano looks, he resembles one of those little reptiles, noting the ashen skin makes the muted red getup pop. Like one of those critters crawling up the wall next to a terracotta sun decoration thing with the faces Eddie loved and bought half a dozen of before returning home on their last trip. Eddie loved those little reptiles and told Frank she wanted to take one home, let it crawl around like at the resort so everything would appear authentic.

She might have liked the reptile, but Eddie wouldn't have liked Siriano. Not at all.

Siriano's God-given name is Rosario, but nobody calls him that. He likes to go by Russell. Frank, as everyone else, calls him by the only name that matters, sometimes said in half whispers, sometimes uttered in frustration—Siriano.

Sitting slung low in the plastic seat, Siriano half-heartedly raises his hands so the guard can unshackle him while he stares at Frank, eyes boring into him.

It is fine; Frank can take it. He can tell a lot about a man from his eyes. He waited forty minutes while the jail worked through count and food service before delivering Siriano to the interview room. He can take the stare, but he isn't and has never been too keen on sitting still when he doesn't have to.

Frank gets started while the guard goes through the rest of his standard operations of unshackling and shackling the inmate to the table. "You like the hat?"

Siriano doesn't answer, doesn't move—just stares.

That's okay. Frank stares back, showing he's not intimidated. He's known many men like Siriano, and they're all the same. They crave power because they're powerless.

You can't be any more powerless than being told when to take a shit or a shower, not that jail is like that, but when doors open and close from a key or a control panel—a cage is a cage.

As the guard leans across Siriano to double-check the wall side of the handcuffs, which is bad practice, putting his body broadside like that in front of an inmate, Frank keeps his mouth shut and ducks his head to the side to look around the guard, to keep the stare with Siriano.

The guard pulls back from Siriano and slips his keys back onto the metal loop of his belt, which jingles in the silence. A hint of stale tobacco smoke wafts from the guard's clothes.

Frank ignores the guard; he's not here for him.

Frank says, "I saw you checking out my hat as you walked in. I like this hat."

He lifts the hat from his head and extends it out for examination. Siriano's eyes shift from Frank to the hat and then back to Frank.

"I thought maybe you were admiring it."

Frank places the hat on the table.

"This woman I knew..." Frank pauses to consider how much to tell Siriano but decides sharing some truths isn't a bad way to start a conversation, "her name was Eddie. We were..." Frank searches for the right word, and once he has it, he finishes, "we were something."

Something isn't the half of it. They were more than something.

"She bought it for me a few years ago," Frank says. "I can tell you it was a son of a bitch to break in."

Frank switches his eyes from the hat to Siriano.

"'Course, don't go tellin' her that. It'd break her heart to hear... and you and I both know I shouldn't be nay-saying a gift."

Frank leaves out the part about her being gone, not mentioning how cancer sucks.

Siriano tilts his head to the side; his right ear nearly touches his shoulder before rolling his head to the left. His way of showing he's listening. But still, he says nothing—just stares.

It is fine and to be expected.

Frank exhales slowly, taking his time to read the ex-crime boss's mood. Siriano's a tough cookie to crack, and he's doing his best interpretation of stone.

"You ever break in a hat?" Frank asks, and when Siriano doesn't answer, Frank goes on, not letting the indifference bother him. "It takes more than you would think, boots too—'course, the secret with them is olive oil; keeps the shine."

The guard double-checks the cuff secured to the table and asks Frank if he's good. Frank tells him he is.

Still staring at Siriano, Frank says, "I see we're not in a speaking mood as of right now, which is strange considerin' you asked me to come here, and I don't rightly know why. But when someone ... that's you ... goes through the trouble of getting me an official message and wants to have a sit-down, even contactin' an AUSA to make it happen, I figured the least I could do, what would be polite, is to come to see what you have to say; maybe find out what you're wantin' to talk about, but I can't think of what you might have to say to me. But I have to say, judging by your normal behavior, this silence is a bit of an abnormality for you."

Frank considers mentioning the beggin' but decides against it.

Frank tilts his chin down as if to punctuate his words and make a point. Then he straightens and smiles.

"And by that, I mean, you're a bit of a talker. I watched you argue with your attorney at your last trial. That was worth a ticket to the show."

The guard at the door, waiting for a break in Frank's one-sided conversation, interrupts and tells Frank, "Knock on the door when you're done; I'll come to get you." He demonstrates the action.

Frank ignores the guard because he's in it now with Siriano. The man may not have said anything yet, but everything about his body language and the way he's been listening tells Frank plenty.

It tells Frank he's about to say something important.

The guard opens the door to leave.

Siriano adjusts in the seat, and the chair legs clank against the gray tile.

"I'll have to wait for him to come back and get me," Siriano tells Frank. Bitterness drips off with each word as Siriano cocks his head over his shoulder, glaring at the guard stepping through the door. "The last time I met with someone," Siriano pauses, "my lawyer, mind you... That fucker made me wait all through lunch. I missed lunch. I like lunch. Lunch is when they serve the good stuff. The good food, or at least something edible, something I can swallow without gagging."

Siriano lifts a finger and points it at Frank. The guard disappears through the door. It clangs shut.

"You know why? It's because they want us fat and happy," yelling the last part at the closed door.

Now that they're alone, Siriano shifts in the chair, getting more comfortable. He throws an arm and a leg out. His demeanor changes. It lifts, and he becomes more like himself, the talker. That vitality and stamina returning to his features. The man de-ages in front of Frank, returning to the man who argued with the judge about what he's called. "It's Russell, damnit." The judge shook his head and argued, "No, it's Rosario." To which Siriano yelled from the defense table, "You ain't my mother or father, and in a country such of this one, if a man wants to be called something, especially a name, which means something in the circles I deal, then you call that man what he wants to be called— it's called respect."

The Siriano who sat at the defense table materializes before Frank.

"Dinner time, they don't care," Siriano says, "because what are we going to do? We go to sleep. Hard to complain when you're asleep. Sure we complain about the food, complain about a lot of things, but who cares? All the important people have gone home for the day. Breakfast, they don't care because it's breakfast. Everyone is all groggy and shit except for the guards. They like to do shift changes before everyone gets up. If you don't take pills, by the time you wake up, breakfast is here, and it's been twelve to fifteen hours since your last meal. So what the fuck are you going to say?

"They tell us to consider ourselves lucky that it's not just cereal. That fucker, that's his favorite line. 'Be happy it ain't cereal,' to which I like to tell him, 'Oatmeal, grits, and that godforsaken fucking farina...' Do you even know what the fuck that is? I didn't know what the fuck that was. I had to have someone explain it to me. And when they did, I told that fucker those are the same damn thing—just hot. You know what it is. It's tasteless is what it is. There's been prisons where the inmates rioted because of the food."

Frank says, "Shitty food gets shitty dispositions."

"I never thought I would say I miss prison."

"This isn't prison," Frank says, "It's jail."

"Yeah, well, whatever you want to call this food, it ain't fit for anyone. Some places ... like the one I was at before all this started, they had good food. I miss that. They had good food for every meal. Good food gets good dispositions—there's some shitty country wisdom.

"Some guys, weightlifters, took to cooking like it was an art, and we were all better off for it. Like they were going to be something, maybe have their own in-prison network show. Like *Beat Bobby Flay*, but it's not the prick from the TV, it's the bitch from cell block B." Siriano laughs at his own joke. "This place only has good food at lunch, which I'm missing. I told them to have you come in the evening, at least then I get some extra time where things are quiet, and I can eat some noodles before bed."

Frank checks his watch, making a show of it. He says, "You wanted to see me."

Siriano stares. He inhales through his nose and studies Frank for a moment. He glances at the hat and then back to Frank.

"I saw you at the trial," Siriano says. "You were standing off to the back. You were hard to miss with that hat. Every time we took a piss break, you'd stand, stretch those damn long legs of yours, always wearing blue jeans. It was those pressed blue jeans that caught my eye every time. You'd slip that hat on your head and walk out the doors. Like you're a cowboy or something. So formal. Every single time, every single break, I watched you do this. You had a routine... I bet you're a man of routines. You have to do the same thing the same way every day. That's you. That's why I wanted to talk to you."

"You wanted to talk to Kelly."

"The marshal?"

Frank nods.

Siriano shrugs. "Okay, well, not you, but then she told me to talk to you, so now it's you, which is all for the better."

Frank nods. "I find as I get older, routines help me get up and moving."

"Routines make you dependable," Siriano says. He motions to the room with a shrug, meaning the jail. "Routines are all we got."

"What did you want to see me about?"

"Legacy," Siriano says. He leans forward in the chair. "You'd think my worldly needs ... my immediate predicament would be my concern. But it's not... My legacy is all I care about now. It's funny when I start thinking about it—here, when I'm forced to live in a place like this, fucking walls everywhere. I would say I like to go out in that rec yard, but it's a concrete box with mesh over my head... still walls. It's not the same as stepping outside. No breeze on my face. No unobstructed sunshine."

"So you don't like being in jail," Frank says, "make better life choices."

Siriano says, "You ever have children?"

Frank doesn't hesitate to answer. "Two wonderful children, a boy and a girl."

He's not thought of them in some time.

"You see them?" Siriano leans forward and points toward Frank with the cuffed hand, which makes the metal restraints clink. "The way you say that makes me think you don't."

Frank sighs, nodding. "Now and then, I wonder how they're doing. And every Christmas and on their birthdays, I send them a card. To be honest, most of them cards go unanswered. Every few years, some come back undelivered. But seeing I have access to some of the best databases in the country and I'm a trained manhunter, I usually track them down, get the new address, and slip the card back in the mail."

"Do they ever write back?"

Frank shakes his head.

"What happened with them?"

"Their mother and me had a misunderstanding ... and they suffered from collateral damage and from not understanding what was happening." Frank licks his lips, pushing back wayward strands of his mustache. "We've not really spoken for over twenty years."

With the look Siriano gives Frank, he wasn't expecting the candidness. He pauses before he continues, blinking a few times, processing the information. "What happened?"

"As I said, their mother and I had a misunderstanding."

Siriano digs further. "Which was what?"

Frank knows what this is. Siriano's testing him, probing him to see what he can trust Frank with. Whatever it is, whatever Siriano wants, must be big because Siriano's taking his time, first doing the vow of silence act and now playing the twenty-question game.

Frank sighs and decides to placate the man. After all, he is behind bars and likely to spend a good chunk of the next twenty years in prison. That and he lost his son.

Frank says, "She wanted to date her doctor boss after nine years of marriage. Blamed my job and said I worked too much, that I wasn't around... I was a marshal back then."

"So she blamed you," Siriano says, "for making a living, for providing."

Frank says, "She should have been blaming herself."

"Why's that?"

Frank doesn't answer.

Siriano tries a different tactic. "What'd you tell her?"

"I said, if you want a divorce, we can divorce. If you want to be married, we can be married. But what we're not going to do is you go off and see if you like this doctor boss of yours, like playing house with him, fucking him, and then decide if you want to come back to me or not."

Siriano processes Frank's honest answer. Then he asks, "Did you love her?"

Frank studies him for a moment, trying to decide if he's going to trust him with this information or not. Figures why not. "With all my heart."

Siriano nods. "I guess if you've not talked to your kids for twenty years, then things didn't work out."

"She preferred to go see how she felt about the doctor boss, and I filed for divorce, which was granted six months later." Frank stands and walks toward the door. He places his hands on his hips and glances out the little square window, giving Siriano his back. "Why did you ask for me to come here?"

Siriano is silent for a long time, but that's alright. Frank knows how to play this game. Siriano wants something. The trick is getting him comfortable with telling Frank what that is without wasting a bunch of time.

Outside the little gray room, the rest of the jail goes on with their day. Prisoners get searched and walk through the metal detector on their way to court. Guards and detention officers walk back and forth, some of them dressed like deputies.

Siriano says, "You know what this place has? It isn't a good dinner or breakfast. We've been over that, but what I mean is ... this place has time to think—solitude."

Frank turns around, hands still on his hips.

Siriano motions to the room and then to Frank. "I know I'm done. You know what I've done. No need to belabor that... I'm fucking done. The feds, they have me for all sorts of things."

Frank scrunches his mustache and says, "They do." He crosses the room back to the table and sits down.

Siriano says, "I'm Paul—although I should say Saul because I haven't fucking converted to nothing. I feel like I'm at a precipice. I'm looking to make a decision I never thought I'd make. Do something against my code. You know, I've always thought of myself as a Caesar, Julius Caesar. That's where I fucking am in more ways than one. Here's how I see it. I'm done. I could've stayed in Germany and enjoyed my fiefdom or come down out of the high country to take what was rightfully mine, and I did that.

I marched on the city. I seized it and then was fucking stabbed in the back. And that was just the start of many: Renaldo Luna, running his thing on the side; Maggie, for not fucking killing Brandy when he should've; my son, although I don't hold him too responsible; the Mexicans; those Sanchez cunts; and that bitch Iris King. They all had a hand in bringing me down and putting me here.

"Now, my son, I don't hold a grudge for that. I would have done the same if I were in his position. I don't speak ill of the dead. But everyone else, fuck them. They brought me down... but what I do blame my boy for was trusting that bitch."

"Who's that?" Frank asks for clarification.

"Iris fucking King," Siriano says. "She played her cards perfectly, but that's what she's good at. She lays it all on the table only to shoot you in the dick underneath. She fucked everyone under the sun. You know, it wouldn't surprise me if that AUSA that gave her her dead husband's folded flag... wouldn't surprise me if she was fucking him. She's a bitch, a cunt, and a whore. But now she's in fucking charge of my organization. How the fuck did that happen?"

Frank leans forward. "You tell me."

Contrary to Frank's expectations, Siriano doesn't blame someone else. He says, "I fell asleep at the wheel. Got comfortable. Let her turn everyone against me and got them all to stab me in the back, just like Caesar. But now, I'm at a threshold, again. It's a crossroads, if you will, where I can end her fucking power trip real quick."

Frank fills in the pieces. "By talking to me."

Siriano means the government. He's ready to turn cooperative witness, something no one ever thought would happen.

Siriano throws himself back against the seat. "That's why you are here. I want to cross the river, the whatchamacallit; that's where I'm at. I am coming down from Germany again, except this time, I'm coming down and bringing everyone down with me. Bringing Civil Fucking War with me, except I'm not going to fall in love with an Egyptian queen and then declare myself emperor. I know, sitting here, my time is done. But I'll be damned if they take what was mine from me."

"You can't have it, so they can't have it."

"Fucking-A, that's right."

Frank clasps his hands on the table. "And you want to talk to me? Why?"

"You weren't my first choice," Siriano says. "That marshal, she said to talk to you. She said you'd be the best person because you have a finger in all these pies ... law enforcement agencies all across the state: the feds, the state, the Indians. They all like you, and more importantly, they recognize your authority."

"They do." Frank scrunches an eyebrow. Kelly knew more about what was going on than she let on. "What did you want to tell me?"

Siriano says, "It's not just what I want to tell you. It's what I want you to do."

"And what's that?"

"Take down that cunt who took over; show her she's not as clever as she thinks she is."

Frank considers the request. "How do I do that?"

"Do I have to do all your fucking thinking? Murder's always a good place, doesn't have a statute of limitations; let's start you there and then see how you do. If you get her on the murder, then maybe I turn government witness and play ball."

Now Frank understands why Kelly couldn't do it. She must have listened to his pitch, but she knows it's career suicide, not that she's really recovered from losing Siriano the first time. But this... this type of thing, she can't investigate.

Frank asks, "Who got murdered?"

"Renaldo Luna," Siriano says. "He was my bag man for a while. He held things together. Ambitious."

"Who killed him?"

"Who, what are you, a fucking owl? That's all you've said. Who this and who that? It's not just about his murder. Although it is; his murder is the moment—stuck in time. It set all this shit into motion which ended up with me here. Locked in this place contemplating doing this ... talking to you ... turning government rat.

"It was my thing, not hers. She took it from me. She doesn't deserve my thing. It's not her thing. It was Renaldo's thing, and before you go asking who again, I'm speaking about Iris King. Renaldo was fucking her. So was my boy."

"Fucking isn't motive." Frank picks up his hat and sets it on his head. He's had enough. "You don't know who killed Renaldo, do you?"

Siriano shakes his head. "I know who it wasn't."

Frank stands, realizing why Kelly asked him to come here. "You've already talked to the AUSA about this, haven't you?"

"Why the fuck do you think I was talking to your girl? They didn't want to hear what I had to say. They didn't care. She, on the other hand, is driving me back to this shithole and says tell me what you want. Says she can't make it happen, but she knows someone who can."

That means Frank. Siriano wants the government to take down his competition.

Coming here was a mistake.

Siriano will never turn rat.

Frank gives it one last go. "So, what do you want?"

"It's not a question of what I want. It's a question of what you can do for me, and I know it's not a whole helluva lot. But what you can do is topple that bitch.

"Now, as far as who killed Renaldo, I'm sure Iris had a hand in it. He was in love with her. So was my boy. Only one way to get to Renaldo was through her. Wilson took over, so I have to assume he was involved... maybe you start there, with his people. When I was kidnapped, it was Alejandro's people... Alejandro was a business partner. Renaldo came from them. Alejandro's people claim they didn't do it. I believe them."

"So, who pulled the trigger?"

Frank doesn't wait for an answer. He knocks on the door. He's heard enough.

Siriano shouts and strains against the handcuffs while stretching toward Frank, "I'm telling you Renaldo's dead; he's missing. You find missing things, animals from what I hear, but it used to be people. Go talk to his mom; talk to Alejandro's people. They'll tell you what happened. They'll tell you it wasn't them but that he's dead. Someone killed him. Iris killed him."

"Maybe, but we don't know that he's dead or where he might be. He could just be missing."

"Renaldo's dead..." Siriano's words become mumbled as he shows genuine emotion and then solidifies into strength. "Wilson's dead... my boy... my legacy is dead, but I'll be goddamned if my legacy will be some bitch sitting in my house. She did it. She killed Renaldo, and then she killed my boy. Maybe she didn't pull the trigger on either one of them, but she's the reason. I don't know how, but she did. I don't know the answers. That's where you come in."

The guard comes to the door and opens it.

Frank tips his hat down toward Siriano and walks through the door without saying a word.

CHAPTER 8:

JERILYN KISSEE

JERILYN KISSEE SWEEPS THE HAIR INTO A pile, humming to herself while checking to see how the girls are doing in the back. Katherine and Kasey are sitting at a round table. Katherine's completing homework. Kasey is playing with her tablet, watching colorful shows filled with puppets and singing. Regina, her mother's elderly office manager, a round, plump woman, sits with the girls, crocheting while holding an absentminded conversation with Jerilyn's youngest, who provides a puppet play-by-play to the older woman.

The hair on the floor belongs to the latest customer, who, while leaving, glares at Jerilyn with a scowl because as soon as the woman was up and out of the seat, Jerilyn was right there with the broom sweeping the floor. Hyper-efficient, almost to a fault, which is something Wayne complains about when Jerilyn scoops up his dinner plate seconds after he finishes the last bite. Jerilyn can't cut hair, but she sure can clean. Over the last two hours ... well,

115

really over the last week, she's made sure the place is spotless since meeting with Brogdon. Before grabbing the broom and swatting the woman's toes, which was an accident, Jerilyn had been cleaning the mirrors at each of the six stations, which her mother calls booths. She wiped the mirrors with a rag, frustrated at the streaks the rag was leaving, talking to her mother.

But the rude customer is so intent on giving Jerilyn a dirty look—even though she'd paid and spent a few seconds checking out the haircut in a mirror near the front door— she opens the front door, the brass bell above ringing as it opens, and nearly collides with a woman, who is entering the salon almost at the same time as the woman's trying to leave. Jerilyn glances at the other woman and recognizes her as a regular. The rude customer, surprised, deepens her frown lines and shuffles around the small, dark-skinned woman.

Jerilyn's mother acknowledges the woman, telling her to take a seat. "Suzanna will be with you shortly; she's finishing up another woman's color."

Suzanna is the busty brunette washing a woman's hair on Jerilyn's left, near the partition separating the small seating area from the rest of the narrow space, which consists of a galley-type seating area with six booths, which Jerilyn's mother rents to other stylists.

"I don't understand why you need this extra money," her mother says. She is seated in one of the chairs, relaxing with her legs crossed and hands cupped around a colorful tumbler Jerilyn made at a time when Jerilyn thought she was going to sell crafts on websites like Etsy. She's picking up the conversation they had been having while Jerilyn wiped down the mirrors before Jerilyn broke away to grab the broom.

It's the same conversation they've had every night this week, and Jerilyn's tired. At first, she could fend off her mother's prying questions, but now, she can't.

Watching Jerilyn sweep, her mother adds, "And why won't you let me just give you the money."

"I don't want to owe anyone anything," Jerilyn says, checking the hair pile. "I want to earn my money. Besides, Wayne's not paid child support in some time. I really do need the extra money."

"But what is it for?"

"I'm not telling you; we've been through this."

"I've offered to pay off your bills," her mother says. "I have the money. You have access to my account. You can see it there. You know what the number is. Just take out what you need; pay me back later."

Jerilyn sighs. "I don't want to owe you money, mom."

"It's not owing me money. It's a gift."

"I don't want to accept that type of gift."

"You accept it at Christmas. You accept it when I take the girls' clothes shopping for school. What's the difference?"

"It's not the same thing. A couple hundred dollars in a Christmas card isn't the same thing as a couple thousand—"

Shit, Jerilyn didn't mean to mention the word thousand, much less let on to her mother that she is trying to raise that much money.

Jerilyn starts sweeping again to brush the conversation away.

To her minor annoyance, her mother pries for more information because that's what her mother does, especially after separating from her father years ago. "What do you need a couple thousand for?"

Her mother used to ask what went on at her father's house. For a while, Jerilyn would manage to stave her off, parrying every question. Still, as time went on, her mother got better with her pointed thrusts, and Jerilyn would eventually break down and tell her what was happening at her father's, whom he dated, and how much he drank. When it came time to open up to her mother, to tell about the times he came back drunk and slapped her around, well, that became easier too because her mother had defeated every bit of rampart Jerilyn tried to raise between them.

In a reflexive defense, Jerilyn spits out the first thing that comes to her mind and hasn't left her mind since she had to short-sell their house and move into a rental, which is a trailer in a trailer park with a shoddy reputation. "Because Wayne hasn't paid child support for some time."

"I don't understand why he doesn't pay. Doesn't he love his children? He must not love his children. I just don't understand."

"It's not his children that he doesn't love."

Her mother snorts in disgust. She's never liked Wayne, not since she first met him when she walked in on him and Jerilyn making out on the living room couch—okay, they were doing more than making out. On the day Jerilyn married Wayne, as she added the final touches to her mother's wedding dress because she, and by extension Wayne, couldn't afford to buy a new dress, much less a ring—the engagement ring consisted of a bottle lid ring wrapped in foil and decorated with glitter—her mother asked her in the back room of the church: "Are you sure you want to go through with this?"

Her mother drops a foot to the metal bar of the seat, uncrossing her leg and then recrossing her leg, gaining the attention of the woman waiting for Suzanna at the front. "He is still working, right?"

Jerilyn pauses in her sweeping and leans into the broom, folding her hands over the top of the handle and wedging it underneath her chin. "As far as I know, but you know what he does isn't very consistent. Last time we spoke, he said he'd booked a new gig, transporting marijuana for Schafer Logistics."

"Marijuana?" Her mother raises an eyebrow. "For Fat Tommy? I know what they say about him. Does he know what they say about him? Is he driving marijuana out of state? I didn't think that was legal. The last thing Wayne needs is to be doing something illegal."

"Mom, he's not driving it out of state." However, she doesn't know that for sure, and Wayne hasn't been as forthcoming about his work for Tommy Schafer as he has been in the past with other jobs. Them being all but broken up, not that either one could afford living separated or that Wayne would let her go, has put a hamper on their already stressed communications. "At least, I don't think so."

"But he's a hot-shot; that's what he does, drives all through the night to rush stuff around, driving things from California to New York. I told you, you should never have gotten involved with a man who doesn't spend every night in your bed. That was the mistake I made with your father, the pilot—like that's something prestigious. It worked for me then, but when I went to bed alone, and he didn't, I learned the ugly truth real quick."

"Don't remind me."

"Did it make being married to him hard? With him leaving at all times to rush off somewhere. It made life with your father nearly unbearable. Have you ever tried to plan a schedule when you didn't know if your husband was going to be there or not?"

Jerilyn has, but not for the same reasons. Wayne would go out. He would say it was with the boys, but it amounted to him going out to bars, drinking and coursing, as her mother puts it, and Jerilyn wouldn't know when he'd get home. And these were on the nights he was in town. And if he did make it home, not sleeping it off somewhere or with someone, Shelia being his favorite resting place or hole, she couldn't count on him to get the girls to school or get up and around in time to make it to work or be where he was supposed to be in the evening.

"Look, him rushing off to God knows where," Jerilyn says. "San Francisco to New York, Canada to Mexico... it made things hard. But I figured it out. I made it work, in some ways. I know, Mom. I know what it's like. You don't have to remind me you and dad didn't and don't get along. I know. I know the history. I lived it."

Her mother stares at her for a moment. "You don't know everything."

"Then tell me, but all you ever tell me are the things I already know, which is that dad wasn't around. Wayne's just like that."

"It's what I was afraid of when you married him. I told you that."

"Mom," Jerilyn says.

"Jerilyn," her mother says with a flat bored tone.

"Wayne's worse. Dad might have stayed a night or two somewhere because of his flying schedule. Wayne drives everywhere. Once, he drove as far as he could through Canada to get something to Alaska. I went with him on that one. You'd think, doing all that driving, you'd get to see something of the world. But no, it's road, country, sure it's pretty to look at, but after a while, Interstate is Interstate. It all looks the same. The same farms, the same houses, the same fields—just different colors, different crops, but all the same."

Jeremy enters the shop and saunters past Jerilyn and her mother. He's heading straight for the pop-can machine. He tosses seventy-five cents into the machine, pounds the side with his fist, Fonzie-style, and a can of pop falls to the slot, Coke. He bends down to pick it up. He turns to look at Jerilyn and her mother, who have both stopped talking to stare at him.

Slack-jawed and pretending ignorance, he says, "What's up?"

That is all her mother was waiting for to continue. "Your sister says she needs money."

Jeremy processes the revelation by popping the tab on the can with a loud crack. Jeremy has a habit of twisting the tabs as he opens them and pulling them off the can. He tosses it to the ground, pretending that he was shooting for the wastebasket near the girls, but missed.

"Hey," Jerilyn says. "I have to clean that up. I just got done back there."

Her brother glances at the discarded tab and shrugs. He guzzles down his first gulp of the Coke and wipes his mouth. "Why do you need money?"

"That's what I said," her mother says.

Jerilyn leans the broom against a chair and turns to inspect herself in the mirror. Her hair's a mess. She plucks at a few strands with her pinched fingers and removes the cigarette she'd stashed behind her ear. She sticks it in her mouth as she runs her fingers through her hair, tucking the strands back behind her ears.

When her mother sees Jerilyn stick the cigarette in her mouth, she leans forward in her chair. "You can't smoke in here."

Eyes on her mother in the mirror, Jerilyn plucks the cigarette from her mouth and sticks it back where she took it. "I'm not going to smoke it."

Her mother says, "You should stop smoking these things."

"You smoked for thirty years!"

Her mother relaxes back in the chair and holds up a curled finger like she did when she scolded Jerilyn or made a point, usually in an argument in which her mother was correct, and Jerilyn was wrong. "And I quit for good reasons. Maybe if you weren't buying those, going to get your nails done, and some other things, you wouldn't need to work here to get that extra money."

The whole time Jerilyn straightens her appearance, she's buying time to come up with an acceptable segue to another conversation, to anything but this.

She watches her mother in the reflection but can't help but look at her appearance. God, she's plain-looking. Two kids can do that to you. Two kids, a deadbeat husband who beats you, and living to survive... Maybe Wayne's, right? Maybe she could clean up some. It would sure help in the dating department. Cutting herself loose of Wayne would help, too—there's some real nutcuttin'.

Jerilyn holds up her hand, turning. "They're press on. I can't remember the last time I got my nails done."

Her mother says, "It was with me as a Christmas present."

"Well, then you should know. Besides, I save money by having Suzanna cut my hair."

From the back, Suzanna says, "And you look fabulous, but don't you think it's getting about time for a trim?"

Her mother scoffs. "I hope people in here don't think of you as an advertisement for my services. My salon's skill. They'd find me lacking if they used you as an example of what we do here."

"Mom," Jerilyn says, protesting as she did as a teenager, carrying the word out a syllable longer than it is.

"Don't mom me," her mother says. "You're like the preacher's kid, except you're not out there causing hell like your husband."

"Raising," her brother interjects.

He should stay out of this.

"Stay out of it, Jere," Jerilyn says.

Her mother glances his way, a sly smile creeping into her stern features. "Raising hell... You're here looking like a stringy mess."

"Sis, I wasn't going to say anything, but you could stand to take care of yourself."

"Don't," Jerilyn says, raising a finger for her brother, the middle, a sibling salute and gesture of sarcastic endearment they've used since high school.

Her mother chastises her. "Jerilyn, don't do that. A lady should be better."

"I learned it from you," she says.

"Then you should unlearn it."

"Like with smoking," her brother says, thinking he's adding humor to the situation. Her mother doesn't pry into her brother's affairs like she does into Jerilyn's. That's always been unfair, at least in her mind.

Her mother turns in the chair to Jeremy. "You smoke marijuana. I don't think you can say anything."

Jeremy sips from the can of Coke. "Marijuana isn't a cigarette."

"I can't believe you two, my two offspring, my children, ganging up on an old woman."

"No one is ganging up on you," Jerilyn says, taking up the broom again and clutching it in her hands. "You're both ganging up on me. Jere's just trying to be funny; believe me, he isn't."

From the back, Suzanna shouts for Jerilyn's mother asking her to come back here and finish up with Mrs. Rose so she can go take care of Ms. Luna. Her mother sets the tumbler down on the counter behind her and says, "Don't think I haven't forgotten you haven't answered my question. You haven't said what the money's for."

Jerilyn mutters, "Whatever," and reaches for the dustpan.

Her brother reaches it first, telling her he'll help. "Here, let me hold this."

With her brother's help, which amounts to nothing more than holding the dustpan in place by pressing the handle into the floor, something even Jeremy can't screw up, Jerilyn sweeps the hair into the dustpan.

"What do you need the money for?" Jeremy asks between sips, letting the dustpan scoot back an inch with every knock of the broom.

"Would you hold it still?"

"I am holding it still."

"No, you're drinking that damn pop. Focus on what you're doing."

"Fine, fine," Jeremy says. "Here, is that better?"

"It is."

"What do you need the money for?"

"I can't tell you."

"You can't tell me? What do you mean you can't tell me? I'm your brother."

"Jere, I can't tell you. I'm sorry."

"Is it for food?"

"No," she says.

"Clothes?" he asks. "Rent?"

"No," she says. "What do you not understand about I can't tell you?"

"Is it something to do with Wayne?"

Jerilyn doesn't answer.

"It does, doesn't it... Well, don't worry about him. He's in jail."

She turns to look up at him. "He's where?" She didn't believe Brogdon would work that fast. She hadn't even filed the first report like they planned to.

Jeremy sips from the can. "In jail, I'm going to bond him out later."

"What did he do?"

"Got in a fight at Shelia's bar and then got into it with the responding deputy. Quite a bit of trouble."

"They're going to let him out?"

"If I pay the bond, yeah," Jeremy says.

"Why would you pay the bond?"

"Because we're friends, J-Lynn," Jeremy says. "Just because you two couldn't make it work doesn't mean I stop seeing him."

"Some friend."

"Look, I came by here to see how you were doing. You texted me asking for money, and then I find out you did the same with mom; I wanted to make sure you were okay."

"I didn't ask mom for money."

"You asked mom if you could clean at the salon."

"Sooo?"

"That's the same thing." He finishes the can and crunches it, dropping it to the floor.

"What the hell, Jere?"

"What, you've got the broom and the dustpan; sweep it in there."

She does but doesn't like how messy her brother is, discarding the trash, littering, and seemingly caring for no one, including the environment, but himself.

"See, it wasn't that difficult," Jeremy says, lifting up the dustpan handle to trap the hair and the crushed can inside the bin. "But seriously, I came by to talk to you, to ask you what mom was asking you. Why do you need the money? But I guess you're not going to tell me, which is fine. You're an adult. You don't need your little brother looking after you. I also wanted to come tell you Wayne was in jail and I was going to get him."

"Why?"

"Why am I going to get him, or why am I telling you?"

"Both, neither, I don't know. Why do you think I'd care?"

"You are married to the man still, and you kinda hate his guts, so I wanted to be upfront with you because I know what you're like when you're mad, and I wanted to tell you I need Wayne's help with something."

"Which is what?"

"I'll tell you when you tell me why you need money all of a sudden. If I had to guess, it's not because you're not making tips at the diner."

Jerilyn looks at her brother for a moment. She shrugs and says, "What do I care if you go bond him out? He's your friend, as you said."

Jeremy whispers the next part so no one, including her mother, hears what he has to say. "I also wanted you to know. I put the package in your trunk like I told you I would. Sorry for the delay. And I wanted to come in and be seen so no one asks any questions that might bring attention to what you're going to do for me. Are you sure you want to do this? You've always said no before. What's changed?"

Yes, she's sure she wants to do this, and everything's changed. She has a chance at freedom, at a life without Wayne. If she has to sell a few bags of marijuana to make it happen and work extra hours at her mother's salon, then that's what she's going to do. Hopefully, she'll get rid of the marijuana as quickly as possible, and she can go back to living her squeaky-clean life.

But all Jerilyn tells her brother now is, "Thank you."

CHAPTER 9:

JEREMY HALL

JEREMY HALL LEANS AGAINST THE DRIV-er's side of his green Marquis, smoking a cigarette, eyes switching from the front doors of the building to his missing side mirror. Fuck those guys for hurting the only thing in the world he cares about. Hell, he might even say loves.

But that's not what has him upset, and anger isn't the primary emotion, as his mother would say. He still owes Fat Tommy and Short Philly money, and they haven't let him forget it. They constantly hound him for the cash. Short Philly has even taken to calling him in the morning at five o'clock, threatening horrible things, mostly grievous bodily injury if he doesn't pay up soon. Short Philly's mind is twisted. Each threat is different from the last, more detailed, too. Jeremy responds to Short Philly with, "If you got up this early to work out, you wouldn't be called fat."

But Jeremy has a plan. Well, it's more the German's plan ... or a continuation of the German's plan: a plan in which Jeremy is an important player. Not just a driver. Not just a seller. It's an excellent way for Jeremy to get back at Fat Tommy and Short Philly, and everyone else gets something out of it, too.

However, to make the plan work, he needs Wayne—and he needs Wayne to go along with it. If Wayne goes along with it, he'll get something out of it as well.

Wayne fucked up the German's plan when he smashed Daniel's face into the jukebox. Shelia said it was an epic fight. But it ended in Wayne going to jail, which is why Jeremy is here today, parallel parked on the main road outside of the jail, watching the passing traffic as he smokes a cigarette.

The jail doors open. Wayne comes out like he's been shoved. He stumbles a few steps, shoulders heavy from his two-week stay—sun bright on his face, lifting a hand to blot out the glare—then he regains his footing and resumes normal steps. He's wearing the same clothes he'd been arrested in. Jeremy knows from experience the clothes you go in with are the same clothes you leave with.

Seeing Jeremy standing there smoking, Wayne stops at the edge of the curb and waits for a car to pass before he crosses the street. Jeremy acknowledges Wayne by tossing his cigarette to the ground.

Neither man speaks to the other. Neither wants to hang around the jail any longer than necessary.

Wayne rounds the back end of the Marquis, and both men open their respective doors, take their respective seats, and close their doors simultaneously as if they'd practiced and synchronized this action.

Once settled in the driver's seat, Jeremy places both hands on the wheel, glances at the missing side mirror, and sighs. Fucking Short Philly.

He turns the key in the ignition. He had left them hanging there while he smoked, the radio running off the battery. Jeremy didn't care what music was playing. He just wanted something playing in the background.

The turn of the key, or a few frustrating turns, brings the car to life.

In the passenger seat, Wayne says, "You shouldn't let it run off the battery."

Jeremy glances at him. "I shouldn't?"

Wayne isn't looking at him as he talks. Instead, he stares intently on the surrounding foot traffic passing by and the businesses outside the window. Wayne adjusts his side mirror to get a better angle.

Jeremy waits for Wayne to say more, but he doesn't.

And the silence kills Jeremy.

This isn't the first time they've been through this routine—Jeremy picking Wayne up from jail—and it won't be the last. Jeremy can't stand his attitude. Sure, Jeremy's learned not to push his friend too hard. Wayne always comes out in a bad mood, and Jeremy doesn't get it. When he's arrested, Jeremy's always happy walking out of jail. Always says, "If you're leaving, why act depressed?"

The last time, Jeremy had his fill of Wayne's silence and said, "You'd think getting out of jail would make you happier." Wayne just huffed. To which Jeremy said, "You can go back in there if you'd like. I won't be upset for wasting my time."

Wayne shifts in the seat, throwing an arm on the window. "That's why you always have problems getting her to start," he says. "One day, that's going to fucking be a problem. Like you'll need to go somewhere or get gone, and it won't turn over. What are you going to do then?"

"It's fine," Jeremy says and pauses as he maneuvers the Marquis away from the curb. "How are you doing? Heard you and Daniel had quite the brawl."

"'Til that shit stick, Brogdon showed up."

"He was doing his job."

"He's a little too enthusiastic."

Jeremy stops the car at a stop sign. "He likes what he does."

Wayne cuts a sharp look at Jeremy. "You sleeping with him?"

Jeremy blinks a few times, turns to look at Wayne, and says, "What?"

"Didn't know if you were sleeping with him or some- thing with all the defendin' of him, you're doing," Wayne says. "Is he sleeping with your sister, is that why you're being nice about him?"

"No," Jeremy says, lost. "I don't know. How the fuck would I know? What the hell's wrong with you?"

"You seem pretty chummy with him is all."

There's a reason, but Jeremy isn't ready to tell Wayne yet; that's the whole point of picking him up. He can't just lay his cards on the table and say, 'There, that's it.' He has to play the hand, raise, and call as he goes, read how Wayne's going to take it.

"You okay?" Jeremy asks.

Wayne is quiet for a few moments, most likely col- lecting his thoughts if Jeremy had to guess, but really with Wayne, there's no telling. In school, they always accused him of being slow. Wayne didn't help matters by leaning into the stereotype and using his brawn to settle matters instead of his words. Jeremy knows better, though. Wayne isn't stupid or slow. Okay, he's slow, but that's because he's thinking.

Jeremy asks a different question. "What'd the judge say?"

Wayne goes back to staring into the side mirror. "Gave me six months to get set up on a payment plan," he says.

"For beating a guy?"

"No, for the child support."

"What about Cooley? Is he going to be a problem?"

"For who? Me? Cooley's a fucking pussycat."

"He's a biker," Jeremy says. "He used to run with a pretty rough crowd before he settled down."

"A bitch biker," Wayne says. "Now he's become an accountant and pretends to be a biker for a religious cult. He's the type of biker who likes to look tough, wearing those stupid rockers and shit, but it's all for church stuff. He goes to court to sit with little girls whose daddy touches them and do toy rallies and shit, while saying look at me, this pretend tough guy—he's nothing."

"So he's not going to be a problem for you?"

"Lori thinks not. She talked to Nessa. She said Daniel lost three teeth on an Elvis record."

"In the jukebox?" They come to a red light and stop.

"Yep. And he's not happy about it, but he did start the fight," Wayne says. "Nessa told Lori I broke his nose and fractured an orbital socket."

Jeremy heard but says, "Did you really drop money on him after the fight?"

Wayne holds up a finger. "First off, it wasn't a fight. The guy suckered me from behind. A fucking blow to the back, but that's the only blow he got in. It was more of a beating—but I'll never admit that in court—in court, it's a fucking fight. A brawl. Mutual combat."

Traffic starts moving.

Jeremy drives, not looking at Wayne. "Okay," he says, pulling the word out like it's putty, "but how did you get a payment plan? What do you owe?"

Wayne says, "The judge thought it was a wash since he hit me with the pool stick first. Who cares if I put the guy in the hospital for a night? He attacked me with a weapon, so fuck him. He's lucky he didn't end up in jail, too, for assault with a deadly weapon. And you know what? He can't be too mad, seeing we just established he started it. I did pay him... At least that dickweasel deputy let me do that before he placed me in handcuffs."

"So, what are you saying?"

"Your sister's going to suck me dry. You know what the judge said? He told me, 'Son, you're in a hole, the worst kind to be in, and if I were you, I'd rather sell my soul to the devil than be indebted to the government for child support. It's worse, trust me.' Like he fucking knows about it. That fucker's probably never been indebted to anyone but those dicklickers who helped get him elected."

Jeremy doesn't have kids. He never wanted them, so he doesn't understand. "What's that mean? What's he mean?"

"He explained it like this," Wayne says. "I owe twenty-eight grand. God knows how it got to be so much. So, I'm away on work. I told the judge she won't let me see the kids. And he shook his head and said I still had to pay. I say I'm working. And he says I still had to pay. I say, 'Do you pay for services you don't get?' And you know what he does? He looks at me, takes his glasses off, and says, the service I'm paying for is for being with their mother. And then chastises me for thinking about my kids as a business arrangement when he just made a comment like that. Fuck him."

"So you have six months to come up with the money?"

"I have six months to get signed up on a payment plan and get ten percent to Jerilyn. He said normally, he only does a month or two for the payment plan, but he's a busy man, and it's a busy time for the court. So he, smiling like the fucking owl-looking motherfucker from those tootsie pop commercials before he bites the lollypop off the stick, says he'll be real kind to me. He'll give me some extra time. He says he'll gives me six months to get on the payment plan and stay on the plan. In the meantime, even though it was mutual combat, he doesn't want to see or hear about me being arrested or in court for anything else."

"What's that mean?" Though, Jeremy knows what that means.

"Sorta like probation. The fucker. He said in exchange for his kindness, I'm expected to drop at least ten percent of the twenty-eight to Jerilyn before I'm back in court."

"And if you don't?"

"That's what I asked when he asked if I had any questions, but he did it in that way that meant I was supposed to shut up, but fuck him. I said 'What if I don't?' He looks at me all stern and says 'Then you're fucked.'"

"He said fucked?" Jeremy asks. "Like in court?"

"Where you taking me?"

"I have a stop to make."

"So, where's that? I want to go home."

"I don't think that's such a good idea. J-Lynn changed all the locks again."

"Shit," Wayne says. "I just want to take a shower and get to sleep. I'm tired."

"You doing anything the next couple of days?"

"I'm working; what else would I be doing?"

"Want to go get a beer? My treat, might make you a little happier instead of this depressed bullshit."

"Fuck you," Wayne says.

"If you smoked weed, then I'd say let's go do that, but we both know you don't."

Wayne doesn't want to answer questions or talk much. It's clear to Jeremy through Wayne's body language Wayne doesn't want to do anything but go home like he said. The guy looks like a sick puppy dog.

Jeremy turns left and says, "So did he say fucked on the bench?"

"No," Wayne says. "The judge didn't say fucked. He said I'd go to jail for a year, and when I get out, we'll try this again. And then he told me that even if I was in jail, the meter doesn't stop, and being free and earning money is a lot better than being jailed and earning pennies on the dollar. He said don't go that route because twenty-eight grand is likely to turn into forty-eight with interest accruing and me not working."

"Trying to screw you."

"No, Jerilyn's trying to screw me. She could just let it go. Let me see the kids every once in a while. Maybe show some fucking kindness toward me. You know when we're good, we're good, but when we're not, we're not. She's such a bitch about things. If she'd just back off some, we'd get along fine. Be like the old days."

"Still," Jeremy shakes his head, "I don't think it would double."

Wayne says, "I don't think so, too. I think he was using whatchamacallit. Hyperbole. Basically, he's saying I'm fucked."

Jeremy tosses out, "So you need money?"

"What the fuck have I been saying? Yeah, I need money, which is why I want to go home, get some sleep, and get back to work. I talked to Tom Schafer. He said he'd hold the shipment I was about to run because he'd been having problems and didn't mind waiting a while. I told him I appreciated it. He said it had to roll out as soon as I could drive."

"What about the court? Think they'll mind you leaving the state?"

"I need money like yesterday," Wayne says. "Being locked up sucks when you're in business for yourself. I had gigs lined up—jobs to do. I don't even know where my truck is. If it's towed, how am I going to pay for that?"

"Don't worry about the truck."

Wayne looks at Jeremy, but Jeremy doesn't take his eyes off the road. He can feel Wayne's eyes burrowing into him. "Why?"

"When you got picked up, Kevin Alexander called."

"Who the fuck is Kevin Alexander?"

"You screw Shelia, but you don't know the name of her boss?"

"The faggot?"

"I don't think you want to call him that to his face."

"But it's the fairy. That's who you're talking about. Why did he call?"

"He knew we were friends. He doesn't like you by the way."

"I know. He tried to ban me from the place, but Shelia doesn't pay him any mind at all."

"He called about your truck, and…" Jeremy lets the last part die to build the interest. It's true. Kevin called, asking why Jeremy's friend busted Daniel's face when they had a job lined up. Jeremy told him it was a fluke deal, but he did have an idea. Kevin said, "No, I'm the one with the ideas … and I think we have the same idea."

Now, Wayne says, "And what?"

"An opportunity."

"Opportunity?"

"A job he wants done."

"What type of job?"

"A job," Jeremy says, not quite ready to spill the details yet.

Wayne eyes Jeremy. Then he asks, "How did you pay for my bond?"

"Do you really want to know?"

"Do I?"

"Kevin covered some of it."

"And the rest? I know you don't have the money."

"My mother. I borrowed some, but with her—she's like a giant clam, and the money is the pearl. I reach my hand in and get what I want. Sure she's willing to give it but not freely. And just like that big clam, she slams her mouth closed, and my hand is trapped inside."

All that's a lie. Thanks to Kevin—the German—Jeremy has a ton of money. He just can't always spend it. Slowly, he's been funneling cash Suzanna's way, letting her wash it through his mother's salon. So while his mother thinks business is booming and Jeremy's a freeloader, he's been reaping a benefit.

Jeremy says, "Hey, I'm here. I have to answer twenty fucking questions about it?"

"Your mom, really, dude?"

"She's asking what's it for, why don't I have any? I tell her what it's for, bonding you out. And then she's like, why can't I get it from my job? She knows what I do, and I say, well, I let Jerilyn have a couple of grand a few weeks back, so I'm a little short at the moment. Tell her you loaned her some heavy amounts of cash, too—under the guise of working the last couple weeks at the salon, and you didn't jump her shit this bad because she wouldn't explain what it was for."

Wayne raises his hand. "Hold up. You loaned Jerilyn money?"

"Marijuana. So yeah, it's as good as money."

Wayne's mouth drops open. "You loaned Jerilyn ... the goody freaking two shoes ... some marijuana ... to do what with it? Sell?"

Jeremy nods. "Yeah."

"What the fuck does she need so badly that she will sell marijuana?"

"Weren't you listening? She wouldn't say."

"Samuel Moody don't mind her selling marijuana?"

"Samuel doesn't know about it, I'm sure."

Wayne kicks back in the passenger seat, looking like a man who's seen everything now.

Wayne says, "That man, he's more than her boss. Every time things got physical, the next day, after she left for work, I'd open the front door to find this old one-armed black dude standing there, a white goatee like Samuel L. Jackson or Frederick Douglass, standing there chastising me about hitting his best waitress. 'Course I'd say, I don't know what you're talking about. He'd say, yes, I did. He'd say, 'I know what you're doing.' He'd say, 'What you're doing within the confines of matrimonial bliss is your business, but when my business affects his business, then it's his business.'"

"What's that mean?"

"If she shows up with a black eye, that's something customers notice, and he can't have that because it's a small town in a lot of ways, and he can't have people asking questions."

"You know why, don't you?"

"I know his business is a cash business for the Sirianos, so I figured the Sirianos use Samuel's place to wash their money. Samuel doesn't need anyone asking extra questions. Other than taking a couple of cash bundles now and then and fudging the books, that guy runs a squeaky-clean operation. Fires anyone who pops hot on a drug test, and he has everyone, himself included because the boss can't be separate from his employees, set up on a six-month testing rotation. Jerilyn used to bitch 'bout how she had to go pee in a cup every so often. I told her she doesn't even drink. She does smoke, and I guess that's something, but it's just cigarettes. She had nothing to worry about. She said she knows but asked have I ever tried to catch pee in a cup?"

"Well, of course, you have," Jeremy says.

"Not as a woman, though. That's the point. So what's Jerilyn need money for so badly she'll sell marijuana and risk Samuel's wrath?"

"She wouldn't say."

"Jere ... don't fuck me around."

"Look, all I know, it's something to do with the kids. She said not having you, not having your child support, things are tight, and she needs money. One of my nieces isn't sick, is she?"

"How the fuck would I know? I've been locked up."

"Anyways, I didn't have the cash needed to bond you out, and Kevin had come to me with an opportunity, and I thought you'd be interested in it. It might help with your situation."

"So you thought bonding me out could be part of the terms, so I'm in this whether I want to be or not."

Jeremy hadn't thought about it like that.

Wayne says, "I don't like being committed to things without my consent." Wayne crosses his arms. "So, what have you signed me up for?"

"First off," Jeremy says, flipping his blinker on and slowing to take a right turn, "the bond was separate. You can still say no. I told him I had to discuss it with you first."

"Why?" Wayne couldn't sound more suspicious.

"Because you'll be the one with the most to lose."

"Jesus, I don't like the sound of this. What the hell did you get me involved in?"

"Calm down."

"Don't tell me to calm down," Wayne says.

Jeremy pulls the car into the parking lot of Gold's Bar and stops across two parking spaces.

"Alright, we're here; I don't see my truck," Wayne says. "Where's my truck?"

"Around back," Jeremy says, turning in the driver's seat. "Kevin has the keys inside. It's safe."

Wayne looks at Jeremy, then at the front doors of Gold's. "You know what, Jere? I like you and all, and thanks for bonding me out, but fuck you."

"It's alright. No one has damaged your truck. Kevin ensured it would be fine."

"I'm sure he did, but let me guess, he wants to see me first to get the truck."

"That would be correct."

"So what's the fucking job?"

"You won't like it."

"Doesn't sound like I have much of a choice, so just spill it, so I know what I need to do... How much does it pay?"

"A lot."

Wayne eyes him from the passenger seat. "What's a lot?"

Jeremy has Wayne where he wants him. "A lot, a lot."

"You know what, Jere," Wayne says, tugging on the handle, popping the latch for the door, "I'm good. Get my keys from him. I'm not talking to him. I'll see if Shelia can take me home. I have a load to take out to Philly tomorrow morning, so I'm going to go home and crash."

CHAPTER 10:

WAYNE KISSEE

WAYNE KISSEE WAITS OUTSIDE THE glass door for Fat Tommy to come to the door, turn the lock, and let him into the building. It's early, the sun is still coming up, and the air is crisp. Wayne jams his fists deeper into the pockets of his ratty letterman jacket, black and gold, threadbare and worn, as his breath crystallizes in the air. He taps his booted foot against the ground.

Wayne stands outside a subsidiary of Fat Tommy's family business, Schafer Logistics. This is the original location. In the '90s, the family business moved to a more central Tulsa location. This place is in a suburb, squeezed into some warehouse space near the railroad tracks off 9th Street. The storefront looks like any kind of cheap mini storage with the same glass front doors dotting the prefabricated metal siding interspaced with brown-orange rolling garage doors every other opening. The building is larger than one story, but everything is on the ground floor. What's not siding is painted cinder block. The color matches the internal beige. The main warehouse space, including the loading ramps, is around the back. Wayne knows the storage area extends through the business weaving through the fabricated internal walls erected to separate warehouse space from office space.

Schafer Logistics owns the building but doesn't fill it all with its operations. Several of the office suites and warehouse spaces sit empty. One office suite houses a chapter of Blue Star Mothers, which Tommy rents to them for one dollar as part of his goodwill commitment to the neighborhood. He says it was something his father started and claims he's passionate about it. Tommy isn't into heavy crime, but as he says: crime is crime, so it does take a bit of sleight of hand to keep everything copacetic with the neighbors.

A pizza place that isn't too bad is crammed into the north corner of the building, and now and then, Tommy allows a chef to open a pop-up restaurant in one of the empty suites just to keep things interesting. The building next door is a vet, and on the other side of that is a transmission repair place that works on all of Tommy's trucks. Tommy is a silent partner, which means he owns it, and the loud partner pays a percentage even if business is slow.

Tommy appears in the glass, a shadowy figure walking down a long hallway with golden carpet and dingy beige walls, tobacco-stained, trimmed in brown and gold.

Tommy doesn't hurry.

So Wayne waits in the cold.

He waits because he's late. He should have been here more than an hour ago, but Lori wouldn't take no for an answer on breakfast or the morning quickie. Wayne could have done without the breakfast, but the coffee was good.

Today, Fat Tommy's dressed in a gray long-sleeve shirt and beige slacks, unlit cigar stuffed in the corner of his mouth. He turns the deadbolt with a click and pushes the door open to allow Wayne into the building.

"You're late," Fat Tommy mutters, removing the unlit cigar from his lips. The end is a chewed, mangled mess. "You were supposed to be here an hour ago. What happened? We've been waiting for you."

"I overslept," Wayne says.

It isn't entirely a lie. He did oversleep, but that's because he crashed at Lori's, and she kept him up late, blowing off some steam.

Getting out of jail has a way of putting Wayne in a lousy mood: going in and coming out. It feels like it's never-ending. It started when he was in high school, with bullshit things, and now thanks to Jerilyn, it continues. Each stint behind bars only solidifies the reality, his reality, that unless he can come up with some serious cash and do so soon, he's bound to go back.

Especially if Deputy Brogdon gets his say.

The fuckin' guy practically rubbed it in Wayne's face when he drove him from the bar to jail, telling Wayne while watching him in the rearview mirror, "I'm going to fuck your life up." The smug bastard.

In handcuffs in the back of the car, Wayne said, "What's your problem, man? Why are you always hassling me?"

Brogdon said he knew why, calling Wayne and guys like him a cancer. Brodgon said Wayne destroys all the good things and people he touches. He said that's why guys like Wayne can't have nice things. He said Wayne's the reason why a lotta guys get the reputation they have, the reason why women don't trust men. He said Wayne's in the same category as those assholes and predators, and he called Wayne an abuser—a domestic abuser.

But hell, the dickweasel could have been describing himself. He chastised Wayne for putting a good woman through hell 'cause Wayne doesn't know how to act like a man, check his temper, or show proper love. He said Wayne's probably never had a role model for a real relationship. He doesn't know how to do it right.

Brogdon said all those things while driving, eyes glancing up at Wayne in the mirror, eyes bloodshot. His eyes were not showing anger; they were showing glee, like every fucker in high school did when Jerilyn and Wayne broke things off. Wayne called those periods cooling down periods. He never really considered them broken up. He'd go fuck someone else, maybe just go on a date or two, and wait for Jerilyn to come to her senses and give him a call. Once he called, but he didn't apologize 'cause it's not his style, and he told her it wouldn't happen again.

Wayne would have shoved a guy like Brogdon into a locker just for the fun of it. Wayne would've picked on the guy—nothing too bad, nothing like kids today, making them want to shoot up their schools. 'Course, those kids don't have guys like Wayne to make sure they know their place. He wouldn't have done anything that would make Brogdon feel like he wasn't part of the group, but he would have made it clear that he was only allowed to be around the group for Wayne to poke fun at, give rides, and make themselves appear better in front of the ladies.

Brogdon would be that guy. A beta male: Wayne once read a book about picking up women and how guys like Wayne are considered alphas. Brogdon's not that. Not a real man. He showed it in the car, giving Wayne shit that way. 'Cause a real man would have said it to his face, not stare up at him in the mirror.

A real man could handle Jerilyn. A guy like Brogdon wouldn't know the first thing about where to fucking begin. The first time Jerilyn lost her shit, Brogdon would hit the road. He wouldn't have had kids with her or put up with her bullshit: her big dreams or her shitty disposition.

Wayne did. He did all those things until he couldn't. He had two wonderful angels with her, kids she wanted but now only uses for the money. Wayne likes to remind her about when she gets on him about the money, about his visitation. "You chose to have them girls. You act like they're a burden."

To hear Brogdon talk, it sounds like he's sweet on Jerilyn, like he has an agenda. Maybe he's trying to get Wayne out of the picture so that he can move in on her. Brogdon wouldn't be the first. It certainly fits with Wayne's first read of the fucker all those years ago, dumbstruck by Jerilyn's tits.

So in the car, staring at Brogdon with contempt, he said, "Are you doing all this for Jerilyn? Shit, man, you can have her. I don't want her no more." Adding, "But she won't want you—'cause you ain't me."

All Brogdon said was, "You don't get it, do you? I'm going to make sure you never see the light of day. I'm going to lock you away so that you can't ever get to her again, hurt her. I'm going to take away any chance of you seeing or having a relationship with your kids."

Wayne asked him if that was a threat.

The dickweasel said, "It's a promise."

Normally something like that wouldn't bother Wayne, but then again, things haven't been going Wayne's way

lately, and the whole time he was in jail, his mind kept going back to Brogdon's eyes in the mirror and how Brogdon meant it. He kept thinking about how the deputy isn't any better than Wayne and how he was bragging about how he's going to fuck with Wayne until Jerilyn's alone and his. Until Brogdon has his shot... Shit, he's probably already called her, but a guy like him, he's a dickhead; he probably wouldn't even use his real number. He wouldn't know what to say. He'd probably talk all about himself, bragging about cop shit, bragging about things he did and had done. All of it nothing. Smoke.

And all those thoughts pissed Wayne off. It pisses him off even now. He knows guys like Brogdon and knows if Jerilyn ever gives in, sleeps with him... fucks him, it'd be a pity fuck 'cause Brogdon wouldn't rape her. Wayne doesn't think he would, but who knows? Maybe he would; maybe he's that type of shitbag. One of two things would happen: Brogdon would take it as a conquest and move on, which is shitty and would hurt Jerilyn, or he'd become so fucking clingy he'd be a problem—a stalker. He would become someone Jerilyn would ask Wayne to take care of.

Then there was the judge laying it on thick. And then there was Brogdon again, the fuckhead, waiting for him near Release with his blue jeans and flannel, hair cut tight and recently trimmed, with his leg up on the wall, wearing boots that have never seen dirt, just waiting for Wayne. Brogdon didn't say anything either. He just dropped the foot, pulled a folded piece of paper out of his back pocket, and handed it to Wayne. He waited for Wayne to accept and then said, "You've been served. This is a Protective Order; read it. It says stay the fuck away from your wife."

He made sure to do it while Wayne was still in handcuffs, still inside the jail.

Wayne wanted to kill him but didn't.

Then the conversation with Jeremy didn't make any of it any better. What was he thinking, trying to get Wayne wrapped into something with Shelia's boss? That guy doesn't like Wayne, and Wayne doesn't like him, the slimy fuck.

Lori made it all better. He knew she would. Just like this morning and every time they're together, Lori, unlike Jerilyn, is happy to see him and happy to help him feel better. She doesn't get on him about being gone, going to jail, nothing.

Not like Fat Tommy, who at the door, studies Wayne's face for a moment, judging him, then says, "Don't do it again."

Wayne steps past him, squeezing in through the door, careful not to touch the door jam or Tommy's skinny out-stretched arm.

Tommy pokes his head out the door, looks left then right, then jams the cigar back in the corner of his mouth and pulls the door shut. He throws the deadbolt.

"This way," Tommy says, walking past Wayne, leading the way.

Wayne follows with his hands still in his jacket pockets.

Tommy takes Wayne to a cheap conference room several doors deep into Schafer Logistics.

"We own the whole building," Tommy explains. "Everyone that works here knows what we do. I tell you that 'cause you've only ever been here after hours, and this is a bit different than the ones we've done before, so don't feel like you have to keep silent or anything."

Tommy shows Wayne into the room. A plump man with a bruised face sits at the prefabricated table. Tommy introduces him as Earl and says he'll be helping out today and all future runs. Earl reminds Wayne of a character actor who was in HBO's *Deadwood* with a brown scraggly beard and hair, a barrel of a body, and red cheeks. Wayne can't think of the actor's name and knows he's been in a bunch of other things, but it doesn't matter; Earl looks like that guy: Carhartt jacket and blue jeans.

Wayne nods to Earl, who throws his head back in response, his right arm stretched out and resting on the table.

Tommy tells Wayne to sit. "Want coffee or something?"

Wayne tells him he does.

Tommy leaves Wayne in the room with Earl.

Wayne, hovering over the chair, asks Earl, "What happened to your face?" circling his face for effect.

"A disagreement," Earl says. He leans back in the seat. "It's why you're going to drive, not me."

That doesn't answer Wayne's question.

Earl adds, "I'll let Tommy explain it to you."

Wayne settles into the seat. "Fine, man."

Short Philly appears in the doorway, just as round as Earl, if not bigger, dressed in a dark blue shiny shirt and nice slacks, clothes probably run in the thousands for him, just like his waistline. "You made it; about fucking time."

Wayne tosses his head back in acknowledgment.

"You're late," Short Philly says. "You want coffee or something? Tommy already offered you?"

Wayne says he did.

On cue, Tommy comes back with three Styrofoam cups of what Wayne assumes is coffee. Outside the doorway, Tommy says, "You're in the way."

"I'm in the way. What the fuck? Wait your turn," Short Philly says. "You get me a cup of coffee?"

"Get your own cup of coffee," Tommy says. "Or go sit down, but get the hell out of the way."

Short Philly raises a hand up in frustration. He enters the room and sits at the table.

Tommy strolls into the room and passes out the cups of coffee, dropping the last one in front of Short Philly. "Here you go, you fat fuck."

"Tommy," Short Philly says, "just don't."

Tommy moves to the head of the table. "Wayne, this run's going to be a bit different from the ones you've done for us in the past."

"Why's that?" Wayne asks.

Short Philly throws himself across the table, hunching his shoulders. "We've had problems."

"What sort of problems?" Wayne asks. He doesn't wait for an answer. He adds, circling his face again, "Anything to do with that guy's face?"

Tommy says, "Yes, business has been difficult."

"Which is why you called me," Wayne says. He uses his hands as he talks. "You all, you run a trucking company, which means if you are coming to a guy like me, if past is any indicator, it's because you either fucked something up or are in a rush. Since I've never been here during daylight hours, I'm guessing it's a bit of both. That guy's face confirms you have problems. I am a hotshotter. I run loads fast and anywhere you want to go. You know that. But what I don't get is why the guy who couldn't get the job done is here."

"He's helping you on this," Tommy says. "And you're right, we've had issues. You haven't been here during the daytime. This location is for running this product all over, legal and out of state. And you've done a couple of runs, small runs, but still, you've done a couple runs to Philly's people. The problems are since the old man went down, we've started running loads in small light trucks, so we don't have to file anything with DPS or have any issues with weight or nothing. We don't want to attract attention."

"But we've attracted attention," Short Philly interjects.

Tommy sighs heavily. "We have. Those small loads have put us behind with Philly's people, and now that we've been hit a couple of times—God knows how the fuck that's happened—it's put my reputation on the line, and we've had to change practices again."

Wayne says, "Good 'cause I don't drive semis for a reason."

"No one's asking you to drive one," Tommy says. "That's fine. With the way the world's going, everyone is having supply and demand issues. When things with Siriano cool down, then we can start running semi-loads again, no one the wiser, but right now, the Indians are circling, and I'm not sure who's doing it."

Short Philly clears his throat, hand to his mouth. "My fucking bet is it's the German."

Tommy motions to him. "Philly, we've talked about this."

Philly's nostrils flare, and he glares at Tommy. "Yeah, we've talked about it," he says, "and I think the guy who benefits is the same fucker who sells marijuana. We've all heard the stories, the rumors. Accidents happen to the competition, people disappearing. And all done by a guy that no one, outside of a certain circle, that fuck's best friend," pointing at Wayne "knows who the fuck the German is. My people are pissed!"

"Philly," Tommy says again, urging Short Philly to calm down, "we don't know that."

"The people we work for, they're fucking livid. These bullshit cocksuckers should show themselves. Let me take a whack at them. I bet they wouldn't be so fucking cocky then."

"You've been robbed?" Wayne asks. "I haven't heard nothing about it."

"That's the point," Short Philly says.

Tommy says, "We've taken pains to keep the information out of circulation."

"But you don't know who is hitting your trucks?"

"No," Tommy says.

"And my people want some product, their product," Short Philly says. "Product they paid for. Product promised to them. We can only blame the pandemic and changing times so much. Iris said she could keep the supply going. She hasn't. We've put them off for a while now, but that's not going to last. Not good business."

"This is why we are taking a chance in sending a bigger load and having Wayne do it," Tommy says. "Wayne, we need you to take a box truck to Philly."

Wayne clears his sinuses. "I don't drive anything but my rig."

Tommy says, "It's not up for debate; you're taking a box truck. It's still small enough we don't have to fuck around with manifest or weight. It's packed with furniture; you're hot-shotting someone's shit as a mover. That's your cover story, got it?"

"I don't drive anyone's rig," Wayne says. "Not semis, not box trucks. I only take my truck. I don't trust others with my safety or freedom."

Short Philly, red-faced and short of breath, slaps the table. "What the fuck do you not understand? You don't have a fucking choice. In fact, you're not leaving here except in that truck, and you're going to make our delivery date. We've made promises, and they need to be kept."

Wayne digests the situation. He throws his chin toward Earl. "Fine, so what's this guy doing?"

Tommy says, "He's going with you."

Short Philly adds, "Trail you in a car behind the truck."

Tommy holds up two bony fingers, joints swollen and out of proportion to the long digits. "For two reasons. One, to make sure you don't have any problems. These guys have had our routes down and hit our guys when they stop, hijacking the truck. We can't figure out how they know our schedule. Don't know if they are watching our drivers leave or have someone inside."

"We don't think it's someone inside," Short Philly says, "which is why it's just the four of us in this room that know anything about what you're doing."

Tommy says, "Earl made the drive out to the farm to get the product, and then he got hit a couple of weeks ago, right before you were arrested."

Wayne doesn't like it, but what's he going to say?

Wayne asks, "And the second reason?"

Short Philly says, "He's going to make sure you fucking stick to the schedule and don't stop."

Tommy says, "I've put an ice chest with water and sandwiches in the cab, two thermoses of coffee, and some piss jugs, so you don't have to stop."

Wayne's not sure he heard that right. "Let me get this straight; you want me to drive straight through? What if I have to shit?"

"Don't," Short Philly says. "Hold it."

Wayne stares at him. "What is this, grade school? If I wanted to do that, I'd stay in jail. I'll shit and stop when I want to shit and stop."

Tommy says, "Come with me." He stands from the table. He leads Wayne and the others out of the conference room to the back warehouse, where a yellow box truck is parked. Entering the space, Tommy says, "We've packed the back end in every conceivable way. It took a couple of days to outfit. We had to bring in a load from a farm."

Short Philly adds, "Cops hit it just after the truck left, so we had to ensure it was clean. It's clean."

Tommy opens the driver's side door and climbs halfway up into the cab. He comes back down with something in his hand.

"Is that a gun?" Wayne asks.

Tommy shows him the 9mm semi-automatic, black, fifteen-round capacity.

Wayne raises his hands. "I don't do guns."

Short Philly places a hand on the back of Wayne's neck like a father would with a child, pulling Wayne closer and turning him so he can see Short Philly's eyes. Wayne sees how serious he is and that Wayne doesn't really have a choice. Short Philly squeezes and says, "Today, this run, you'll carry the gun ... and if you get hit, you'll use it."

CHAPTER 11:

GABRIELLA LUNA

GABRIELLA LUNA WATCHES THE SUN come up. It's bright and blinds her, the light blasting across her windshield, catching the cool dew on the glass. The orange-yellow rays show how chilly the air is outside the car and the promise of the new day's warmth. It means the morning is here, which means she's still here, which means she hasn't slept, hasn't eaten, and hasn't been home. She's been sitting here, across the street from Gold's Bar, waiting to kill Kevin Alexander.

Gabby parked outside of the strip club across the street to lie in wait, to watch, and to think. Nobody asked her why she was there or what she was doing except one stripper, a lovely blonde girl who looked twelve but claimed to be twenty, who was maybe one-hundred pounds. She reminded Gabby of herself when she met Alejandro. She's a young, lithe thing with a strong body, healthy hair, perky tits, youthful ignorance.

It reminded her of a different time.

The girl came by after two in the morning. Gabby watched her exit the club, look around as if looking for a ride, smoke, and then flick a cigarette to the ground. She then noticed Gabby in the car. Gabby hid the gun in her purse as the girl strolled over to her vehicle, a silver Toyota Camry. She walked with one arm bent up, palm to the air, fingers out, with her overly large purse that doubled as a clothing bag hanging from her arm, a strap hanging over the side. She was dressed in a fluorescent orange Sherpa jacket resembling a feather boa rather than something a guide in the Himalayas would wear. Certainly, nothing Gabby's ever worn. She moved gracefully in her high heels, never once stumbling, feet shuffling forward quickly in short, small strides. When she reached the car window, she bent at the waist, with the firm posture of a dancer, and knocked on the glass, her delicate and boney fingers balled into a loose fist.

Gabby sat there, staring straight ahead, trying not to make eye contact, mentally sending signals she didn't want to talk, wanting the girl to go away. The girl didn't mind or couldn't read Gabby's mind. She knocked again.

Once Gabby rolled down the window, the girl asked if Gabby was okay. She had a thick country accent, "I noticed you sittin' over here when I went into work, which was at four this afternoon, and now it's after two in the morning, and you're still here—everythin' alright, hun? Need anything?"

The woman was fishing for Gabby to open up to her, tell her yes, she needed help—help to kill a man. Gabby didn't say that.

Gripping the edges of her purse in her lap, Gabby looked the girl's way and told her she was okay.

She thought about what lie to tell the girl, thinking of telling her how she was thinking of going in and applying for a job but she hadn't decided yet if she wanted to work there. She figured that wasn't very believable. She didn't fit the mold, didn't look like the skinny things coming and going out of the place, not anymore. Maybe she could have when she was younger.

So instead, Gabby said she got into a fight with her boyfriend and needed time to think. "I didn't know where else to go."

That was believable. Passing headlights revealed Gabby's tear-soaked cheeks, which helped sell it, and Gabby couldn't help but stare at the girl who studied her.

The girl nodded and said in an all-knowing tone of voice, "To see if he shows up here, right? I did that once; tried to catch the bastard outside my best friend's house."

Careful to keep the purse closed to not reveal the gun, Gabby retrieved and then wiped her cheek with a napkin and nodded, pretending to go along with the girl's misplaced conclusions.

The girl showed Gabby appropriate sympathy, turning the corners of her mouth down dramatically to make a sad face. She patted Gabby's shoulder through the open window, telling her, "Be strong, girl," which was both uncomfortable and awkward for them both. Then a car honked, breaking the moment, and the girl turned, face transforming into an ecstatic smile. She said that was her ride without turning to look at Gabby and shuffled off in those heels in those same small strides.

Leaving Gabby alone with herself and her thoughts. Leaving her to wait to kill Kevin Alexander.

Gabby doesn't know why after the whole night, she hasn't either done it yet or left.

At first, she was waiting for business to slow down. Then she was waiting for him to come out of the bar. Kevin Alexander did come out a couple times. The guy's hard to miss, can't dress. He smoked a couple times and enjoyed the cooler air. And now she's just waiting, and she doesn't understand why she's postponing this—why hasn't she done it yet?

It should be easy.

Kevin killed her boy.

That's all she needs to know.

She should just drive across the street, get out of her Toyota, go inside, and shoot him. That was her original plan, but that didn't happen. She didn't do that. She couldn't do that. She doesn't know why. It makes her feel like she's failed as a mother. Flavia told her the truth about her boy. Gabby believed her. She didn't have to see any evidence. Her heart isn't a court of law. Her son is gone, and Flavia provided the answers, the names. Flavia told her where to find Kevin Alexander and gave her the gun to do the deed. All of it should have been clear, straightforward.

'Course, Gabby can't help but feel Flavia wound her up like a doll and set her loose. So maybe that's why she hasn't done it yet. Maybe there's another reason. Maybe there is no reason at all.

Gabby glances down at the small silver revolver in her lap. Five rounds. A metal cylinder. Black hand grip. Small. Smith and Wesson. Light. Something Flavia thought Gabby could handle. Something Gabby can handle.

In her mind, Gabby saw it so clearly. She sees how she would do it. She sees how it would happen. It would be like that scene in *The Godfather*. But instead of going to the bathroom to retrieve the gun, instead of having dinner with the man, which Gabby doesn't think is something she could ever do—she would sit down with Kevin Alexander; she doesn't want to hear his voice or know why he killed Reni—she would just walk inside, find him at the bar like Flavia said, then she would shoot him, placing all five rounds into Kevin's chest. She would drop the gun. Maybe sit down and have a drink; wait for the cops.

Unlike the movie, Gabby wouldn't run off. There wouldn't be a car waiting for her. She wouldn't flee to Italy. No, she intended—intends—to stand up for what she did and tell the world why. "He killed my son."

That's what she would say.

"My boy, my wonderful boy. He killed him and made him disappear."

That's why yesterday Gabby went to Whisper's Salon—Rumor Hall is the owner and an old friend, and Suzanna did her hair—she wanted to look her best.

Gabby's been a customer for years. She and Rumor used to have beers together. They would talk about men who didn't love them, the men who they couldn't stop loving or seeing. Often they were the same men. They talked about kids and single motherhood, schools, jobs and about the salon, about gray hair, and about the right hair coloring to cover up aging. They talked about how nothing stopped time or changed what's happened.

After the haircut and Rumor argued with her two children, Gabby asked Rumor to help her with her make-up. She said she had a big date. Rumor obliged. So Gabby watched the woman's deadbeat son, the poker star wannabe—not that Gabby ever seriously considered someone a star for sitting around a table and bullshitting—leave in a rush to go pick up a friend from jail, if she heard right. The daughter, who worked the broom, wiped the stations and tidied up while managing two little girls in the back. She reminded Gabby of her younger self, of those conversations with the girl's mother, and of Renaldo.

Then Gabby went home, changed into something nice but comfortable, and drove to Gold's. First, she parked in the parking lot of the bar, three spaces from the front door, under a camera. Later, she moved across the street to ... wait? She still doesn't know why. He killed her son.

But he's a son, someone's son, right?

All night, Kevin never left the bar to go anywhere. He must sleep inside somewhere.

At six in the morning, Gabby's about to give up. She can't go in there. She can't kill him. Not today. Maybe tomorrow.

As she's about to leave, shifting to drive, something catches her attention. She sees a lifted pickup truck with a loud exhaust pull off the main street and park in the bar's parking lot. A well-dressed young man wearing sunglasses gets out and goes inside. A minute later, a man on a motorcycle with a bald head, or balding, hard to tell from here, wearing a black motorcycle vest and blue jeans, arrives and goes inside the bar. Finally, a green Marquis rolls up and parks by the bar's front doors. The driver gets out and stretches. He leaves the car running; Gabby can hear the music from here. He sucks up the last of whatever he was smoking and tosses it to the ground. Gabby recognizes the boy's face. She knows him, watched him drink a can of Coke at Whispers, and watched him rush out to bond a friend out of jail.

Rumor's boy.

Why is he here?

Slamming his driver-side door shut, muting the music, he joins the others inside.

Gabby shifts back to park and waits.

The three are inside for less than ten minutes. Gabby watches as they walk out of the bar, all dressed the same, like they are going to work. Dark blue coveralls, tan jackets. Two of them are holding something flimsy and green in their hands. She knows it's each of the men she observed arriving because of how they walk. The young, good-looking man carries a shotgun, holding it low at his side, trying to conceal it by his leg, but Gabby spots the telltale shape. The young man gets in the passenger seat. The bald man comes out of the bar with his hands shoved in his pocket and gets in the backseat behind the driver. Rumor's boy, the driver, stops at the car door and slips the flimsy green thing over his head, pulling it all the way down to his neck, revealing it's a ski mask, then he rolls it back up to his forehead like a beanie.

Guns. Masks. Matching outfits. What is Rumor's boy doing? What's he into?

Rumor's boy—Gabby searches her memory for his name—Jeremy. He slips in behind the wheel. The bald man in the back playfully slaps the back of Jeremy's head, skewing the beanie/ski mask. Jeremy backs out of the space and maneuvers his vehicle to the parking lot exit. He throws his blinker on and takes a right onto the main roadway.

Gabby doesn't know why, but she follows, pulling out of her spot and edging into traffic, taking a left to follow them north. She's careful to keep her distance.

While she drives, she thinks that Jeremy and Reni were the same age. How they weren't friends, but to their mothers, there was still a connection. The two boys probably never said two words to each other, but their mothers did, bragging or, in some cases, bitching about what each son was doing. Rumor never talked much about her daughter. She's younger than her brother. The daughter always seemed to have a boyfriend; if Gabby remembers correctly, she fell hard for some shitty high school sweetheart. Both boys had their troubles. Rumor used to complain about Jeremy's marijuana use. She couldn't keep it out of his mouth. She tried, Gabby knows, but working all the time made it tough to be home, which was something Gabby was all too familiar with. Reni wasn't doing well in school and was skipping class. She suspected he was running with a rough crowd. She couldn't understand it and would tell him, "Why? I give you a good home, food; why do you act like it's nothing?"

Reni didn't understand the value of what his mother was doing, the value in the good home, the good food. All he seemed to care about were sneakers and looking nice, always spending his money on shoes and clothes, and if he wasn't able to afford it, he just took it, shoplifting, which resulted in several phone calls from police officers asking Gabby to leave work to come pick up her son, or leave work to take her son to court, or leave work to make sure he did his community service.

It was Rumor—when Reni was having these hard times in school, and after Gabby caught him smoking marijuana—who suggested Gabby introduce him to his father. Rumor is the only other person who knew who Renaldo's father was. She said, "Sometimes a boy just needs to know his father."

But Alejandro didn't want Renaldo to know he was his father. Alejandro wanted nothing to do with Gabby or the boy. He had his own family. He didn't need them, but Renaldo needed him. That's what Rumor said.

"So, fine," Rumor said, "don't give the bastard a choice. He doesn't want to know him, then make it to where he doesn't have an option." She explained that Gabby could just start leaving Renaldo at the restaurant while she worked. It was in the same building. She could keep an eye on him and make sure he got his homework done. Rumor said, "The best part is when Alejandro finally comes around to the boy, 'cause he will, he'll feel like it was his decision, not yours."

And that's what happened.

But maybe Reni didn't need to know who his father was. Knowing him led to his death and disappearance. Knowing him led to Renaldo killing his father. Maybe Gabby made a mistake. Maybe if she hadn't done that, Reni would still be alive. Maybe he would have been a businessman like she knew he wanted. Reni loved selling things, used to trade shoes for other shoes like some kids did baseball cards.

Driving behind Jeremy's Marquis, Gabby is careful to not be seen. She keeps a few spaces back. She watches as Jeremy drives to a suburb and watches as they park around the corner of a building. Gabby pulls into a nearby gas station to watch them watching something. Then she sees a yellow box truck and a small Chevy Impala pull out from behind the building across the street where the others have parked and watches as it enters the main roadway.

The Marquis falls in behind the Impala. Gabby falls in behind the Marquis. They travel like this for some time. The Impala on the box truck's tail, the Marquis a few cars back keeping pace, and Gabby behind them.

They travel north toward one of the highways that cross the state and go out of state, I-44. The box truck could have gotten on any of the other highways, but it took city streets and traveled the speed limit to make a straight shot for I-44.

Traffic thins and then compresses. Now the Marquis is near the box truck's passenger side, obscured by another car and a pick-up truck with hay forks. Gabby can only see the corner of the vehicle, the rear taillight. She's directly behind the Impala, which is still behind the box truck. She can see both drivers in their side mirrors. The driver of the box truck looks bored. Drives like it, too. The fat man who drives the Impala appears to be alert. His suspicious eyes scan everything yet see nothing. He doesn't notice the Marquis, doesn't look side to side, and barely checks his rearview mirror. He never sees Gabby.

Then everyone comes to a stop at a traffic light. The fat man unscrews the lid of a thermos and fills the lid with something hot, probably coffee. Gabby watches him in his mirror, his window down, as the filled green metal lid slips out of his fingers. It must splash across his crotch. She hears him curse as he jumps in his seat and swats at his lap, taking his eyes off the box truck.

Gabby's so distracted by the man in the Impala that she nearly misses the appearance of the younger man who's carrying the shotgun, pulling his evergreen ski mask down over his face. The sight surprises her. It's surreal. The man walking with a gun, wearing that ski mask, marching between the car and the box truck. He doesn't look around. He's intent on circling the box truck to get to the driver's side. Gabby notices another ski-masked figure, already standing in front of the truck, a silver pistol pointed at the driver of the box truck, yelling at him, giving him directions.

The yells reach the fat man in the Impala, who looks up from swatting at his burnt crotch and yells out, "Shit." He jumps in his seat and scrambles, searching for something.

The light changes, and a couple of cars take off through the intersection. Several don't.

The ski mask at the front of the truck yells louder. His voice sounds stressed. He says a name that Gabby doesn't understand. Then there is more screaming and yelling. The shotgun man hasn't reached the driver's side door. The man in the front of the truck pops off a round through the front windshield. Glass breaks. There's an exchange of gunfire. Gabby doesn't know guns but can distinguish the two different types of gunshots, which nearly run together. The man in front of the truck jerks three times. Blood appears on his tan jacket. His gun lowers. The shotgun man reaches the driver's door as his ski mask partner falls to the pavement. The shotgun man reaches up and rips the door open. There's a single pop and yell of defiance. The shotgun man shifts to the side and lets off a load from the shotgun that catches the driver's side door and window of the box truck, shattering glass.

Then the fat man in the Impala is out of his vehicle, bumbling with the door and his jacket, raising his gun, shouting, and calling the man a son of a bitch. The shotgun man whirls around toward him, eyes protruding from the mask, wild.

The fat man shoots at the shotgun man twice, his small handgun popping in his hand. At the same time, the shotgun man lets off a thunderous boom. The shotgun man takes the two rounds. Gabby can't see where. The round from the shotgun catches the fat man in the stomach, turning him, causing him to shoot three more times, and dropping him. The shotgun man staggers, dropping the barrel of the shotgun to the pavement, scraping it on the pavement as he takes two stumbling steps and collapses backward.

CHAPTER 12:

KEVIN ALEXANDER

KEVIN ALEXANDER SITS WITH HIS LEFT leg crossed over his right knee on a plush white couch, sipping coffee from a white mug.

This is Iris's house, and Kevin is in her living room, where the furniture, like most of the house, is decked out in black, gold, and white: hard and impractical. It makes the whole room feel like it is pretending to be something it's not.

Perhaps that's the point.

Kevin, dressed in jeans and a baggy black sweatshirt, baseball hat low over his eyes, sits across from the fireplace, staring at the emptiness under the white marble mantle, as cold and black-hearted as Iris. He waits for Iris to come down the stairs and start her morning. She's up there, awake, enjoying whoever was in her bed—Kevin knows who because he peeked.

The fireplace, like this house, like him, like Iris, is more than it seems and less than it wants to be.

173

He lifts the brim of his hat when she appears. She steps off the stairs, raising an eyebrow at his presence in her living room. She says, "How did you get in here?"

Kevin, sipping coffee, greets Iris. "Good morning."

"How did you get in here?" she asks again, tightening the sheer blue kimono robe draped around her lithe body. She grips the edges of her robe. "Why are you here?"

Looks have always been important to her, and Kevin's not blind. She possesses a certain attractiveness even if she isn't his preference. Creamy skin, reddish-brown hair, delicate features that border on the feline, sharp bone structure: she's a small and fragile thing of beauty that's cursed several men. The one Kevin knows is upstairs now is no different, and his presence plays perfectly into Kevin's plans.

Looking at her, Kevin slurps the coffee from the mug loudly just to be annoying. "I've proved it time and time again. I can get in anywhere. I can do anything. I haven't found anywhere I can't access. Homes are no problem."

"Why are you here?"

Kevin sets the mug down on the white saucer resting in his lap, cradled and supported with his other hand. He isn't an animal, and this isn't the first time he's made a morning surprise appearance in Iris's home—she has rules.

It makes him wonder why she hasn't increased her security or at least improved it. The least she can do is try to make it challenging for him.

The first time he got into her house, the urge hit him, and he laid a stinky bomb in her downstairs powder room, that's what she called it, which stunk up the house something awful. It nearly gave him away before he was ready because Iris came to investigate the smell. When he walked out of the bathroom, zipping up his fly, she confronted him and asked if he used the powder room. He said no, there wasn't any powder.

She looked at him and said, "The bathroom under the stairs."

Kevin said, "Oh yeah—figured you didn't need a steaming pile of shit on that nice fluffy white rug over there." She called him disgusting. He said it's a thing.

She told him to go back to the powder room and flush the toilet. "Don't forget to wash your hands." She didn't move from her spot until he accomplished the tasks. Every subsequent time he's come here, the urge hasn't hit him. Maybe it's the fact she's fine with him being here; she trusts him, but for the life of him, he can't think of why. It must have something to do with Iris being Iris. She doesn't hide anything because what she doesn't want people knowing, she keeps to herself, in her head. Everything else is left out and open to interpretation. Once she realized he would continue to show up in the morning unannounced, she explained the rules to him: cups with saucer, leave shoes by the door, spray the bathroom with the floral spray after use.

This morning he made coffee and finished her newspaper, which sits folded next to him on the couch. Kevin taps the paper and says, "We have a problem."

Iris flares her nostrils, a tell, one Kevin's noticed in his time with her. Everything about Iris is an act, a ploy, nothing more than a means to an end, a way to get what she wants. Nothing is genuine. Nothing is true, and Kevin doubts she's ever shown the truth to anyone. She's a cold-hearted bitch and not only does she know it, but she also delights in it—wears it like armor. Nothing stops her from getting what she wants, including death, not the death of her husband or death in general, as in taking another's life—except Kevin took the life. Iris is perfectly capable of killing if the need arises.

Iris used to brag to Kevin about how she had her husband wrapped around her finger. He died by a series of circumstances she, and by extension Kevin, set into motion. She told Kevin he did what she wanted because he got laid. She said her marriage was a marriage of convenience and delusion on his part and that her husband's death was an accident.

Kevin can confirm. Franklin Hayes, Kevin's best friend growing up, wasn't supposed to kill the DEA agent.

Kevin watched Iris's husband's death derail her and her plans. It threw her into a tailspin. It fractured some of her armor to the point she nearly revealed parts of her true self, but she adapted, hardening into the woman she is today. Most of her plans turned out for the better in the end.

Iris's strength is her ability to see when something isn't working and change. She abandons failed ideas when necessary and doesn't waste time or resources on plans that don't work. She adapts better than anyone Kevin has ever met.

Kevin adapted, too, and learned a valuable lesson about trust. Who can he trust? How does trust work? He learned he can't trust anyone. And if something needs doing, it's better to be the one willing to do it than trust someone else to do it.

Something Iris doesn't do because, if she can manipulate someone to do her dirty work, she does.

That's why Kevin will be her downfall. She just doesn't know it yet. Because she's never given Kevin his due, she doesn't recognize his value. She doesn't think he deserves more. She doesn't see what he brings to the table and what he has done for her, how he made her endgame happen. If it wasn't for him, she would not be sitting where she is now on Siriano's metaphorical throne. Iris doesn't appreciate who Kevin is or what he's done for her, all that he has accomplished in her name; she judges him. He can feel it in the way she looks at him. She judges him for the way he looks, for how he lives his life, for who he is, and for where he comes from.

But then, Kevin judges her back, so perhaps he shouldn't take it personally. He has been undermining her from the very beginning, just as he did with her predecessor and former lover Renaldo Luna, a man Kevin never liked. Siriano trusted Renaldo, and Wilson and Iris destroyed him because of it. But Kevin killed him.

Killing Renaldo was sweet. The look of surprise and acceptance on the man's face as he walked into his apartment, seeing Wilson seated at his table, a pile of Kevin's shit on the rug, Iris behind him walking him to his doom, and Kevin there to the side, placing the gun against the man's temple. In those final moments, Renaldo realized he'd been played. He started to say, "Yeah, sure—" he was going to say 'okay' because that was his thing—"yeah, sure, okay"—but Kevin didn't give him the chance. One shot is all it took to depose Renaldo and take Siriano's throne. Kevin did that. Kevin disposed of Renaldo's body. Not Iris. Not Wilson. Kevin. Kevin pulled the trigger. Kevin did everything necessary to ensure the transfer of power. He did it all, and he did it because he wanted to.

Kevin did it because Neil Smith chose him and trained him. Siriano trusted him to fulfill sensitive tasks, especially when the old man was locked away in prison. Wilson befriended him and saw how useful he could be.

But Siriano, the others, too, made a mistake. He didn't choose Kevin. He didn't choose Wilson to run his empire in his stead. He chose the runt from the streets, an urchin, Renaldo, who did not value the Siriano way. Renaldo was never content and was infected with ambition. Siriano should have excised him long before Wilson and Iris decided he needed to go. That's why Kevin was so willing to help. The infection needed to be cut out.

The problem with infection is that it spreads. First to Iris and Wilson, and now to Kevin, which is how the German was born. A childhood nickname Franklin, who killed Iris's husband, bringing the chaos full circle, gave him.

So perhaps, Kevin shouldn't criticize Renaldo. Maybe they are the same. Two men who came from nothing, who touched power and learned to love it. Renaldo wanted to belong, prove himself to people who only saw his skin color. Kevin doesn't care about belonging. He realized long ago he is different, and the differences make him unpredictable.

Kevin doesn't want scraps. He doesn't want the ruins of an empire, Siriano's fractured organization. That was Wilson's hubris. Iris's too. They want what Siriano had. Kevin doesn't. He wants something new, something that's his. Something as different as he is.

And to get it, he'll do what needs to be done. Over the last two weeks, he's allowed old hatreds to fester, to provide him an opportunity to eliminate Iris and his infernal stress. After all, isn't wanting to be one's own boss the goal in life?

Standing at the bottom of the stairs and processing the situation before acting, Iris asks, "What sort of problem?"

"A load was hit," Kevin says. "It was public."

"When?" Iris studies a painting on the wall, a snow leopard in action, leaping toward the viewer, claws extended.

"An hour ago."

"And we already know? Usually, it takes time for us to find out about it. Didn't the last one take over three hours for the driver to get to a phone? I believe he said he had to walk in the dark on the side of the highway until someone gave him a ride."

Kevin nods. "This one was different. Like I said, it was public."

"How public?"

"Our driver killed one of the hijackers—left him dead in the street. There's more, but I won't trouble you with the details."

Iris turns her attention from the painting to Kevin, eyes trying to lock on his. "This is not good."

Kevin denies her the satisfaction of eye contact. He picks up the mug and sips the coffee. "You're telling me."

He glances up to see how she's reacting.

Iris is good at hiding her emotions, but when things don't go according to her plans, she sometimes loses her cool. The nostril flare is one sign. There are others. Iris does have her weaknesses.

Her greatest weapon, her femininity, is also her strongest liability.

That's what Kevin plans to exploit to its fullest.

He swirls the brown liquid in the cup, teasing spilling it on her white couch... messing with her some. Everything he does is to increase pressure. He can feel her intense gaze and her need to leap across the room to stop him from staining the couch.

He adds, "Which is why I'm here."

Iris places a hand to her neck and runs the hand to the back of her neck, massaging her muscles. She studies him for a moment. "I assume you made coffee?"

Kevin sets the mug on the saucer. "In the kitchen."

Iris turns away from him in dramatic fashion, the hem of the kimono twirling. She moves toward the kitchen and disappears from view. She says in a louder voice, doing well to hide the hint of concern in her voice as she asks the question, and *it is* the question, "How long have you been here?"

Kevin follows her into the kitchen. "Long enough—who's upstairs?"

He finds her standing on tippy toes, reaching for a mug and saucer in a white cabinet. Her robe comes undone, showing flashes of pale skin, revealing her nudity underneath. Modesty has never been her strength. And she's not particularly concerned with what Kevin may see.

Iris pulls a mug from the cabinet, drops to her heels, grabs at the folds of her robe to keep them together, and says, "That's none of your business."

Kevin sets his mug and saucer down on the countertop near the sink. He leans against the countertop, reaching for the toothpick holder near her spice rack.

"Do you cook? You don't strike me as someone who cooks," he says, pulling a toothpick out of the holder and slipping it between his teeth. "And I'd beg to differ with you on this. I think it's some of my business."

"None of it is your business. Your business is to make me money and make sure things run smoothly. I believe current events show otherwise. They show you are doing neither."

She rotates around to reach for the coffee pot. She starts to fill her coffee mug with a generous portion of what remains in the pot while holding her robe closed.

"The way I see it," Kevin says. "You use people."

Iris doesn't let on if she's offended by his comment or not.

Kevin says, "You sleep with them, you trick them, you use them—men mainly—but you're pretty good with everyone. Equal opportunity offender and all."

Iris sets the coffee pot back on the burner. "I suppose you have a point?"

"I'm getting there," Kevin says. "So yeah, I feel like it's my business because I'm supposed to make you money and make sure things run smoothly—both ain't happening right now—and I have to ask myself why?"

"You're suggesting I'm the reason?"

"No," Kevin says, which sounds convincing. "No, but who you sleep with tends to affect business."

"Who I sleep with is my choice."

"You think it's a choice? Did Renaldo think he had a choice? Wilson? You used them. You slept with them. Used both of them. Renaldo. Wilson."

"You let him die."

"Did I?" Kevin asks. "The way I saw it, that was all part of the plan. A plan I didn't know about. Either you trust me, or you don't. You didn't then. I don't want it to become a habit."

Iris's lips crease into a smile. "I should have told you the plan."

"You should've, *love*, but you didn't. And that crazy friend of Wilson's cold-clocked me when it shouldn't have happened. This brings me back to my point. Not only did you use them—you used me."

"I didn't use you," Iris says. "Wilson couldn't know what I was planning."

"Because you wanted to take over."

"That's one way to look at it," Iris says, not denying the charge, "but not everything went the way it should have."

"You're talking about our third stakeholder."

Iris doesn't answer.

"You're talking about Flavia, about her shooting Vega."

Iris nods. "It caused quite a problem with Vega's people, specifically his brother Virgo. He's quite upset with her."

"Vega, Virgo, who the fuck names their kids that?"

"It doesn't matter."

"Oh, it matters."

"You came here to tell me what you told me," Iris says, hands cupped around her mug. "Why are you still here?"

"We need to talk about what you are doing."

"What am I doing?" she says with an icy look.

Kevin points up. "You use people—so, tell me that's not Omar Sanchez up there, Flavia's husband."

Iris smiles but doesn't show her teeth, barely breaking her lips as she speaks. "I assure you it is not Omar."

"Are you sure about that?"

"Positive."

"Because if you were fucking Omar behind Flavia's back, that could cause problems—and that, *my friend*, would affect business and, in turn, me."

Iris takes a drink, using the silence to pause the conversation.

She says, "And if it were Omar upstairs, it would be his decision."

"Not if he was a *target*," Kevin says. "A guy like him, with someone like you, he wouldn't know what hit him. He'd be no different than the others. He'd be a helpless little duckling on the pond waiting for you to come along and blow his little feathered head off."

Iris sips her coffee and sets the mug on the saucer, which is on the counter next to her. She undoes the sash around her waist, flashing a full-frontal view of her nude body, and then reties the robe. "I think you need to get back to work, figure out who is hitting our truck."

Kevin points the toothpick at her. "I think you need to be honest with yourself and realize someone's out to get you, and you need to think long and hard about who that could be and why."

"You think Flavia would make a move against me."

"Not if that's not Omar up there." Kevin points the toothpick at the ceiling. "But yeah, I think she's capable. She has the manpower. She doesn't like this arrangement you two hammered out, and she never really followed directions. Had you let me in on your plan, I might've been able to do something about that."

"You think Flavia could be the German?"

Kevin sticks the toothpick back in his mouth. "I think that's what Short Philly and Fat Tommy think. They know what the German is capable of 'cause they keep getting hit. They know what rumors everyone has heard about this German," waving his hands, "how ruthless the German can be, how carefully the German runs his ... or *her* little business. They think these hijackings have to be an inside job. Someone who knows the schedule. I can't think of a better person with a better motive."

"It could be you," Iris says.

"Could be," Kevin says, dismissing her while suppressing a smile. "But why would I go against you? You aren't fucking my husband. We all knew the schedules. We all agreed on when a run goes. But this last one I had no hand in other than approving it happening as part of your council. Flavia's people delivered the truck from the farm—which the police hit by the way—to Fat Tommy and his people. Flavia pushed for a larger run to Short Philly's people. Flavia openly questions your ability. Remember, it was your lover who killed her mentor. You have to ask yourself who has the motive—who do you think it is?"

Iris looks to be considering the question. "Do we have an idea of who's hijacking our trucks—the actual players?"

Kevin smiles. "I do."

"How?"

"Pattern of behavior, plus a little digging on my part. The German has a middleman who he ... or *she* ... uses as a face of his or her business. He drives a Mercury Marquis, apparently pretty distinctive. I heard it was left behind in this last heist. Fat Tommy and Short Philly have experience with this guy. I'll start there."

Iris waves a dismissive hand at him. "Then take care of the situation."

"Don't worry. Consider it handled."

CHAPTER 13:

FRANKFORT CORBIN

FRANKFORT CORBIN SITS DOWN FOR HIS regularly scheduled dinner with his adopted daughter US Deputy Marshal Kelly Chambers, at their steak place in Sapulpa. She affectionately calls Frank Uncle Frank and has since Eddie introduced them when Kelly was young, but he's more her adopted father. After her mother's death, the dinners became a necessity for them both, and they make time for them when they can.

This afternoon, they sit in the corner booth of a little rectangle-shaped space off the main hall of the restaurant. The booth has red cushions on a painted black wooden frame. The tabletop has advertisements for local businesses laminated onto its surface. The advertisements creep up the cream-colored stucco walls with pinned business cards for various businesses, then blend into western memorabilia that's somewhere between cowboy and Indian. Of course, that's most of Oklahoma, a land split between cultures and thriving in the nethers. It's men on horses wearing cowboy hats, others in headdresses with spears and arrow-heads, with their slumped shoulders, these Turquoise soldiers. Brown leather tack, both in paintings and antiques. With canvas wolves, shadowed or bathed in ghostly light, howling at the moon.

Once settled into the booth, Frank removes his hat and places it in the seat next to him. He's wearing a beige vest over a drab forest green button-up work shirt with sun-faded blue jeans, and a gun on his hip. The vest is a canvas work vest, zipped to the top button of his collared shirt. Frank likes to wear the vest when he's in town conducting business, such as interviews, to hide his gun and to blend in as much as a country boy can in the city. That and he likes having the extra pockets. It makes for a good place to hide his hands while at a crime scene so that he doesn't touch anything, what Mitchell calls "museum rules."

Frank orders black coffee to go with his red meat. Kelly orders caffeine-free soda, a Sprite, or as Frank refers to it, "sugar water," to go with her steak, which he has a hard time understanding. He says, "You know, you drink, and you're not on the clock. You could order a red wine or some locally brewed Choc beer to go with your steak. It'd be a better pairing."

"You know, you could drink," Kelly says, giving him some attitude while unwrapping her straw, "then you could order whatever you want with your steak."

Frank doesn't drink. She knows this.

Kelly sinks the straw into her clear-colored soda.

Frank picks up a piece of celery that comes with the hors d'oeuvres served with every meal. The hors d'oeuvres, like the memorabilia, ride the line between American redneck and Lebanese steak house. He dips the celery into the hummus sitting in a small silver boat in the middle of the table. "I just can't see why you drink that junk."

Kelly, wearing a simple business suit, black, with a white undershirt, sips her drink before picking out a pickle from the boat, tossing a chunk of celery to the side like it's poison. She pops the pickle into her mouth. Frank has a love-hate relationship with pickles.

Kelly says, "Because it tastes good. You should switch to decaf."

"I don't drink decaf," Frank says, sipping his coffee. "It don't taste good."

Kelly tries to hide it, but his scripted response makes her smile. This is a conversation they have had before and most likely will have again. She asks, "How'd your first official day back go?"

Frank's first day started when he received the call from Mitchell telling him about the attempted hijacking. That was after he came back inside from sitting on his back porch drinking coffee, which is his morning routine. He had left his cellphone on the kitchen table on silent, the phone's always on silent, while he went about his routine and enjoyed the sunrise. It used to be a time when he and Eddie would watch them together. Now he watches them alone because he can't count on the Austrian Blue Heeler Kelly got him a couple years back to be an adequate morning companion. The dog doesn't appreciate the sunrise the same way. He just runs around, fetching the tennis ball Frank pitches between sips. When Frank came back inside, he noticed the little black brick buzzing against the custom-made kitchen table Eddie picked out about fifteen years ago when she made Frank transition from the card table he'd been using to something she deemed nicer. The thing cost so much that Frank can't bear to part with it even though it's the ugliest thing he's ever seen and doesn't go with anything else in his house, kitchen chairs included. Besides, if he sold it, he feels like he'd lose money on the deal.

"When I arrived at the scene, I nearly hit Mitchell with my car door," Frank says. "So I guess it started off alright."

"I still don't understand why you all were there."

"We are cops, no matter our description," Frank says as if that explains why he was there. It doesn't really explain it, but it settles the matter long enough for him to tell her that "Mitchell couldn't wait to explain to me what had happened. Like him being out for months recovering from his hip was dull or something. He was rip roarin' and ready to go, appearing at my window like a *sprite* ready to explain to me why two livestock agents had been called to a shootin' in the city. I guess a *highway* robbery is interesting if it's something you care about, but I don't know. Maybe I'm getting to the point in life where I'm just okay having dinner with you and that being my day, not investigating murders and shootings."

Kelly nods like she understands. "Is it related to something you're workin' on?"

Frank shakes his head. "Call it a favor for a friend. You remember Raley Freeman?"

"The OSBI Agent you tried to set me up with," Kelly says, chomping on a carrot that comes from the same silver boat at the center of the table as the other appetizers. "I remember him. Oh, how could I forget?"

Frank wiggles his mustache and then runs a hand down the drooping edges. "A *yes* would have been sufficient."

"Deputy Vanilla Do-Dah and I aren't exactly what you'd call a well-made match."

Frank cradles the small ceramic coffee mug in both hands. "You were single. He was single." He takes a sip, and coffee drips from his mustache before he runs his lower lip over the strands. "Both of you about the same age; it was worth a shot. Besides, it's a better idea than you and that reporter—what's he, like ten years older than you?"

"A bit more."

"You going to tell me how much of a bit?"

Kelly doesn't, and Frank waits for her to supply more, studying her face, watching her twitch her nose and make a visible effort to keep her mouth shut, smashing her lips together.

"Must be hard for you not to say something," Frank teases. "Not normal for you. Goes against your nature..."

Kelly blinks, remains steadfastly silent, and says nothing.

"I know you have something you want to say... not speaking isn't an easy thing for you."

As much as he tries, Frank's childish jabs can't elicit a response from her. Kelly just stares blankly at him, glass on the table, fingers pinching the straw, big brown eyes like her mother's staring up at him while sucking the Sprite from the straw, gurgling it some as she does.

Frank says, "You're not going to tell me, are you?"

"I don't see how it's any of your business. I'm an adult. He's an adult. And we like each other."

"Love may be more accurate," Frank says.

Kelly says, "You think so, huh?"

Frank nods and sips his coffee. "I do." He pauses for effect. "Speaking of the reporter, you heard from his daughter any?"

"She went her separate way from the boy she left with. He was, quote, 'too serious.' She's somewhere down in Texas. Says she likes the warm weather."

"She staying out of trouble?"

"For the most part," Kelly says. "That boy, Maggie, he did send a postcard to Sonny saying he hoped for a great baseball season this coming year and no hard feelings."

"Tellin' her dad she left him without sounding like he was grovelin'?" Frank says.

Kelly says, "Something like that. It was sweet."

"He's a killer," Frank says. "I did some checking, found out he's connected and takes money for killing—not what I'd call sweet by any means."

Kelly says, "Well, it doesn't take away the fact he helped Sonny and his kiddo reconnect."

"She's livin' in a different state. That's not quite what I'd imagine as reconnecting."

Kelly's fingers touch her mother's necklace at the base of her neck. "I thought about living somewhere else, so I didn't have to listen to you judge me for dating a man I actually like."

Frank hums to himself. "Love—I don't know why you can't admit it."

"Probably for the same reasons you tease me about his age. I'm protecting your feelings."

"What feelings?"

"The ones you keep deep down in that vest of yours."

Frank scoffs. "You don't have to protect me."

Kelly shakes her head. "Yes, I do."

"Why's that?"

"Someone has to. Might as well be me. Sure as heck isn't going to be Mitchell."

"He's an alright boy."

"He's a handful of years younger than you. He's not what I'd consider a boy."

"Well, he isn't a girl."

"Uncle, you know what I mean."

Frank lets it go. He says, "Mitchell's just biding his time until he can retire."

"You didn't answer me," Kelly says. "You do that when there's something you either don't want to talk about or really want to talk about. Why are you two investigating a shooting?"

"Couple of reasons."

"I thought you said it was a favor for Raley?"

"That's one of the reasons," Frank says, motioning to her with the mug to punctuate his point. "Another being we help out where we're needed. My investigation about some cattle gone missin' dovetailed right into an investigation of Raley's." Frank pauses to eat another piece of celery. "Turns out, the cattle were butchered for food for this marijuana grow out in the boonies. The Mexicans workin' the place weren't allowed off property to go to town to go grocery shopping. What food they did have was either delivered dry goods, like rice and beans, or they grew on site."

Their meals are delivered to the table, two plates with meat dripping with oily liquid smoke and foil-wrapped baked potatoes with sour cream in some little paper cups. The waiter drops crackers and butter next to the hors d'oeuvres.

Frank lays eyes on his steak. "The Mexicans got a hankering for some farm-to-their-table meat."

"So what's that have to do with today's events?"

"A whole hell of a lot, as it turns out," Frank says. "That's what Mitchell was so excited to tell me."

"I heard it was a mess out there," Kelly says. "Like something out of a movie."

"Or the evening news," Frank says, referring to Kelly's starring role in last year's news cycle when Siriano was kidnapped from her custody outside the courthouse in front of a bunch of cameras. "Mitchell called today's events, 'a fucking mess.' Told me when I got there, we had two men dead, witnesses everywhere, and a missing truck. Then asked me if I wanted to know what the kicker was."

"What was it?"

"*Damn*, you're just as eager as he was," Frank says. He takes a slow drink just to build anticipation. "I'll answer you where I didn't answer him. With him, I just palmed the crest of my hat and slipped it onto my head while giving him the look."

"But you're not going to give me the look," Kelly says, narrowing her eyes. "You're going to answer the question."

Frank nods. "Mitchell told me the truck we watched roll out of that compound a couple weeks back before the raid was the same truck involved in the shooting. Same tag number."

Kelly absorbs the information.

Frank continues: "At the time of the raid, I figured OSBI would track down the truck and seize its contents. It wasn't mine or Mitchell's worry, but I did tell OSBI Agent Raley Freeman ... not *Deputy Vanilla Do-Dah* ... 'no way that truck left that compound empty.'"

Kelly says, "But since then, you've had other things to worry about."

"Funny you should say that. What do you think's been on my mind?"

Kelly cocks her head to the side and stares at him. "How did your visit to Russell Siriano go?"

"Now, remind me again why I was there?"

Kelly dips her knife into the butter and slathers it on the top of her potato. "You think I set you up?"

"I don't think so. I know so," Frank says, knife gripped in his right hand. "You set me up. Now I'm not too upset about that, but I don't appreciate it very much either."

"Someone needed to listen to him," Kelly says. "I couldn't do it. What'd he want in return?"

Frank cuts into his steak and runs it through a puddle of liquid smoke before slipping it into his mouth. "You telling me you all didn't talk terms?"

"He said he was interested in cooperating, but he didn't tell me what he wanted in return. He bitched about the US attorney not listening to him."

"How did you get to me?"

"I said I might know someone who could help but couldn't make any promises," Kelly says. "He thought you were my father."

"The man's request was odd. As equally self-serving as it was intriguing. The man doesn't want justice."

"So, what'd he want?"

Frank takes a big bite, chews awhile before answering, and then chews some more. "He wants me to find out what happened to a fella named Renaldo Luna who used to work for him before he disappeared. Siriano believes he was killed."

"What'd you tell him?"

"I haven't decided what I'm going to do," Frank says between bites. "The man's a snake, and in my experience, bitin' is just what they do—he can't control it any more than a rattler can. But no one should disappear from the face of the earth without a trace, no matter how criminally involved he is, and since visitin' Siriano, I've learned that's exactly what happened to Renaldo Luna. One day he's here, checking out of the hospital against medical advice. He'd been shot in the head. I couldn't believe being shot in the noggin didn't kill him."

"I've heard of such things happening."

"Then supposedly he shows up at his old boss's and mentor's house where he allegedly murders him. The only witness to the crime was the dead man's bodyguard, who didn't do too good of a job guarding the man. He stated it was Renaldo who killed the man. But the not-so-good of a guard is now dead, so he was unavailable for comment or follow up, and ... here's a kicker for you ... he'd been involved in the strange chain of events having to do with Siriano's kidnapping."

"You're talking about Pablo Jimenez," Kelly says. "Omar Sanchez said kidnapping Siriano was his idea."

Frank sips some coffee. "So, maybe Siriano is on to something. But it's hard to believe Renaldo would kill a man that, by all accounts, he loved like a father."

"It seems like an odd turn of events unless his old boss was the cause of the gunshot to his head," Kelly says like she's reading Frank's thoughts.

"It's kind of poetic. But the next day, after all that mess, Renaldo's gone, disappeared without a trace. No one's heard from him since. I visited an old friend at the DEA who I've been meaning to go by and to visit her new baby.

She gave me some background information, but I'm not sure how much of it I can use. You federal folks keep a lot of information close to the vest, partly 'cause there's intelligence that's valuable for other investigations and partly 'cause there's a form for every form, and after a while, it gets tiring, and you just give up and keep things to yourself. The friend did confirm some of Siriano's rambling, saying she was sure Iris King had something to do with Renaldo's disappearance. She dropped the pretense after a while, telling me he was probably dead. She asked me, 'You know who moved into Renaldo's apartment?' I shook my head. She said, 'Wilson Notaro.'"

Kelly comments, "Now, isn't that strange?"

"It was strange and seemed to confirm what Siriano was saying. I even considered calling Renaldo's mother to see what she might have to say, but I wasn't sure if that was the right move. It'd mean I'd officially taken up Siriano's cause, and I'm not ready to commit to something like that. Probably because I've been suspended with pay pending the shooting review for killing that man who raised an old rifle during that raid, and any investigation I've done has been unofficial at best and dangerous at worst."

"Considering your bread and butter are Cattle Rustlers. Mine are convicts."

"I did find out the man I shot was from Mexico, so I guess Mitchell had it right," Frank says. "But as far as the shooting goes, I didn't delight in the killing. The man left me no choice."

"Good thing the county you were in is large but has a small population. The District Attorney was quick to deliver a verdict about the shooting." When Frank doesn't

say anything, Kelly reaches across the table and takes Frank's hand. "Uncle, he cleared you."

Frank glances at her hand, her fingers massaging his knuckles. He looks at her mother's eyes staring back at him. "Doesn't make what happened any better."

"There you go talking about those feelings of yours—remember you don't have those."

Frank says, "OSBI took a few days, but they didn't see anything wrong with the shootin' either since it was going to be one of their boys who was going to get shot."

"Are you going to tell me about the hijacking? How's that truck tie to the grow?"

"Funny enough, it all ties back to Siriano. That grow was registered to him, as you know—I'm thinking Flavia Sanchez was running those Mexicans out there."

"Who rented the truck?"

"Boy named Wayne Kissee, supposedly a hot-shotter."

"Why would a hot-shotter rent a truck? Wouldn't he have his own?"

"That's what Mitchell said. We did some asking around. Sounds like Wayne might have been running a load for Schafer Logistics, who—"

"Who has been running this and that since the moonshine days."

Frank dabs the corners of his mouth with his napkin. "But you want to know what I found *interesting* about this whole fiasco?"

Kelly gives him the look.

Frank says, "The witness who got the tag of the truck was Gabriella Luna."

"As in?"

"The same—his mother."

"You going to talk to her?"

"That's the question I've been pondering all day," Frank says. "Seems the universe is trying to tell me something. Your mother always told me I needed to listen better. I guess at this point. I don't see how I can't. It's what she'd want."

CHAPTER 14:

JERILYN KISSEE

JERILYN KISSEE SHIELDS HER BODY WITH the hollow brown door as she cracks it open to peek inside Samuel Moody's office. She was late to work again, and Samuel sent word through the main line cook and his nephew Rufus Moody that she needed to come to see Samuel when she got in. Rufus yelled to her as she tried to slink into Moody's BBQ and American Diner unnoticed, "J-Lynn, he wants to see you—couldn't cover for you this time." Jerilyn nodded and tied the apron that completed her uniform, short black shorts, and a tight-fitting T-shirt, both contrasting against her pale skin, with flats even though Samuel likes heels. Her hair, thick as it is, is twisted up into a bun, held with a pair of chopsticks she bought at a garage sale a few years back, wrapped in an ornate green cloth with nylon knots—black, red, and gold—that decorated the edges of the fabric to simulate little lanterns.

Jerilyn peers inside the office. Samuel is behind his desk writing down this week's produce order and making marks

201

in a ledger. He writes in pencil with his left hand. Noticing her, he looks up from what he is doing, smiles wide, and sets the whittled pencil down to the side. With his prosthetic right hand, he gestures for Jerilyn to sit, motioning to the metal folding chair in front of the desk, which is unfolded and waiting for her.

Samuel gently closes the ledger and adjusts the desk lamp, which casts a yellow light on the malted brown office interior and provides the only light in the office crammed full of stored items for the diner. The two chairs and the desk take up most of the space's small footprint. The office has seen cleaner days. Samuel prefers the single lamp despite having overhead lighting, which he keeps off and disconnected because, as he says, he doesn't want to see all the little flaws: his sorta mantra for life. The office color matches his general makeup, dark skin with yellowing around the eyes. He has a bald head, which is dented and scarred from his time in the army and events of his past he doesn't talk about. Today, he wears a baby blue raggedy sweater, a crisp white apron with a grease stain on the bottom left where he wipes his hand, and elastic waistband blue jeans.

The click of heels against linoleum snags Jerilyn's attention, and she glances back before entering the office to catch her friend and coworker, the only other waitress for tonight's shift, Lori Hawkins, passing through the kitchen with a tray full of dishes, ribs curling up off one plate. Lori mouths good luck to her before Jerilyn steps into the office.

"Shut the door," Samuel says. "You can leave it cracked if you want. This won't take long."

Jerilyn slips inside and around the door. She leaves the door cracked. She fidgets with her name tag, trying to control her breathing. Her heart hammers inside her chest. She doesn't like being in trouble, and she knows she is in trouble. She wants to please—something Wayne has taken advantage of in their entire relationship. Wayne's never happy, and no matter what she does, she upsets him. "Jerilyn, you didn't put the dishes away right," or "Jerilyn, the towels weren't folded like I like them." Jerilyn doesn't like to upset anyone, but part of her growth away from Wayne has been learning to deal with disappointing others. She can't make everyone happy. Why try anymore?

She can only control her happiness. That's a hard truth to realize.

Samuel's been good to her, but Samuel was bound to notice her being late and take exception to it. Luckily, Jerilyn has friends that look out for her. Samuel may not always be the easiest man to get along with, but he's reasonable, except, sometimes he loses his cool, and then he loses control. It results in his unexplained injuries.

She's seen it happen when a customer got too fresh with Lori, squeezing her butt cheek as she passed his table. Jerilyn did warn Lori that her cheeks were hanging out the bottom of her shorts and how that causes unwanted attention, but Lori said that's what Samuel wants and how she likes them ... and then the customer called Rufus a dumb n-word doofus, which didn't go over too well, but Rufus isn't a fighter. Though, he is an artist in the kitchen. Samuel, he's a fighter; he was before the military and now even more so since his return. He heard the commotion. He said nothing to the guy. He just came out from his back office. He marched to the table and took the man by the back of the head, and before the guy knew what was happening, Samuel slammed his face into the salad bowl

sitting on the table in front of him so many times that he shattered the bowl and the plate underneath. With his one hand, Samuel yanked the guy out of the seat. He had lettuce hanging off his brow and a tomato in his cracked teeth. Samuel kicked the man's ass and threw him, flying, out the door into the gravel lot outside, where Samuel proceeded to stomp on the man's back until Rufus grabbed Samuel around the waist and pulled him away.

Samuel's never been like that with Jerilyn but knowing a man can inflict that much destruction on another weighs on her mind. Samuel seems to sit comfortably behind his desk. If things get too bad, he'll have to get clear of the desk before he can get to her.

Jerilyn takes two steps toward the seat. "I'm sorry I was late—"

"—don't tell me it won't happen again; we both know each other too well for you to insult me like that. Just take a seat."

Jerilyn sits and keeps her hands in her lap, fiddling with her apron strings. She says, "I'm sorry."

"I'm sure you are," Samuel says. "And so am I."

"Things have been crazy lately."

Samuel sighs, nodding like he understands. His face communicating it is crazy for everyone, and Jerilyn figures it probably is. Who is she to think her life is any different? But her life is different. It feels different. Feels like Lori doesn't have to put up with this bullshit. Lori doesn't have kids. She doesn't have Wayne in her life. Jerilyn doesn't feel like Lori has to put up with the things Jerilyn puts up with. No one should get smacked around just because something bad happened at work or some guys cut Wayne off in traffic.

In a tired voice, Samuel says, "Are you going to elaborate any or leave me in suspense? If you don't elaborate, I'll just have to take your showing up late as something personal, and after all you and I've been through, I don't want to be sore at you for something as minor as being late to work three days out of the five. Rufus covered for you yesterday and Lori the day before that, but damnit, J-Lynn, I have a few things I care about—pet peeves if you will— and being late's one of them."

Jerilyn drops her eyes and stares at the teeth marks on the yellow number two pencil. "I know."

"I know you know," Samuel says. "J-Lynn, you and I've done a lot of good work together, so I'm willing to forgive you, but I would like to know why you've been late. Tell me what's going on with you. Lori said you've been talking to some deputy, and you've seemed distracted ... and I'm not going to get into what my good-for-nothing daughter said she heard you doing last night at a TU frat house—selling weed, what's wrong with you?"

Damn Shelia for calling her and suggesting the frat boy as a potential client. Jerilyn doesn't know why Wayne ... or her shithead brother go to that damn bar and talk to that coked-out hussy.

"I need money," Jerilyn says.

"I know you need money; we all do. But you know what this place is and how I run things. I don't need trouble here."

"That's what the business with the deputy's about. He promised to help me with Wayne—"

"For how much?"

Jerilyn doesn't want to admit the truth to Samuel, but he's been a sorta father figure for her for a long time. He's protected her when no one else would. Even lit into Wayne one time when he left her with a black eye. "Five thousand," she says.

Samuel blinks once and takes a moment to sip his coffee as he stares at her before speaking again. "You could have come to me."

Jerilyn pulls the apron string tight around her finger. "I know I could have."

"Why didn't you?"

"Because you would have said yes. I don't want your charity. I want Wayne gone; besides, you would have taken other steps…" Jerilyn lets her voice fade.

"The boy needs a beating for the way he treats you," he says, nodding. "But you're right, I would have done things my way, and Wayne wouldn't be a bother no more."

"That's not what I want," she says. "He's still good deep down."

"So are tootsie pops, but they still can break a tooth if you're not careful." Samuel sets the coffee cup on the desk. "What's this deputy say he is going to do for five grand?"

"Get Wayne locked up for a few years."

"Kill'em?"

"I don't know," she says, twisting the string of her apron around her middle finger again. "Didn't make it sound like that's what he was going to do, but he did mention he was capable of it."

"Well then, what's he going to do? What did he make it seem like he would do for your five grand, fix some reports and such—lie?"

"Not how he made it sound," she says. "More like pay more attention to Wayne; not let him get away with as much as he does."

"So, in other words, this white boy—because let's be honest, he's white—is asking you to pay him to do his damn job. You should have come to me."

"I want to do this on my own."

"Like sell marijuana?"

She nods.

Samuel says, "That's dumb shit. You ain't a dumb shit. Your brother is. That's probably where you got it, this marijuana. He's mixed up with all kinds of nonsense that's going to catch up to him sooner or later, but I know, or at least I thought I did, you're smarter than him."

"It's just a pound," Jerilyn says, speaking with her hands. "I sell that; I make up the last bit."

"Where's the marijuana, now?"

"My house," she says.

Samuel gives her a look.

"Top of my closet, so the girls don't come across it."

"Why are you doing this?"

"For the girls, of course. If Wayne were out of the way, maybe they'd have a good life. He's holding them back, holding me back. If the deputy can get him locked up and out of the way for a while, give them a chance at a real life, then it's worth it."

"It's not worth it if you go to jail for possession with intent."

"I hear you, and I know where this conversation is going. It's not what I want. I can't accept the money from you. I have to do this on my own. No one else. That's why I didn't ask you. That's why I didn't ask no one else to help me."

"Good, because I'm not going to offer it to you. I just want to know that you're doing the right thing—you're not—but I guess I can understand what you're doing and why you're doing it. I never wanted my place to be a front for some dipshit honkey, but here I am. Why did I do it? Because it was good money, and it kept me afloat. Problem is, no matter what business is, I have to pay my percentage—ten, by the way. Good month, I pay ten. Bad month I pay ten, it don't matter none how many people come through the door. Only saving grace now is that the man I worked that deal out with is in prison, so as far as I'm concerned, it's up for negotiation. Now, there's been a nice Spanish-looking lady coming around who seems agreeable. She knows the restaurant business, so maybe I can stop paying my *tithe*—that's what the man called it like he was God. I called him on it, and he said he didn't want to be God, compared himself to a Caesar—and start paying something a little more beneficial to me. 'Course, the man only really used me for my hogs."

Jerilyn stays quiet.

Samuel lifts his left arm and points a finger at her. "People try to take advantage of others. They've been trying to do that to me my whole life, and since I got back from Afghanistan, they've continued, but in spite of all that, I've made a life for myself here, and I have things I care about. I can't have a waitress, no matter how fond of her I am, coming into work late without any repercussions."

"I was working at my mother's," Jerilyn blurts out. "I'm sorry, as soon as I was done there, I got the girls to the neighbors and rushed here."

"It don't matter none where you were or what you were doing, J-Lynn. Commitments are important. When you promise to do a thing, you need to do it. Your first commitment is to those girls. Then I'm next, 'cause I put money in your pocket. Anything extra you do should come after those two things." He holds up two fingers. "What you're doing is cheating me and cheating the girls by stretching yourself so thin. There's bound to be repercussions somewhere, and I hope you don't suffer them."

"I'm sorry," she says. "How many times do I need to say it?"

"I know you're sorry, and so am I," Samuel says. "What I want you to do is go home early tonight—I've already called Ramona in. She'll be here within the hour—and then show back up tomorrow at noon to make up the difference."

"I need the money—the tips!"

"I need the money, too, so I guess it's going to hurt the both of us. But let that pain be a reminder in the future to pay a bit more attention to the clock and be here when you say you are going to be here."

A tear rolls down Jerilyn's cheek as she stands to leave.

Samuel raises that left arm, palm up toward her, fingers out. "Now, as far as the marijuana goes, bring me whatever you have left. I'll make you whole so your brother doesn't come try to get the money you owe out of you."

"You can't do that," she says.

"I can and I will," he says. "Just bring me the rest. I'll take it off your hands. Then after some time, we'll talk about what to do about that deputy because a man of honor doesn't take money from those he's supposed to protect to do a job he's already being paid to do. I understand your need, so I'll think of a solution that's agreeable to all parties involved. But don't do stupid shit no more, J-Lynn."

Sniffling, she nods.

"Now get," he says.

Jerilyn exits the office. Lori's waiting for her at the back door. "I'm so sorry, J," she says.

"It's not your fault," Jerilyn tells her.

They step out the back door, and Lori hands her a cigarette. "I feel like it is—I asked Rufus where you were. You should have seen the look he gave me. But I thought you were in the back. I wanted to tell you something. I didn't think you were late again. That's not like you."

Jerilyn sticks the cigarette in her mouth, and Lori lights it for her. "I was working at momma's trying to make some extra money."

"For that deputy you told me about?"

Jerilyn puffs on the cigarette. Snorts the smoke. "Why'd you tell Samuel?"

"I don't think it's right, that's why. A guy like that is a creep. I think he has the hots for you. I don't trust him. He's trouble."

"I can handle myself."

"I sure hope so," Lori says and then adds, "but you can't do that to Wayne, get him locked up over nonsense."

Jerilyn almost asks her what business it is of hers. But they are friends, and Jerilyn only told Lori about it a few days ago when she was late the second time.

"Lori, it's not nonsense. He's a deadbeat who hasn't paid child support."

"You all are still married."

"We're separating," Jerilyn says. "And what's it to you?"

Lori looks away while withdrawing her cigarette from her lips. Smoke falls from her mouth as her shoulders slump.

"Look, I need to go home, drink some wine, and take a bath. Maybe I'll feel better after that. The girls will be with the neighbor for a couple more hours. I'll get them after I've collected myself some and figured out what I'm going to do."

———

WHEN JERILYN PULLS up at the house, the lamp in her living room is on. She turned off all her lights when she left for work. Burglars wouldn't leave a lamp on, so whoever it is in her house wants her to know he's here. Still, not much scares her anymore, so she goes up the front steps and sticks her key in the lock. She unlocks the front door and opens it to find Deputy Brogdon sitting on her couch, bleeding, right arm in a makeshift sling of a ratty-looking T-shirt, gauze wrapped around his neck, and a shotgun across his lap. But it isn't gauze; it's paper towels and duct tape, the silver lines shiny in the lamplight.

Jerilyn shuts the door.

Brogdon coughs once and winces in pain then asks, "Where's your brother and dipshit husband?"

Frozen in the doorway, unsure what to do, Jerilyn cocks her head to the side and narrows her eyes. "You're hurt."

"I'm shot to shit," Brogdon says, glancing at his bleeding shoulder. "But that doesn't tell me what I came here to find out. Where are they? Where would they go?"

"What happened to you? You look terrible."

Brogdon deflects. "Too much to explain. Lost a chunk out of the side of my neck, but nothing that can't be stitched back up. I got lucky there. The shoulder, on the other hand, is fucked. I'll need a hospital to get fixed up if I can." He moves his arm below the elbow, but the motion brings a lot of pain. "No way I can raise my arm. It isn't like the movies. All the blood vessels, the bone, lungs. A wound like this is lucky it didn't kill me."

"What are you doing here?"

"I'm here because instead of helping me, your brother dumped me out on the side of the road. I told you, I need to find your brother and husband."

"I don't know where they are."

"Yeah, you do," he says, "and if you don't, then you're going to make sure they come to me." He rotates the muzzle of the shotgun so she can look down the barrel.

Jerilyn considers the different ways she can play this. This is the sort of thing both Wayne and Lori warned her would happen if she cozied up with the deputy. Wayne never thought he was any good, and Lori worried for Jerilyn's safety. Taking her time to acknowledge the threat of the shotgun, Jerilyn removes her key from the lock and shuts the door behind her. She reaches into her purse and withdraws her crumpled pack of cigarettes. She taps one out and drops the pack back in the purse. She digs the lighter out of her right pocket.

Lighting a fresh cigarette, eyes on Brogdon, Jerilyn says, "Why?"

"'Cause they took something from me that I need back, and I can't go to the hospital for a gunshot without people asking a ton of questions. I figure I have about a day before I lose credibility."

"That still doesn't answer my question. So you what, you want to kill him?"

Brogdon nods and clicks his tongue against the roof of his mouth. "Now you're getting it. I'll say I was defending myself. Say you called me to come over because your husband lost his mind. I come over. He shoots me twice, and I kill him. 'Stead of calling the police right away, you panic and patch me up as best you can and drive me to the hospital."

"You think that's going to work?"

"If you go along with it, yeah, I do."

"What if I don't?"

Brogdon digs a piece of paper off the couch and throws the paper on the floor. "That's a search warrant for your place. My boys and I served it yesterday. It's for marijuana. Your brother's a known dealer. We found a pound in your closet." Brogdon holds up a folder resting on the cushion next to him. "Here are a few photos printed out to show you I'm serious." He flips the folder twice, drawing Jerilyn's eyes to the folder. Brogdon adds, "You have quite the underwear drawer."

"I wouldn't do threesomes 'cause Wayne wouldn't entertain the idea of adding another guy."

"Well, that's just not fair."

"So he brought me a lot of toys to try for him to watch. They're gifts. I don't feel the need to give them back."

Leering, actually leering, Brogdon grins. He tosses the folder on the floor next to the paper. "Also, there's surveillance photographs of you last night selling some of that marijuana at a frat house to an undercover officer."

"Goddamnit, Shelia," Jerilyn says. "She called and asked if I knew where my brother was, too, 'cause friends of hers wanted to buy some tree for a small party. The party wasn't small, and the guys had already bought most of what they wanted elsewhere. So yeah, I might have sold a few grams to make the trip worth it, but that's hardly the crime of the century. I spent more time doing nothing, fending off half-assed attempts of hitting on me. 'Where you from darlin', 'cause you look like you could use some cuddlin'' and that type of country ass bullshit. One guy even dropped the line about me being an angel. I told him I ain't an angel, far from it, but you know that. I told him he wasn't big enough for me, man enough. He didn't like that. I sipped a beer and then left when it became clear all the boys, who I think were my age as it were, all they wanted from me was for me to get undressed. They thought it'd turn into some porno or something, a big group of guys and me, them taking turns ... or some guy takes me back to the room, another in a closet with a camera or something. I didn't trust them. I might be the same age, but I have two kids. I know where that shit leads."

Brogdon agrees and starts to say before she's finished talking, "You're a good-looking woman—"

"I'm a good-looking woman who has mouths to feed, not fuck off at some party when I could be working."

Brogdon says, "So then, you're not going to have any problems with what I'm proposing. You're going to help me, or I'll bury you."

"What about our arrangement?"

"What about it? You bribing me to get rid of your husband? Surely, you can see how that will look."

Jerilyn drops her purse on the side table next to the door where she and the girls keep their shoes. She digs the pack out of her purse and taps out another cigarette, dropping her spent butt on the floor. Brogdon looks on the whole time, probably peering down her shirt as she's bent over. Once she finds the pack and has the cigarette out, she straightens and plants the cigarette between her lips. She touches her lighter, the flame warm against her skin, to the tip, and smoke fills the air around her with a hazy cloud. Talking while lighting the cigarette and smoking, Jerilyn says, "You know I was thinking about that story you told, and I've done some cooking in my life, even on some camp-fires and such where I used a cast-iron skillet."

Jerilyn withdraws the cigarette from her mouth and holds it just inches from her lips, crossing an arm across her chest to support her elbow.

"I don't think it would've bent like you said if it was used to beat on a girl. Maybe a steel one or something you might buy at Target. Either you embellished it or some-thing, or you made it up... Either way ... it hurts your credibility."

CHAPTER 15:

JEREMY HALL

JEREMY HALL BACKS THE YELLOW BOX truck into his father's barn, glancing into the rearview, seeing how the scene could play out if it were a movie; guys involved in a heist, back at their hideout, are upset with one another because things didn't go right—everything went fucking wrong—and let the carnage unfold. It'd be tense as hell. He imagines how it would work, have a roving camera, use a jib, some dollies or something, maybe even go handheld for a continuous effect. But Jeremy hates the handheld effect because it causes too much kinetic movement. He wants the audience to focus on the tension, the suspense, not the epileptic camera movements. Jib and dollies, steady and smooth would be the way to go. But the whole scene reminds him of *Reservoir Dogs*—that's the plot, right? Except for one thing, those guys were in on it. Here, it's just him and Wayne at the barn, and Wayne's pissed. He wasn't in on the heist. He had no idea what was going on. Plus, both are now covered in Brogdon's blood.

That was a trip. Brogdon was shot down by Wayne's backup, some fucking fat guy in a tan jacket. Jeremy didn't see it happen, but he saw the aftermath: Brogdon opened Wayne's car door and Wayne took a shot at him; Brogdon shot out the driver's side window, and Jeremy dove through Wayne's passenger door, ripping his ski mask off, and had to yell at Wayne to get him to stop. Wayne just looked at him like he couldn't believe it. Jeremy wasn't sure if it was Jeremy's appearance Wayne couldn't believe or the fact that everything that had happened was happening.

Wayne said then what he says now through the open window waiting for Jeremy to back in and park the box truck, "What the fuck—*Jere*?"

That's when Brogdon and the other guy went at it, breaking the moment between friends and causing them both to look at Brogdon fall flat on his ass, but Brogdon wasn't dead. He groaned, took a couple of deep breaths, and swatted at his neck, which was bleeding. Then Wayne froze up—wouldn't move or couldn't. So Jeremy pushed him out of the driver's side door, causing Wayne to fall to the pavement. With Jeremy taking control and giving directions, they both scooped Brogdon under the arms and loaded him up into the truck. Jeremy pushed Wayne, who pushed Brogdon in the truck first and then climbed in behind him. But Wayne either wouldn't or couldn't drive, or he wasn't in any sort of condition to drive, so Jeremy had to climb in behind the wheel and drive the truck, but he knew how this would look. He knew what was going to happen. The truck's all shot to shit, and people were watching, since it was rush hour and all. He knew it's just a matter of time before people catch on to them. Jeremy also knew—knows—he can't go home. Neither of them can.

So Jeremy panicked for a moment, slammed his foot down on the gas, and drove the truck from the scene, sideswiping some cars in the process. But in doing so, he left his Marquis, his baby, behind with the driver's side door open, car crooked in the lane, engine running, and side mirror missing.

At the time, Jeremy figured they needed to lay low somewhere until they can figure this out, figure out what the next move will be because there is always another move. But Wayne, coming out of his catatonic state when Jeremy bounced off a honking one-ton pick-up truck didn't like Brogdon being in the car with them. Brogdon was bleeding all over the place, and Wayne bitched about it, telling Jeremy that Brogdon had to go. Jeremy asked where's he supposed to go. Wayne said he didn't care, just get rid of the guy. Jeremy told Wayne, "I'm not stopping." So they didn't stop. A few blocks over, they dumped Brogdon out of the truck; Jeremy slowed down to a crawl, and Wayne just opened the passenger door and pushed the poor bastard out of the door. Then he slammed the door shut. He didn't look back. Jeremy did though, looked in his side mirror, and he saw Brogdon roll and stay down.

After that, Wayne didn't say anything the whole way out past Inola where Jeremy's father owned about sixty acres right off the highway with a big barn still maintained. The barn houses the tractor equipment for the acreage. His father bought the barn with all the airline money he made flying all over the place. It's where Jeremy has stashed every truck they've hijacked because no one comes out here. No one asks questions. No one but him knows it's here.

Now, Wayne says, "What the fuck—*Jere*?" Sulking outside the truck, pacing, as Jeremy slips the truck into park. He looks up at Jeremy through the window and leans back as Jeremy opens the door, stares at him as Jeremy leaps off the step. "You didn't answer me. What the fuck did you get me into? What the fuck were you thinking?"

Jeremy's trying to work out mentally what his next move is. "Not right now, man."

Wayne twists his nose, like a rabbit, showing he doesn't like the answer, and when Wayne doesn't like something, he becomes violent. He lashes out, and he does so now. He grabs Jeremy. He clenches his overalls, clasping the lapels, and drives Jeremy into the side of the truck, smashing Jeremy's back into the truck hard, wth a sluggish thud noise.

It fucking hurts.

"You better fucking say something to me about what happened." Wayne tightens his grip on the fabric bunched in his ham-sized fist. "You don't just get to say, '*not right now—man*,'" he mimicks Jeremy, "you better fucking explain what the fuck you've gotten me into. I don't want any part of this, but now I don't have a choice. What the fuck were you thinking? What were you doing there? What's going on?"

Jeremy grips Wayne's wrists and looks him in the eyes. In a steady voice, Jeremy says, "Wayne, you need to calm down, think. Think about things."

"Calm down, think?" Wayne lifts Jeremy off his feet. "Calm down, think! No, motherfucker, you better start talking. That was Daniel Cooley. I fucking killed him. I shot him. You hear me. You understand what I'm saying. I shot him. What the fuck is going on?"

Jeremy struggles to remain calm because getting upset with Wayne isn't going to help the situation. It will only make things worse. Wayne's bigger, stronger. He can break him. Wayne may be slow to think things through, sure, but he can be reasoned with. Made to understand.

In a controlled, small voice, feeling the pressure of the truck against his back and the tightening of Wayne's grip on his neck, Jeremy manages to say, "I tried to bring you in on it, but you wouldn't listen to me."

"Listen to you?" Wayne says. "*That's* what you were trying to bring me in on?" Wayne pounds Jeremy's back against the side of the box truck but the intensity lessens and Wayne staggers. "Fuck!"

Jeremy fights every instinct inside of his body to stay calm. He needs to wait Wayne out.

"Look, I have an idea," Jeremy says. "Well, some of an idea, part of an idea, part of a plan, it's been forming since we tossed Brogdon out of the truck."

Wayne acts like he hasn't heard him.

Jeremy stares into Wayne's face.

Wayne's eyes narrow. They're red and wet around the edges like he's been crying and playing it off. His nostrils flare. He snorts.

For a long time, both men are silent.

"Good, breathe," Jeremy utters. "Take in air, feed oxygen to your brain. It will help you calm down." Jeremy can't break eye contact. "Wayne you're my friend. You're upset; I get that. You need to see reason. You're not going to kill me. We can get out of this together, but we need to work together."

Wayne holds Jeremy there for a few moments longer, which causes Jeremy to doubt how deep their friendship runs. Then Wayne lets go, and Jeremy drops to the ground. He doesn't expect the release, and since his feet aren't touching the ground, he falls hard and lands in the dirt.

Jeremy lies there, not moving. Wayne steps back and punches the side of the truck, denting it.

"Work this out together," Wayne says. "Jeremy, you don't get it. You don't get who you're messing with. You've fucked us, fucked us both. Do you know who that shit belongs to, who I'm running for? Do you know what I'm running?"

Jeremy kneads the base of his neck where Wayne had him, massages out the soreness. "Yeah, that's why we hit you."

That's the wrong thing to say.

Wayne responds by kicking Jeremy in the side. Jeremy rolls as the blow drives the air out of his lungs. Wayne stalks forward, advancing on Jeremy to kick him again.

Jeremy holds up a hand. "Stop!"

Wayne bats the hand out of the way.

"Wait, just listen," Jeremy says, scooting.

Wayne stops.

"Wayne—just listen to what I have to say." His voice is strained, and the talking makes his ribs hurt more. He groans through each sentence as if a hot poker is lancing his side. The heat radiates through his body to his brain. "You have to see where we sit at the table with all this. We have a good hand. But you have to listen. Just listen to me. You beating me up isn't going to make it any better."

"Beat you up?" Wayne says, advancing again, "Who said anything about beating you up? I'm going to fucking kill you."

Jeremy retreats, stumbling backward and landing on his butt. Wayne doesn't slow. Jeremy scuttles in the dirt of the barn's floor. Arms and legs kicking up grit, fleeing from Wayne, creating some space. But he's not going to get away from Wayne this way. He knows this. It's like a horror movie, Wayne's going to keep coming, and when he gets to Jeremy, all he's going to see is red.

Jeremy has to try to get through to him one last time.

He crawls to his knees. With both hands up, he shouts, "Stop, just wait!"

Wayne doesn't stop. He treads forward. "Why? Why should I? Do you know who I work for? They knew this was going to happen. They knew, Jeremy. That's why Earl, the fat guy, that's why he was riding behind me. You fuckers, and I'm assuming it was you all, you all hit him a couple of weeks ago."

Jeremy mutters, "That's why he looked familiar."

Wayne says, "You don't know? How don't you know?"

"I don't get involved," Jeremy says. "I don't hurt no one. I drive. I don't do anything else. I won't. I haven't. I told them I couldn't do anything violent; it's not in me."

"Yeah well, you're doing something now. That's you though, a big waste of fucking space, a nothing, nobody. Your head is always in the clouds: thinking about movies, thinking about writing, telling stories. You don't live in the real world."

"What's the *real* world? Where you beat my sister... Why, because you had a bad day?"

Wayne slows as the crack about Jerilyn bounces around his skull making him angry and confused. Wayne lets the insult go. "You know what? All you want is be some nobody on the page, tell some stories. Well, congratulations fuckhead, you got stories now, plenty of them, and if we make it out of this, you might get to tell them. But we aren't going to make it. You just got us both killed. How do you not see that?"

With raised hands, Jeremy says, "We both can make it out of this."

"No, *Jere*, no, we can't. That's what you don't understand. You think you can use your imagination to get out of this mess. You think you can think your way out of this. Well, you can't. Whatever idea, whatever you think you've come up with, it won't work.

"And to tell you the truth, Jere, this may sound harsh, but you're too much of a fucking dreamer to make anything happen. Who are you; you're a nobody drug dealer. You always tell me that's just what you're doing but not what you're doing for a career. You tell me, *You're going places*. But you aren't. You weren't. Never will."

"What, like you?" Jeremy says. "You're nothing too. Not going anywhere. Look at you, you're a fucking cliché; you can't even be an archetype."

Wayne flexes his fingers, clenching them into a fist. He doesn't understand a thing Jeremy said. Why would he? Wayne's never been a reader, and he doesn't watch TV beyond sports. Why would he know the first thing about any of that? Wayne's mouth twists into an O. "What?"

"That's the point," Jeremy says. "You're too fucking stupid to even understand what I just said. I'm going to be somebody, you fuck. You won't. I'm going to get out of this town. I'm going to stay gone. And I'm going to be someone."

"Well, you're somebody to someone now, aren't you?" Wayne says. "Fat Tommy, Short Philly, these guys, they don't fucking play around, Jeremy. You need to think this through. With your car back where you left it, they'll know it was you. They're going to come for you. And they'll think I had something to do with it, and then they'll come for me."

"I know that," Jeremy says. "You don't have to tell me. But I was doing it for you. Tanner would have killed you."

Wayne scoffs. "Who the fuck is *Tanner*? Brogdon? Are you talking about that shit stain badge-wearing pussy cunt? You on a first-name basis now with him? That guy, that fucking guy is a problem. Now *he's* a nobody who doesn't know when he's beat, when he's met his match."

Jeremy says, "We've done a lot of jobs together. He's alright when you get to know him."

"He wants to fuck your sister—told me as much," Wayne says.

"And you don't?"

Wayne blinks. "I'm different."

"Not that different," Jeremy says. "You act like she's this terrible weight around your neck, but when push comes to shove, I—your best fucking friend, your only friend—I know you love her. You love the girls. You act like you don't, but you do."

"I do love them," Wayne says in a quiet voice, not disputing what Jeremy said.

"I don't know what all's happened between you two, but I know some."

"You don't know shit," Wayne says. "You don't know what you're talking about. You don't know your sister. You don't know how terrible she can be, chipping at me all the time, nagging me, acting like I'm not trying. I am fucking trying. I'm trying to be everything she needs, and she makes me feel like I'm nothing. Do you know how that feels? Do you even understand?"

Jeremy shakes his head.

Wayne says, "No, how could you? You aren't married. You have no earthly idea what it takes to have a family, raise kids. If your sister would just recognize I'm trying, we wouldn't have the problems we have. If she truly didn't want me around, I'd leave. I'd pay my part, and I'd go, but every time, every *goddamn time* I leave, Jere, she calls me back in when things get hard. She did that in school; did it when we were kids and does it even now. Back then, it was some guy bothering her or going to get her some cigarettes or beer, using my feelings for her to get what she wants. Now it's a roof over her head, a new dishwasher, some fucking clothes. It's no different. That deputy has something cooking with her, and at some point, it's going to blow up in her face like a black cat."

Jeremy nods. "Tanner ... *Brogdon*, he's not just some pretty boy. He can handle himself. We should have at least taken him to the hospital. It was the right thing to do, not leave him in the street."

Wayne waves a hand. "If he wants to go to a hospital, then he can fucking get himself there. He can handle that himself."

"Wayne don't be like that."

Wayne pokes Jeremy's chest with a finger. "No, *you* don't be like that. You've fucked us. Both of you. Why the hell shouldn't I wring your fucking little neck right now?"

Jeremy slaps the finger away. "I didn't know this was going to happen. None of it. We haven't hurt anyone before. We just do what we do, but it's at night, early morning time, usually at some empty gas station parking lot."

"Well, somebody got hurt this time."

"No one was supposed to get hurt."

"Well they did, so what made this one different?"

"The guy that puts it together, he was insistent we hit this load. He said we had to do it. He said that this one was the most important one we've ever done, said it would be hard. This is why I tried to bring you into it. I knew it might go badly if you didn't know. Why couldn't you be in on it? But you wouldn't listen to me. You wouldn't hear me out. You *refused*."

Jeremy watches the revelation shoot across Wayne's face. "Waitaminute, you wanted me to do a job for Kevin Alexander, the fucking dick jumper at the bar—*he's the German?* Everyone's afraid of that fucking guy. That's who you're working for?"

"It's been good so far."

"Selling weed's one thing Jere, but armed robbery, hijacking shipments, that's a big fucking leap. Jesus, how haven't you gotten clipped yet?"

"It's been good so far."

"Well, it ain't good now. It's far from it. What am I going to do? I don't want any part of this, but you're my friend. I'm with you now. Do you know how that's going to look? Do you know how a guy like Short Philly's going to take that? He's not going to like it. A guy like him, he'll bring the whole house down to swat a mosquito. What do you think he's going to do now?"

"I haven't thought about it like that."

"Then you haven't thought about it. Your mom, Jerilyn, the kids..."

"Surely, he wouldn't..."

"Short Philly plays by different rules. *God*, how are you so *fucking stupid*? How did you even get into this?"

Jeremy hikes his shoulders. "There was this guy who staked a couple of games back in the day when this other guy Renaldo was running games, and before that, some chick named Iris ran some games. I played. I won. I won all the time. They'd bring me in to play guys, but it was a setup. They were marks. I cleaned them out. This guy, he liked me. He was like my patron or some shit. Then when I went big-time, he kept staking me for those big tournaments, then I started losing. The guy I was playing for sent Kevin around, but Kevin didn't want to trash a good thing. He talked to the guy staking me, convinced him I was more useful to them back home. But whatever Wilson Notaro had going on, I must have been separate from their shit because the feds moved in on everyone, and he got killed.

"Jesus."

"After Wilson died, Kevin had me start selling marijuana to work off my debt. He said I still had to pay the organization. You know I didn't want to come back here. I had gotten out of here. I'd gotten to Vegas playing a card game. Why would I want to come back here? I didn't have a choice. I owed them. My debt is still there. Just smaller. Kevin likes me, likes how I work. I've kept his secret. I did what I was told. I didn't go to the cops. And in exchange, he's let me run his business, and I've done well for myself, but it's all tied up in product. Kevin's a weird dude. What he does is he gets something on you, and then when you're not looking, he uses what he knows to cash in. Same with Daniel. Same with Tanner. Each one of us ows him big time for something … so big that when he asked us to do this, we couldn't say no."

Wayne listens and then says, "I've heard the stories about him—the German."

Jeremy says, "Some of those stories are true, but most of it is him and his minions, whispering in people's ears, playing up shadows. It's easy to believe something's out there in the dark when you have someone pretending to hear the monsters scraping across the floor. You remember when we were all kids and you used to do that shit, pretend something was out there? You were just fucking with me. Kevin's like that. He's like a fucking spider with webs everywhere. The guy knows things he couldn't possibly know. And he uses people who no one pays attention to, who are ignored. It's why he's gone as far as he has."

230

CHAPTER 16:

WAYNE KISSEE

WAYNE KISSEE STARES AT THE NIGHT sky, looking at the pinpoints in the blackness, waiting for Lori to bring him a beer. He needs to think, and coming here, to her house, seemed like the best option. No one would think to look for him here. Maybe Sheila would, but she's not looking for him, and Wayne had to get away from Jeremy. He had to figure out what his next move is going to be because Jeremy doesn't get it. He may think he can sit around and wait, but Wayne gets it. He has to move now. There won't be a later.

"Damn him for dragging me into this."

After Jeremy fell asleep on a couch stuffed with marijuana in the back of the truck, Wayne took one of the trucks parked out back, wondering if this one belonged to Earl. He thought of Earl, the shooting, Fat Tommy and Short Philly. He could see their determination... see how sick they are of the hijackings and how serious they're going to handle it from here on out.

Lori appears at the back door wearing his ratty letterman jacket. It's all she's wearing. Her legs extend out of the jacket half-zipped up her chest. She's smiling, the makeup from work still heavy on her face, lips bright red in the pale light. Her pose is meant to entice him to come inside, spend some time with her in bed.

He plans on doing that, but right now, he needs to think.

Wayne looks at her and removes his hands from his jeans pockets, saying, "You know I'm thinking, coming here may not be the best recipe for thinking, but I didn't know where else to go. I can't go home. And I can't let this go on too long. They're going to think I am involved."

"Just explain what happened," Lori says between yawns. She worked late, but if Wayne remembers correctly, she wasn't supposed to close. She didn't explain why she closed. He needs to ask her. She says, "I'm sure they would understand."

"If I do that, I might as well shoot Jeremy myself," Wayne says. He gazes at the sky. "We've been friends forever. He introduced me to Jerilyn. But I don't know, maybe I should. Maybe I should shoot Jeremy. It'd serve him right, bringing me into this. He could have just told me what was going to happen. Then maybe I could have done something about it. Prevented it. Changed the game. But now I can't do that. He should have told me. He didn't. And then he had to go tell me who the German is—"

"Who?" Lori asks.

Wayne closes his eyes and shakes his head, and in a patient voice, because she has no way of knowing, he says, "The guy he works for."

Lori carries the beer low at her waist. She steps forward and offers him the beer. "I'm glad you feel like you can trust me."

Wayne accepts the beer, forcing a smile on his face. "I don't know what to do," he says. "This is bad, Lori, this is really fucking bad. Jeremy's fucked me. I don't know how to get out of this one."

Lori listens and nibbles on her lip as she thinks over what options Wayne might have. She's smart, smarter than he is, smarter than Jerilyn. That's what attracted Wayne to her in the first place.

He remembers the first time they got together. Jerilyn had gone out of town for a funeral or something, or maybe to just get away from him, one of their little breaks, and Lori came over asking for her. He said she's not here. Lori just looked up at him in the doorway, a little smirk on her face, bit her lip like she's doing now. She said she wanted to talk to Jerilyn about a business opportunity. Lori said she wanted to start an online business and wanted to bring Jerilyn into it. Wayne told her Jerilyn wasn't there and explained why. Lori didn't back down, didn't leave, or step off the porch. She asked him, "You want to hear about it?" Wayne told her he did but really, he just wanted to stare at her some more. She'd always been attractive to him, but somehow in that morning light, without the kids around, without Jerilyn, she looked radiant.

Inside the trailer, Lori sat on the couch, with her hands in her lap, staring at him, and she laid the whole thing out for Wayne. She showed him what she'd done, the online website—he had to dig out the battered laptop he and Jerilyn shared. He told her he bought it from the library when they were dumping obsolete inventory,

except Wayne stole it... Although stealing's a loose word; he checked it out and never returned it and threw away all the notices that came in the mail. She showed him the products, explaining how she took a class at the community college on running a business and how to work a website. Then Lori told Wayne her ideas and how she was going to make the things she wanted to make, leatherwork. She explained that her father had a hobby and taught his daughter everything he knew. Wayne thought Lori was an artist. Wayne didn't know how the things she made looked so good. Jerilyn and she might be friends, but Jerilyn was never smart or ambitious like Lori. She might bitch about how Wayne never made anything of his life, but neither has she. Lori, however, she's going places, going to be something.

At the time, Wayne didn't understand what was happening to him. He understands now. The feelings that flooded his body weren't about having sex with someone. What was happening felt like the butterflies everyone describes, except in his case, they felt like eels, squirming around inside his gut, all the way up to his throat, and all the way down to his cock, giving him strength, making him hard, filling him with electricity he's never felt, not for Jerilyn, not for Shelia, not for anyone else.

And when it came to the moment of crossing the line, it wasn't Wayne that made the move. He just stared at her dumbstruck. It was Lori; she did it. He thought afterward that she seduced him. One minute, she's talking, and he's listening, and the next, she's unbuttoning the top of her shirt, rubbing the base of her neck, her clavicle, skin glistening in the morning heat in the hot trailer, and then she's reaching for his cheek, her hand caressing him. He remembers wondering what the hell she was doing. And then she was kissing him, forcing his hand to her body, down the shirt, into the cup of her bra, making him feel her, feel how firm and soft she is. Jerilyn was never like her.

They fucked on the couch like the world was going to end at any moment, didn't even get undressed all the way. She climbed on top of him, undid his zipper, then pulled her jeans, he remembers they were jeans, down to her knees like she was going to use the restroom, half-sat on him, half-crouched, and let him enter her, hanging on his neck, kissing him. She came like that, whole-body clenching into a ball, bringing him with her so he came. It was wonderful, except the eels were still inside him, still making him hard, so they went again and again. Fifteen times that day, making her visit an all-day affair.

Their relationship, whatever it is, is built on trust. Wayne's never lied to Lori, even if she has been the *other* woman—whatever that might be. Seeing each other has been secret. It wasn't secret because Wayne didn't want people finding out; it was secret, to hear Lori tell it, because she didn't want Jerilyn finding out. They are best friends. Lori might not have a problem sleeping with Jerilyn's husband behind her back, but she certainly has a problem with hurting Jerilyn's feelings if she ever were to find out.

Lori says, "You could talk to Tommy and see if he'd listen to what you had to say."

"Tommy's with Philly, and Philly doesn't like Jeremy."

"How do you know? Tommy's always seemed reasonable. My daddy used to work with him from time to time, making custom mud flaps for his trucks, the stenciling and carving on that type of rubber isn't that much different from the leather."

Wayne shakes his head. He sips the beer. Then he says, "I know because when I was there talking to Jeremy about how he fucked me, him thinking we can talk our way out of this goat rope, Jeremy's phone rang, and the way he shot his hands in the pocket was so fast you'd think his pants were on fire."

Lori licks her lips, trying to read Wayne's face. Talking to him the way she is—maybe she's just humoring him— until he gets tired of talking and takes her up against the side of the house, the brick at her back. That might be why she's wearing that coat the way she is, with nothing underneath. She does that from time to time. Wayne will get to talking, and she'll listen patiently, and then mid-sentence, she'll reach over, shush him, laying her index finger to his mouth, and then she'll start kissing him, fondling and brushing him, getting his pants undone, seizing him how she wants when she wants.

She asks, "Who was it? Who called?"

Wayne finishes the beer and hands the empty bottle back to her. "That's what I asked him," he says, watching her stroll to the trash can back toward the door. She lifts the plastic lid and drops the beer inside; it clanks against the glass of other bottles, and she turns back toward him with the lid in hand, as he keeps talking. "Who is that?' I still can't believe he still had his phone—that's some stupid shit. It's the first thing you need to get rid of when people are going to be looking for you."

Lori puts the lid back on the trashcan and asks again, "Who was it?"

Wayne doesn't answer her question right away, he's getting there. She needs to be patient because, as he explains what happened, his mind's working out what to do next.

"All he did was look at the screen and deposit the ringing phone back in his pocket. I stared at him. I said, I just asked you a fucking question, you not going to answer? He stared back like I'm a dumbshit for being suspicious of him. He goes, 'Oh, it's Short Philly.'"

As she walks back to Wayne, she says, "What, why was he calling Jeremy? How did he know to call Jeremy?"

"That's what I wanted to know," Wayne says, nodding. "I said, 'Why is Short Philly calling you?' Then, Jeremy said, 'He's been doing it for a few weeks now, threatening me.' I couldn't believe it. He's been threatening him. I just stared at him, watched him stupidly shuffling side to fucking side."

"Wait, what did he do to get Short Philly to call him like that?"

"I'll tell you what he did," Wayne says, pacing now, getting worked up over the whole thing and talking with his hands. "It dawned on me what he did. It's what he always does. He thinks if he plays the odds, the angles, he's going to win. His imagination gets the better of him. Like always. Like it always has. He's so fucking stupid. You hear of being pussy blind… Well, he's risk blind, and he likes it. He likes the game. Likes the idea of winning. Gambling. I guess you would have to have some affinity for it to go play poker like he did. I said to him, 'You fucking didn't?' He says, 'I thought if I could make some extra cash, I could pay down on my debt to the German. I thought I'd get out of this shit, this robbing people.'"

Lori cuts Wayne off, halts his pacing. She says, "He bet with his boss's money?"

Wayne stares down into her eyes, staring down into the folds of the coat, his mind running a hundred million miles a second. "He claimed he won, then lost."

"How bad?" Lori grabs Wayne's hands. "How bad did he lose?"

Wayne clutches her hands and squeezes. "Well, he said he only walked out of Tommy's cleaners down five hundred."

Lori squeezes back. "That's not bad."

"But he said he had to buy back in on a line of credit. They didn't think the money was his, which it fucking wasn't, and he's a dumb fuck for thinking he could bet with his boss's money like he's out there representing the German, and they've heard of the German and how he is... He bragged about all the bad things, rumors, whispers, whatever people think this guy's done. What did he think was going to happen?"

Lori asks, "What did happen?"

"Jeremy said Tommy and Philly gave him all his money back," Wayne says. "He said they revoked the credit line and *he* owed them a substantial chunk of change."

"Fuck, that is bad."

That's what Wayne's been trying to tell her. "I know. He's supposed to be my friend. I don't see how he could do this to me. Screw me like this. He set me up. I don't know what to do."

"Look at me," Lori says, drawing her elbows back enticing Wayne forward, into her. "Look at me," she repeats, softer this time, peering up at him, the glow of the moon on her face.

Wayne looks at her, her breath warm and sweet against his cheeks, her lips nearly touching his, their foreheads touching.

"I hear you," Lori says. "I hear what you're saying. I get how you think you're fucked, I do, but I also think we're in a position here. We have the marijuana."

Wayne doesn't understand what she's saying. "We don't have the marijuana. Jeremy does."

Lori shakes her head and talks to him as if he's a little kid who needs the whole thing laid out for him. "We know where it is." Her eyes stare into his eyes. "And, we know Jeremy's been selling the marijuana he's been hijacking."

"I would assume so. It would make sense. It's what I would do."

"It's what I would do, too," Lori says. "And I think about where he might have got that pound for Jerilyn. Jeremy's too good at selling, and he's not going to give away a pound of good product. He had to unload some of that stolen shit, and he had it sitting around. My bet, knowing him and the way he is, and knowing her, he was going to tempt her with more if she was able to sell it. That's what he does. She doesn't know it, but I do. You do. And she's a looker. People will buy from her that wouldn't buy from him or his guys. I bet he even had Shelia give her a tip last night."

"What tip?" Wayne blinks. "Jerilyn sold marijuana last night?"

Lori grips him tighter, drags him closer. She kisses him, tongue flicking across his lips. "Jere's a weight, bringing everyone down, trying to turn them into him, that's what he's doing. It's not enough he's screwed up his own life, he has to screw up hers."

Wayne says, "What is she thinking? Why would she do that?"

Lori's face tells him she knows exactly why. "Samuel sent her home yesterday because of it, because she's been

late to work three times. I listened through the door. He knows about the weed, and he wanted her to give it back."

"What about our kids?" Wayne says, trying to process what he's hearing. Jerilyn selling for Jeremy. Samuel is involved now. Lori's face indicates she knows more but isn't saying. "What's going on? What aren't you telling me?"

"I like Jere, but this is too much, even for him. You have to ask yourself and he has to ask himself, what if they find out she has their weed?"

Lori's brain is working now, the same way it worked when she started her business, which is doing well. She's examining all the possibilities, processing the moves like she's playing a board game. Lori's six moves ahead.

Seeing all that, Wayne, in a searching voice, inquires, "How would they find out?"

"But what if they do?" Lori says. "What then? What if DHS comes into the trailer and finds it? What if some of Brogdon's friends pull her over or catch her selling? Hell, what if Brogdon uses Jeremy to get whatever it is he wants from Jerilyn?"

"What he wants from Jerilyn? Jerilyn's talking to Brogdon? What's she doing that for?"

Lori doesn't say. "If we take a moment to think, we've got the cards here."

"What fucking cards, we got nothing," Wayne says. "I killed a man, and we've got a truck full of stolen marijuana that isn't here, it's there. What cards do we have? We have nothing."

"We have everything."

"Explain it then."

"You know where the truck is. We've got the truck which means we got the product. We know it was an inside job, and we know who did it because we know who the German is. Now, don't you think that's valuable information?"

"So we, what?" Wayne says, still confused. "Trade information and marijuana for a pass? I don't know if Short Philly works that way."

"You and I both know that's exactly how Short Philly works," Lori says, peering up at him. She kisses Wayne again, longer, with harder contact. He feels himself rise. She should feel it too. She says, "He'll see the light. He'll get it. We just have to be smart about it. But it's time for you to decide. Now or never. You could walk away, but you might as well go home and blow your brains out. Jeremy's worked this out. It's like a script or a story to him. All it took was a little logical puzzling, and he got it. The German's not looking to kill him. It's Fat Tommy and Short Philly who want him. So trade weed and info for your life. And use the weed to get out of this."

Wayne listens, and all he says while glancing back at the house, the inside, warm and bright, "It could work."

But like before, with Jeremy's other plans, not just the ones over the last few weeks, but the plans throughout his entire life... like when bullies would pick on him or a teacher gave him a bad grade and Jeremy wanted Wayne to change his mind... Wayne had to be on board. He had to agree.

Lori gives him a now or never look, the same look Jeremy's always giving him, the same one she gave him on the steps to the trailer the first time they had sex. "The phone's inside. Who do you want to call first?"

CHAPTER 17:

KEVIN ALEXANDER

KEVIN ALEXANDER THUMPS HIS FINGERS on the tabletop, rolling them across the laminated surface one at a time in succession, explaining himself, saying, "I was Wilson's man. He was my friend. I liked him. I got into this because of him. I'm loyal to him—*was* loyal to him."

Kevin glances out the window at the parking lot, at the sun breaking the horizon, the light white and refreshing. It's the next morning, the day after the failed job, almost 24 hours since things went to shit. With that in mind, trying to push his plans forward despite missteps very much out of his control, Kevin sits sprawled in a booth at the Morning Joe Cafe, Alejandro's old place, chewing on a toothpick while drinking coffee. He is dressed pretty much in yesterday's clothes—he hasn't slept—and is talking with Flavia Sanchez, the third prong of Iris King's little triumvirate.

Last night, after it became clear there were difficulties and he needed to pivot his plans, Kevin called Flavia and

243

asked about setting up a meeting, telling her they needed to talk. Hesitantly, Flavia agreed to a meeting. She said it had to be at her restaurant. He knew she would agree to the meeting because Flavia doesn't like farming things out. She's been against Schafer Logistics, Tommy in particular, and would prefer someone from within to make the runs. "Throughout all of this, you've always been the dissenting vote," Kevin reminded her and then commented on her choice of venue calling it her *home turf.* He said, of course, she was meeting someplace she's comfortable with, messing with her when he said it, but she didn't laugh.

In a very serious voice—she's always serious—she said it was her only stipulation and then reminded Kevin he was coming to her, so she wasn't going to put up with his bullshit. "So knock it off, and don't waste my time..." leaving the rest of her threat unstated.

So all Kevin said on the phone then was, "What was it that Renaldo used to say? Yeah, sure, okay. Fine," agreeing to meet her at the diner, fully intending to waste as much of her time as he could.

Now Kevin tries to answer her question, explaining why he asked for the meeting without coming right out with it. "For a couple of reasons. Firstly, because it's the next logical step. I don't have enough capital to openly challenge *her* without your support, so I very much need your support."

"Support for what?" Flavia says.

Kevin would admit that she is pretty if she dressed right, but she doesn't. She's wearing denim overalls and a white T-shirt, and has her dark and lustrous hair, which matches her hard-like-stone eyes in both color and intensity, pulled over one shoulder, resting there. She looks like an Indian Princess instead of a line cook making eggs for a living.

All around them, dishes clatter in the kitchen and bells ring above the door, signaling people entering and leaving. Kevin can hear the coffee pot, hear the coffee brewing, then hear it being poured. Wait staff buzz around, two girls and a busser. All of it is loud and distracting. All of it happening around them without her intervention. Without Omar though—he's usually in the back.

Flavia says, "The little doggie wants to bite at his bitch's leash. I don't want any part of that."

Kevin sighs. "I'm not biting at a leash."

"But you are a little doggie, going from master to master," she says. "You were with Wilson Notaro before, no? And now you're with her, and you're what, here to be with me next? Is that it? Sounds like a little doggie going from master to master."

"I'm not a dog," Kevin says. "That's not what this is."

"I don't care what *this* is; *she is* a bitch," Flavia stresses. "So why are you here, truly *here*? Why are you talking to me? I'm nothing to you."

Kevin relaxes in the booth and throws an arm over the back of the seat. He plucks the toothpick from his mouth. "I'm here to talk to you about some things, and I want to ask you something, something that's been on my mind lately."

"What things? You don't like how you're treated, so you want to fuck the bitch who fucks everyone else? You want my help? That's not very novel. I didn't think you swing that way."

Kevin shrugs. "I told you, Wilson was my friend."

"And she killed him," Flavia holds up a finger signaling for him to stay quiet. "Or had him killed, it doesn't matter which. You did nothing but fall in line with whatever game she was playing. So what? What's that have to do with me?"

"You have the manpower to continue forward."

"Manpower? Is that all you want?"

"Not all, no," Kevin says, picking up his coffee, sipping it and staring at her. "And for you to listen to what I have to say."

Flavia doesn't visibly move but Kevin observes her body shift in impatience. "I *am* listening to what you have to say, and you haven't said anything worth listening to," she says. "You said for a couple of reasons. What are the others?"

Kevin sets the mug down, places the toothpick back in his mouth, and rolls it to the side with his tongue. "A couple of reasons are personal, and I'm not sure I can share them with you," he says. "A couple aren't."

"But there are some you can share."

Kevin says, "You're not used to following others, are you?"

"I think..." she hesitates, "you—if you don't know the answer by now, the answer to that question—your question, a stupid question at that—is we should go our separate ways. I have things to do."

"Hold on," Kevin says, taking the toothpick from his mouth with one hand. He still taps the fingers of the other hand against the table. "It's been a long night, and I'm tired." He pauses to assess her mood. "You haven't gotten up yet, so despite all your bluster, you want to hear what I have to say. Just admit it or end this now. You know that I know something that you need to know, but I don't want to give it away without something in return. And whatever I know that you already know, you can't bring yourself to ask because despite what you say, what happened with Wilson caused us all problems, you included, so spare me this hard-ass act and talk with me."

Flavia tilts her head to the side. "What do you think I know?"

Kevin smiles. He motions with his hand on the table. "Look—I'll level with you, I'm frustrated, okay? You can understand that. I'm frustrated with how things are going: how *she* treats us. We're nothing to her, and I think she's made that pretty damn clear. You and her, I know that you two don't get along. Hell, we don't get along," meaning him and Flavia. "She asked you not to get involved and what did you do?" He finishes the question with a couple of well-placed well-timed taps.

The effect is what he desires. Flavia relaxes in the seat. Her shoulders lose some of the uptight tension that kept her so rigid, and she fights to suppress a smirk as she answers: "I got involved."

"Right," Kevin says, stopping the rhythmic tapping to make pistol fingers at her. "Right, you got involved. You," pulling the word out, "shot Pablo. That wasn't the plan. That's not what you were told to do and that wasn't what was supposed to happen. That caused some problems down south with your cousins. From what I hear, they don't view us as two separate organizations any longer. They see us as one, and they see us as someone they don't want to do business with. That was because of Pablo."

"He was worthless," Flavia spits. "He needed to go, and my cousins don't care about him."

"No, they cared about Vega."

"His brother will come around; he's a businessman."

"And Pablo wasn't," Kevin says, but the way he says it is both question and statement. "Because he wanted to start a war?"

Flavia jerks her head once. "He was a coward."

"And you shot him. That wasn't the plan... So what if he *was* a coward, he was needed."

"Not to me, not my plan, it was her plan. Our plans aren't the same."

"See that's what I'm *saying*. You have a plan of your own. You make decisions for yourself. No one else does that, no one else but you. We're alike in that regard."

Flavia chuckles. Kevin cocks his head to the side. When she gains control of herself, smiling, she says, "We are not alike in any way."

"No?" Kevin says. "We aren't? Okay, I'll give you that. Maybe we aren't. Maybe we are. Ultimately, it doesn't matter. We still need to talk. We still need to talk about her and what's going on."

"What's going on?"

"A lot," Kevin says. "I know you know, so ask me. I'll confirm."

"What do I know?" she says, trying her best not to let on, but he sees it, and he's going to use it to crush Iris.

Kevin takes the toothpick from his mouth and points the sharpened end at her. "How about this, tell me how you felt when you found out *he* went to the cops?"

The question catches her off guard. Her eyes narrow. "When who did?"

Kevin says, "That's how it happened by the way," jabbing the toothpick at her. "It's the only way it could have happened. I've looked at it, done some deep thinking, just like you have. I know you have. You've thought about this. How could you not? How do you not ask the questions, the *question*?"

"What is *the* question?" she asks with contempt in her voice, revealing she knows.

"How did the cops find out about where you all kept Siriano? Someone had to tell them. So who knew?"

"Who did?"

"Our side didn't know," Kevin says, touching his chest. He leans into whisper, turning on the dramatics. "That was kind of the point of the kidnapping, right? We aren't supposed to know where you kept him. We had to meet with you, where you wanted."

"Iris knew, she had to have known," Flavia says.

"Fair point," Kevin concedes. "But she didn't go to the cops. She wouldn't do that. She had her own thing cooking. She wouldn't have wanted them a part of that plan. It's how she got her husband killed. And I know she didn't tell Wilson. I'm sure."

"*You,* you could've known."

Kevin agrees. "But I don't talk to cops."

Flavia sips her water. "So get to the point. Spit it out," she says. "Say what you're going to say. You're enjoying this too much."

"I'm not enjoying anything," Kevin says. "I'm laying a foundation. You don't build a wall without leveling the ground. That's what I'm doing, I'm showing you my hand, so to say, so you can see where I'm at, what's going on here." He motions back and forth over the table.

The bell above the door dings. A customer enters and sits at the bar. Kevin and Flavia sit in silence the whole time.

Then all Flavia says, turning back to him, is "Lay it quicker."

Kevin gnaws on the end of the toothpick for a moment. "You don't feel like she's trying to use us? You don't feel that?"

"Who?" Flavia says, frustration creeping in at the edges of her voice. Kevin knows he's brought her to her breaking point. "All you do is ask questions. You came here to tell me something, but you have said nothing, and you won't say what it is you want."

"Iris, *the bitch*," Kevin says. "You don't feel like she's using you, using me? The same way she uses people to get what she wants with little regard for what they want? That's not a problem for you? You just want to take orders, take orders from her? Damn you, damn the neighborhood, damn everything you've worked for, everything *Alejandro* worked for?

"Do you want me to say that I don't like her?"

"No, I want you to ask me the question you want to ask because I know the answer. And you know the answer, too, which means you don't like her."

Flavia leans back in the booth. She studies him. "You want me to ask you about my husband?"

"I do."

"You want me to ask you if you think he's the one that went to the cops?"

"That's certainly a question we know the answer to."

"You want me to ask you if Iris is sleeping with him?"

"Well, that's certainly a question worth asking. Are you sleeping with him?"

"No," Flavia says. She looks away with pain on her face, a look of betrayal. "Not since..." she almost says it but catches herself, "...Pablo."

"Look, the reason I'm here is I'm supposed to find the guys that have been hitting our trucks. But I can't find these guys anywhere."

"You know who they are?"

"I do," he says, crossing his arms. "One guy, named Jeremy Hall, is known around town to work with the German. He left his car behind."

Flavia says, "Is this where you tell me you're the German?"

Kevin raises an eyebrow. "Me?"

"Yes," she says, "you, who else would know our shipment schedules? Who else gains? And who else thinks chickenshit like that means anything?"

Kevin crosses his arms. "If you agree to work with me, knowing if I am the German or not doesn't matter. It's irrelevant. You need to understand this, understand some things. First of all, I need to find this Jeremy Hall."

Kevin doesn't say who he actually needs to find before things get out of control, but Flavia doesn't ask him why he needs to find Jeremy.

Kevin says, "It's partly why I called for this meeting, I'm trying to get ahead of Jeremy ... or his friend Wayne, the driver. These guys, they're like best freakin' friends forever, been together a long time. This Wayne guy is married to Jeremy's sister. What I'm saying is if these two mooks decide to go to Fat Tommy and Short Philly... well, let's just say Jeremy knows things, which, at this juncture, could and *would*, theoretically, hurt me, if I were this German guy. It would hurt me greatly if they came out. Before today, not

that big of a deal. After next week, it probably would mean nothing. But if these things came out right now, I'm sure Short Philly would shoot me in the head and not give me a second glance. It's a delicate time. Things have to happen when they're supposed to happen."

"And things aren't happening how you thought?"

"If it were me, being this German, I should've never let Jeremy operate with so much freedom. Look, after visiting Iris, I promised to take care of Jeremy, which to be honest, I always intended to do. So I returned to my bar and waited for his little wrecking crew, or what was left of it, to return. One of them dying wasn't a big loss. That man was too violent and men who are violent are too hard to control, something my buddy Neil used to say to me. And living the way I do, who I am, I've found that to be true.

"I had a plan. I'd wait for them there. I poured a drink, told my staff to come in later, and delayed opening the bar, all of which isn't how I do things, but it was going to be a special visit. When Tanner—that's the other guy involved in this, tiger of a guy and my sheriff deputy 'cause I've always liked a man in uniform; if you don't have one you should get one—when he and Jeremy walked through the door, I would be waiting for them, in the dark, gun in hand. I'd shoot them both, claim they were burglars, and I was just a business owner standing my ground."

Flavia says, "But that didn't happen."

"No, it didn't," Kevin says. "That didn't happen. Usually after a job, my guys come right back to the bar. That didn't happen this time. So, although, technically, my plan had been flawless, I've primed them with the other jobs and kept anyone worth anything from knowing who they were to me. There would be no connection, nothing the cops could prove. But these guys, they never showed up. 'Course no one's been killed before, much less hurt, so maybe that's a reason. Now one of them's dead, and the other two are gone, nowhere to be found or seen. They're not answering phones. Not reaching out. Nothing. But life goes on, no reason to let things out of my control cause so much stress."

"What are you trying to say?" Flavia asks. "What does that have to do with what's going on? With me?"

Kevin throws an arm back over the back of the booth, not letting on how stressed this power play is making him. He stops tapping and raises his fingers in a halting motion. "Hold on, slow down, I'm getting there."

"Get there faster," she says. "As you can see, I have work to do." She jerks her head to the right, to the open diner full of people.

Nodding slowly, Kevin says, "I get that." He starts rapping his knuckles on the table again. "But what I'm asking of you isn't something I want to ask without vetting you to make sure this won't blow back in my face."

"What you are asking me is how angry am I?"

"Might be," he says.

"You're telling me you're the German, and you've been hitting my trucks."

Kevin holds up a finger. "Not just your trucks, my lily."

"Our trucks," she corrects. "And you're saying you know—I don't know how you do, but the hint about the deputy was about as subtle as your appetite—that Omar talked to the cops about where Siriano was."

"Did he?"

"You think he did, and that's why you are here. You think that he shouldn't have done that, no matter how much danger I was in. He shouldn't have done that." She pauses. "And you aren't here for manpower."

"No, I'm not here for manpower," Kevin admits. "I need Fat Tommy and Short Philly to stay out of it. You need to tell them that. That's why I'm here, but that's not what I'm asking. I'm here to tell you I'm the German, but I'm also here to tell you I'm done stealing from you. I never wanted to steal from you. I only wanted to steal from Iris. And now that I know what I know, I think now is the right time to make my move. What I don't need is our third-party friends losing their cool and using me for target practice."

"But that's not what you wanted to ask me."

"No, it isn't. All of those are reasons. I told you that I had a few."

Flavia guesses his motivations and reasons some more. "You want me to ask you if I know my husband is having an affair with Iris."

"No, that's not what I came here to ask you."

"Then what is it?" she says, her eyes glistening with tears. "It wasn't to ask for my help. It's clear you just want me to stay out of the way."

"I do," Kevin says. "No, what I came here to ask you is: you and your husband were inseparable..." He holds up two crossed fingers. "Like this. Regular lovebirds, working in this business. What changed? What drove your husband away, made him weak enough for Iris? You all not sleeping together? Getting along?"

Flavia nods, saying, "We *are not* sleeping together or getting along," and in a very frank voice and as Kevin had guessed it all along, she says, "He talked to the cops."

CHAPTER 18:

GABRIELLA LUNA

GABRIELLA LUNA PARKS HER VEHICLE across the street from Gold's Bar, in the strip club's parking lot as she did the day before, and she immediately notices the cop in the cowboy hat reclining in his Ford Bronc, with his hat pulled low over his eyes and face. All she can see from where she is is his angular chin and drooping mustache. Then almost as if he feels her eyes upon him, the cowboy cop lifts the rim of the hat with his index finger to reveal his eyes, which lock with hers. The cop stares at her for a few moments, sips something from a gas station cup, probably coffee, sets the cup down, and exits the Bronco. He tugs at the edges of the vest that hides his gun and badge. Checking himself in his reflection in the Bronco's window, he fixes his hat and traverses the parking lot toward her. At her passenger door, he knocks on the glass, peers inside, and waves at her through the window.

Dressed in yesterday's clothes, make up all but nonexistent with her hair a mess, Gabriella doesn't want to talk

257

to him, but just like with the stripper from the other night, she relents against her best intentions, and she presses the button on her left to unlock the doors. With a clunk, the black nubby plunger in the door lifts.

The cop opens the passenger door and bends over to look at her through the car. He dips his hat toward her empty passenger seat. His sharp eyes, half-hidden under the brim of the hat, rove through the cabin before settling on her, studying her. In his eyes, Gabby sees intention, a keen intellect, and tremendous awareness. He has beautiful eyes, eyes that communicate everything he ever feels he has to say. He possesses the eyes movie directors would want to film, the eyes of a western movie star, eyes that would fill a movie screen.

Gabby doesn't know who he is; he's a cop, the gun and badge tell her that. And she remembers seeing him yesterday, with the gun and the badge. She remembers telling him who she was and remembers the face he made as she said it. But he didn't explain himself; he didn't talk to her, not really. At some point, he told her his name, introducing himself, but she doesn't remember it. She only remembered it was some sort of city name.

He didn't do the talking yesterday. It was the OSBI agent, Raley Freeman, who interviewed her. But he did so with this cowboy-looking cop standing behind him, eyeing her over his shoulder, appraising the interview, with his arms crossed and eyes half-closed. His eyes were burrowing into her the whole time she spoke to Freeman, looking without looking. This cop never said a word. He barely moved. He stood there and listened. Calm. Quiet. Peaceful.

"Do you mind if I sit?" he asks.

His eyes, those hard eyes, should see how annoyed she is with his intrusion. They should see how widely her nostrils flare, demonstrating her irritation. But playing nice and coating her voice in severe politeness, she asks, "If I did?"

The cop grins broadly, seemingly missing it all, or maybe he doesn't. Maybe he discerns it all and disguises it well. "I'd sit anyways."

His temperament, the nice guy routine, the cowboy get up, is all meant to disarm her. She feels this. Believes this. And in a way, it works. She's intrigued by him.

"Then, by all means, sit," Gabby says, taking her hand off the steering wheel to gesture to the passenger seat, careful to keep her purse with the revolver on her thigh and within reach and to keep it from falling to the floorboards.

She doesn't know if he knows there's a revolver in her purse, but he acts leery of her bag, glancing at it, or maybe he's just assessing the situation, or her, or maybe her imagination is getting the best of her. She doesn't know. She hasn't experienced this before, not like this. She hasn't done anything wrong, not yet, but still, the thought of murdering someone, because that's what it is no matter how she justifies and rationalizes it, makes her feel guilty.

And with the way this cop is looking at her, scrutinizing her, the same way he did yesterday, she senses he knows she is here to kill a man. Maybe she gave it away yesterday. Maybe she is giving it away now. Maybe he knows a gun, the one Flavia gave her, is in her purse, and knows it's inches from her reach. She doesn't know how he knows.

She doesn't understand this man. She didn't understand why he was there yesterday, and she doesn't understand why he's here today. Now. How could he be here?

Why is he here? Why does he act like he isn't surprised to find her here? Does he know? He couldn't.

The cop removes his hat and folds his large frame into her passenger seat. The cowboy boots look ridiculous against her floorboards and drop flecks of dirt onto her mats.

"What brings you here this morning?" the cop asks as he settles into the seat. His right arm disappears between the seat and the door as he adjusts the seat, sliding it back to create legroom. Then he pulls the lever on the side, dropping the seat back a few degrees. "That's better." He places the hat in his lap.

Gabriella watches all this. "I should ask you the same question."

The cop chuckles. "You could, you could. And maybe you should." He talks with his hands, but not in an erratic way, more in a self-assured and calm way, using his hands as punctuation or to stress his intonation. "But I do believe I asked first. But seeing how I'm a gentleman and you are a lady, I'll answer your question. I'm here to watch the bar over yonder." He points the brim of the hat toward Gold's Bar. "See that motorcycle over there ... that belongs to one of our dead guys from yesterday."

Gabriella cocks her head to the side. "One of our dead guys?"

The cop grimaces and apologizes, lifting the hat toward her as if to slow her down. "I'm sorry, a force of habit. I didn't mean he is *ours* ... yours ... I mean—"

"I know what you mean," she says. She glances in her side mirror, at the brick wall of the abandoned box chain store building behind her car. Maybe it was a Staples or a Walmart. It's been empty for years, and she can't remember.

The cop takes a moment to reset, sighing before he speaks. "Why are you here?"

Gabriella answers honestly. "I... I don't know."

"You don't know," the cop says and then, more to himself, repeats the question, "Mhmm, why *are* you here? It's mighty strange to find you here. Maybe if I knew you better, maybe, it wouldn't be strange. Maybe you like *strange,* and that's why you are here."

Gabriella frowns at the crassness of his remark, but she doesn't take offense. She reads him as a man who voices a majority of his thoughts but not all of them.

The cop analyzes her reaction and says, "No... no, that's not right. It's early, and they aren't open, so I don't think that's it, no ma'am. No, it seems strange to find you here. *You* belong someplace else. Being here doesn't strike me as something you should be doing. But then, that thought makes me want to know the answer even more. Why *are you* here?"

Gabby's shoulders tense, bunching into a knot. It makes her back hurt and prompts her to roll her neck side to side, stretching. She blusters, "You are right, you don't know me."

"But I want to," he says, waving the hat at her once. "I want to get to know you."

"Why? Who are you?"

He hums to himself, wriggling the mustache. "Well, I'm Frank, of course. Frankfort Corbin."

"What kind of name is that?"

Frank smiles, a kind, pleasant smile. "You got me. Maybe my parents liked the name. I don't know. It's unique, that's for sure. My father had been in the army, so maybe he was stationed in Germany, and Frankfort is better than anything else over there, I don't know. They always called me Frank, except when I was in trouble, and then it's like with any child I suppose, I was Frankfort Xavier."

"Xavier?"

"Catholic," he says. "They were, not me; I don't know what I am."

"You dress like a cowboy."

"No," Frank says. "I dress like a representative of the cattle industry. Completely different things. I'm a lawman, so I dress the part. I suppose though, with popular culture being the way it is, I can see how you would misunderstand, and I don't take any offense to it, no *siree*."

"So, what are you?"

Frank wears pride well, he's a hard worker and happy to do what he does. "I am an agent of the Oklahoma Department of Agriculture. You ever hear of Fish and Game, Wildlife, Game Wardens? I'm like that for cattle and such, which is all just fancy window dressin' to say I hunt cattle rustlers."

"I don't know what that is."

"It's okay, most folks don't. They think, like you did about me being a cowboy—the outlaws and troublemakers of the old west by the way—they think rustlin' is a thing of the past, but I can assure you, it very much isn't. You can just think of me as a Cattle Cop, most everyone else does. No reason to call me 'agent' or anything, not like with Agent Freeman with OSBI, who you talked to yesterday."

"You were there yesterday."

"I was."

"Why?"

"Freeman called me."

"Why?" she asks again.

"The truck used in that crime is part of a rustlin' investigation I'm working. He was doing me a professional courtesy. He wanted me to come see what I could see. That way he didn't have to explain everything. I live in town, and I've been on leave, so it wasn't a bother."

His words hint at something, especially the comment about the leave, but Gabby doesn't understand or know what.

"Are you good at what you do?" she asks. "What did you see?"

"I saw some things," he says. "But it's not about what you see, not all of it, 'cause seein' is only part of it, you have four other senses you can use, not to mention the unofficial one of feeling. Sometimes crimes like that—it's about what you feel. How you feel. What the intangibles are telling you."

"Like your gut?"

"Right, like your gut. Makes you ask questions you might not ask like: What happened here I'm not seeing? How did this transpire in this way? What is missing that should be here? Or my favorite, which one of these things isn't like the other? It's as much about what you can put together through hard facts as constructin' a story and arrangin' it together in your imagination. Every good cop has imagination."

"What about the bad ones?"

"The bad ones don't," he says. "Some cops just can't see it. You know, they look at it, and they think they know what happened, but they can be completely wrong, which is why you see them on the news gettin' in trouble. Not that it doesn't happen to everyone now and then, even the good ones, but especially the bad ones 'cause they don't know when to walk away. Their problem is that they don't think. Don't ask themselves questions they should be asking. Don't use their noggin. No brain. No imagination—imagination is intuition, reasoning, wisdom."

"An understanding?"

Frank tells her that's it. "Displays knowledge, which the bad ones don't show off. What they're showin' is their ass. Thinking about what they do, how they do it, why they do it, from time to time, would have taught them when to walk away. Taught them when to go forward, too. It's like *wres*-tlin' a bear: do I stand here and let the grizzly get me? Or do I run off? Sometimes you have to stand your ground. Take your shot. Hope you do the right thing and don't get chewed up in the process if wrong. But then, sometimes you just walk away. You look at the situation, and you see it for what it is, usually bigger than you or has nothing to do with you, and you decide this isn't worth it. It's too big for you or it's none of your concern."

"What are you saying?"

"I'm telling you how I see things. If you read into them any more than that, then share your thoughts with me. I'd love to hear what you have to say."

"You heard what I had to say yesterday."

"I heard the story for sure."

"But you think there is more?"

"Isn't there always?" he says. "I mean, there's always more but sometimes it's about asking the right questions. It's about having imagination, seeing the story behind the story"

"Questions like what?"

"Like what's the revolver for? The one in your purse… What's it doing there? You don't strike me as a woman who'd carry that Air Weight around."

She says, "It's mine," a little too fast.

"That's not what I asked you… although I'd argue it isn't yours."

Gabby doesn't question his assertion. "What do you want from me?"

"To know why you are carrying that around," he says, and when she doesn't answer, he adds, "and to know why you were followin' that truck."

"What truck?"

"The one from yesterday. You were following it. You didn't just find yourself there by accident to witness all that. By the way, how are you doing with that? Seein' something like that, what you saw, a man killed, isn't an easy thing, not when you're up front for the show."

"I'm fine," she says. "But I didn't sleep much last night."

She didn't sleep any. After the cops released her, she went home. She tried to eat but couldn't. She tried to sleep and couldn't do that either. She stared at the ceiling all night, cursing herself for not doing what she had sat out to do. And every time she blinked, she saw that man being shot. Her mind replayed the events over and over. When she did finally drift off, she dreamed of her son. He came to her, spoke to her, and asked her to forgive him. She told him about his father, doing it in all the ways she ever imagined doing it. Then he told her he killed his father and apologized for doing that by leaning over her and kissing her forehead. When his lips touched her skin, he was shot. In her dream, it was in the head, and she awoke in a panic.

She couldn't sleep anymore after that. Though, she could still feel where he kissed her.

In a soft, understanding voice, Frank says, "It'll get better, but I know you weren't there by accident."

"How?"

"We're not stupid, slow sometimes, but not stupid. First thing Raley did was pull the video from the starting location, someplace called something logistics. Then he pulled all the video from that place to where everything happened, looking at everything all the way ... and what did I see when he showed it to me?"

"Me," she admits.

"You. Now why did I see *you*?"

"I... I don't know."

"Oh I think you do, and I think I'm seeing it now."

"What do you mean?"

"Well, that fellow who got shot, not the one in the car but the one trying to hijack the truck, his motorcycle is over there. TPD Patrol-man found it. I've been sitting on the bar, a favor for Raley, waiting to see what I see. No one has come or gone, which is strange 'cause, as far as I can tell, that place is always open. Though, it wasn't yesterday. The bartender, a woman named Shelia who showed up about an hour ago to find the door still locked, says her boss told her to take the day off—now that's mighty strange."

"Maybe he was sick or something."

"Maybe," he says, seriously considering her words. "Do you know who happens to own that place?"

"No," she says. It's a lie, and she doesn't fool him.

"Kevin *Germaine* Alexander," Frank the Cattle Cop says using the full name. She didn't know his middle name. Flavia didn't tell her. "You know Mr. Alexander?"

"No," she says. "Should I?"

Frank shrugs. "Don't know. I think maybe you don't know him, but you want to get to know him."

"Why's that?"

"You want to get to know him 'cause he's the one who most likely killed your son."

Gabby tries her best to hide her surprise, only allowing a slight twitch in her smile, but her words escape her mouth with a sour tone. "He what?"

"Don't play like what I'm telling you is shocking, although it coming from me might be. I guess I can see that."

"Who are you?"

"Frank. We've been through this already. Let's not misunderstand each other and go back around."

"You know about my son?"

"Renaldo," he says. "I knew who you were when you said your name."

"So, it means something to you?"

Frank nods. "Your son sure meant something to you, too."

"What do you know about Renaldo?"

Frank stares hard at Gold's Bar. "I know he's no longer with us," he says, holding up his hand to stave off her questions. "Hold up, I'll get there. I'll explain… It's a guess, but I have information that indicates Renaldo got himself killed. My info says Mr. Alexander most likely did it."

"He did?" she says, begging for confirmation while stating a fact, with millions of thoughts racing through her brain. "How do you know? No one else believes he's dead."

Frank looks at her. His look tells her he does. "Mr. Alexander didn't do it alone though, from what I'm hearing two others were involved. Now—one of these people is already dead. Can't kill a dead man twice. That's for sure. Otherwise, justice would be a bit different. The other is a woman named Iris King. From what I hear, she was sweet on Renaldo."

"I've heard of her, yes."

Frank pauses.

Then he says, "Iris King has gotten herself wrapped up in some nasty business—same business Renaldo was in, same business as Mr. Alexander over there."

"Why are you telling me this?"

Frank looks down at his hat, twisting it in his hands, examining the band, the sweat stains.

"Because I lost someone dear to me," he says, voice small, "and I know what that feels like. It felt like my heart being ripped out and stepped on, and there's nothing I can do about it. Every morning, I wake up, and the pain's there, maybe fading some by now, but it's still there. It's still aching. Now, the woman I loved, she knew she was dying, so I got to deal with those emotions over time. I can't imagine having her ripped from me without ever knowing it was going to happen." He motions to her, again. "Like you... like with Renaldo.

"No one should ever disappear from the Earth. With what I do, I hunt men, and I've been doing it a long time. First as a marshal and now as what I am. I hunt man but do so under the pretense of hunting cattle. Lots of men try to hide, try all sorts of strange stuff... Thing is, it's hard for a man to disappear, truly disappear, never to be seen again. In my experience, and maybe it's 'cause I'm me, a cynic—although that woman who I mentioned, she always thought I was a bit of an optimist—most men don't disappear for good, not like with Renaldo, unless they are dead. I think your boy is dead, and I think you think that, too."

"I know it."

"How? Mother's intuition?"

Gabby shakes her head. "Someone told me."

"Same *someone* who handed you that gun?"

That stops her. "What do you mean?"

"I mean, you followed that truck. I think you followed that truck for a reason. You had to start somewhere, and I think you started here. Only way that explains how you were where you were yesterday and why you are here today, which means you have that gun for a reason. You had it yesterday. You have it today. You have it because the man," Frank points at the bar with the hat, "who owns that bar over there killed your boy.

"Now, yesterday, you talked about how the whole thing went down. You talked about the man—his name was Earl, by the way—how Earl got shot and how Earl shot another man. That vehicle next to the motorcycle belongs to a sheriff deputy named Tanner Brogdon, not that it matters to you, but I think he was that man. You mentioned how the one who owns the motorcycle yelled out the name Wayne, and you mentioned how the driver and another masked man helped the one Earl shot into the cab of the truck. Just so happens, the man driving the truck was named Wayne Kissee, and the man who is the registered owner of the vehicle left behind is Jeremy Hall, whose sister is married to Mr. Kissee."

"Why are you telling me all this?"

"No reason, really. Maybe the thought is if I tell you the truth of something you can tell me the truth of what you're doing. If you don't want to tell me, that's fine, but I'm going to ask you to move on and leave Mr. Alexander to me. Otherwise, I'm goin' to have to arrest you for obstruction. I think you saw those men I mentioned, all but Mr. Kissee, start their trek yesterday from here, and if that's the case, then I feel like Raley, my friend, would like to hear that, considerin' you left all that out when you spoke with him yesterday. You left it out cause you'd have to explain that gun that we found in your purse and why you were here, and I think you thought we might not understand. Raley might not, but I do." Frank looks away and then adds. "I've lost someone, too."

Gabby listens to what he has to say and is silent for a long time. Then she says, "You remind me of a river."

Frank's face expresses genuine surprise at her assessment but also an eagerness to listen to what it is she has to say. "A river?"

"Yes," Gabby says. "I see you as a man who likes to tell others what he's thinking, but you aren't telling others your thoughts just to tell your thoughts. You're telling them how it happened, how it is. That's what you're doing. Your thoughts, they are deeper than that, and you keep them secret and to yourself, like the water in a river. Sure, we see where it is going, what it is doing, but under the surface, we don't see the current; we don't see the fish swimming or the erosion happening. You are like that. You communicate in that manner. It makes you very effective at talking to others. However, it makes you difficult to talk to because you see what's in front of you and you hear what they are saying; where others only see—only hear—what they want to hear."

Frank pops open the passenger door and slips the hat on his head, but he doesn't exit the car. Looking over at her, he says, "This is too big for you."

Gabby reaches down for the purse for reassurance. She grips the straps tightly. "He was my son. You said it yourself. No one should ever disappear."

"I did say it," Frank says. "But there's no reason to lose yourself in the process."

"What do you suggest I do?"

"Allow me to deliver justice, not your revenge, and tell me what you know—who told you what you know."

"And what do I know?"

"Who it was that handed you that gun and pointed you in that man's direction."

Gabby is quiet for some time as tears roll down her face. She says, "He was my son."

Frank says, "He was—but he's not forgotten, not in any way, and I'll see that the people who took him pay for what they did, but the only way I can do that is by doing it the only way I know how."

"What do I need to do?"

"Leave the grizzly be and let the hunter take care of him. This is too big for you, but not for me."

CHAPTER 19:

FRANKFORT CORBIN

MITCHELL LAMB ROLLS INTO THE parking lot at the same time the Luna woman leaves. Mitchell pulls his Dodge pickup truck alongside Frank's Bronco and parks, driver's window to window. "Was that who I think it was?"

"It was," Frank says, removing his hat and setting it in the passenger seat. He watches the Luna woman exit the parking lot and travel south down the main road. Their eyes lock as she passes his position, but then she turns her attention back to the road, so Frank turns his attention to his partner.

"What was she doing here?" Mitchell asks, digging some chewing tobacco from a disk-shaped can with two fingers, which he holds out the window, pinching the contents trying his best not to drop any as he deposits the substance in the corner of his mouth.

"She didn't say," Frank says. He sips some cold coffee. He had a patrolman drop it off a couple of hours ago, the

273

same one that ran the plates for the motorcycle and the tag on the deputy's truck. "You know you need to stop using that stuff."

Rolling the dip around in his mouth, Mitchell gawks at him, "What?"

Frank says, "That's disgusting."

Mitchell shrugs and deposits the hockey puck-shaped can back in his door pocket. He asks, "What am I going to do? I like it. I need to have at least one vice in my life. You have a vice... that damn coffee."

"I had a vice, and I cut it out."

"You're talking about the drinking."

"I'm talking about the drinking."

Mitchell peers into his side mirror, adjusting the glass with the same two fingers he shoved the dip into his mouth with. "You really think this bar has anything to do with yesterday's events?"

Frank nods but stays quiet.

Mitchell says, "You know Raley's only letting us sit on this thing because he didn't think it was a lead worth following. I mean, Germaine, the German, who would be stupid enough to basically be called their name as an alter sadistic secret ego."

"Someone vain."

"It's just a coincidence you found the dead guy's motorcycle."

"It wasn't me."

"Fine, it's just coincidence you had some poor uniform schmuck find the motorcycle. Frank, if you do good police work, the least you can do is take credit for it. Finding the motorcycle, a possible motive, and connection, as in a possible ID for one of the other suspects, is good work.

Thinking these guys are hitting trucks of weed for some boogie man named *the German* and the guy that owes the bar happens, *happens*, to have a middle name similar, isn't."

"Says the man who sucks on dried cancer-causing leaves for a good time."

Mitchell shoots Frank a smile. A piece of tobacco coats one of his canines.

Frank says, "You're flirting with cancer. The drinking wasn't going to give me cancer."

Mitchell holds up one finger, then turns in the seat and digs his cellphone out of the cup holder next to him. He holds it up and shakes it. "Cancer."

Frank concedes. "Fair enough."

Shaking the phone again to make his point, Mitchell says, "And if this little doohickey doesn't, the coffee sure will."

"The jury's still out on the coffee," Frank says. "What are you doing here?"

"I thought I'd take a nice Saturday morning drive; I had no idea you'd be here. I saw your truck and thought I'd stop off to say hi, shoot the shit, see if you needed anything."

"Are you here to relieve me?"

"Nah," Mitchell says, dropping the cellphone back in the cupholder. "I came here because I wanted to go to the strip club but seeing that they aren't open, I guess I can hang out in the parking lot with you or stay here by myself while you go take a piss or something."

Frank just looks at him.

"Frank, you're no fun when you're all serious when you've been up all night. Yeah, I'm here to relieve you for a few hours," Mitchell says, dropping the act. "You know

they say staying up all night is equivalent to being drunk. You have to be careful with your driving. Your decisions—"

"Who's they?"

"They, them, universal you, I don't know—they. The doctors. The people who looked at our careers and scoffed at it saying they'd rather make money than do what we do. Why do we do what we do?"

Frank stays quiet.

"They, them—those people smarter than us, they say when you don't sleep, your brain acts like it's drunk. It makes for poor decision-making. Don't make poor decisions."

"Poor means bad?"

"I don't know, it's whatever they say. Go read a white paper if you want to know, considerin' you're wanting to do all this investigatin'."

Frank stares at him.

Mitchell yawns and scratches at the stubble on his chin. "So, you going to tell me what it is you have to do? Raley called and said I needed to get over here, *pronto*, his words, to relieve you. He said you called, and he sounded surprised to find out about the bike, but seeing it's you, I'm sure he half expected it. I would have. You're a damn fine investigator. Second only to your loveable—"

"Laughable."

"*Lovable* partner," Mitchell says. "I know that face you are making. I know you. You are working on something. Not everyone sees it. My wife doesn't believe me when I tell her these things. She thinks I'm full of it. I say, 'Frank's mind works differently. He sees things I don't. He sees how pieces fit together before he has the puzzle piece.' How do you do that?"

"God-given gift."

"Yeah, well she thinks my gift is bunk, but it's not. I tell her I know you. Hell, we spend more time together than she and I do."

"Isn't she happy I'm male?"

Mitchell rolls his eyes and comments that's not necessarily an argument anymore. He says, "Frank, I know you. You have this whole thing figured out. Sure, it's … what's that word … supposition? It's supposition, circumstantial at this point, but that's because you aren't the dick working the case. You're the guy asked to help out, to do some of the heavy lifting, to see what you see."

"Well, I saw."

"And what did you see?" Mitchell doesn't wait for Frank to answer because, as he said, they are partners, and he sees things in Frank no one else sees—his gift.

Frank says, "I have something I need to follow up on."

"Does it have anything to do with the woman who just left?

It does, but he's not going to share his thoughts with Mitchell. Investigations are about fact, but sometimes, when coincidences keep happening, fact becomes feeling, and Frank follows his feelings.

So Frank doesn't answer Mitchell. He rolls his upper lift under his teeth, biting at his lip while brushing his mustache with his lower lip.

Mitchell gives his classic 'don't fuck with me' stare right back to Frank.

Frank grips the wheel and gear shifter to slip the Bronco in drive.

Mitchell says, "Frank?"

Frank pauses what he's doing to turn back to Mitchell, hand on the gear shifter, foot on the brake. "Yeah?"

"We chase cattle rustlers."

Frank says, "I know that."

Mitchel breaks the look. "Okay, I know you know," he says, alternating peering into the side mirror and glancing at Frank. He adjusts the mirror to get a better look at the bar, while saying, "I wanted to make sure. I know we work on these taskforces from time to time, and that's why Raley wanted us to come see that God-awful mess yesterday, but this isn't any of our concern. I'm serious about what I said a couple of weeks ago. We shouldn't be doing this stuff, hiking to some ridge to look over a grow or any other type of criminal crap. We should be thinking about retirement. Shit, Frank, you're already retired from one thing, can't you just slow down? You shot and killed a man. You didn't have to do that. I mean, you did at the time... What I'm saying is, we didn't have to be there that day. You didn't. There are younger men out there more willing even if they are less able. Maybe it's time we take a step back."

"What are you saying, Mitchell?"

Mitchell stares at him for a long moment, rubbing his chin with the hand holding his spit cup. Then he spits, slow, into the cup, the dark brown fluid moving as slow as turning a honey bottle upside down and letting it fall, Mitchell's way of buying time to organize his thoughts. "That you have that look you get when you're on to something. Like a goddamn bloodhound."

"What's that mean?"

"That there's this look you get, smug, almost like you know some punchline to some joke that no one else has heard—this gleam in your eye."

Frank dips his chin in agreement. "That's who I am, who *we* are. You're no different. It's in our blood. I'm doing the Lord's work, same as you."

"Fighting crime is the Lord's work," Mitchell says before pausing to spit into his dip cup again. "What you're doing isn't any of your concern. What you need to do is talk to Raley, tell him whoever it is, whatever it is you *think* you know, and go on with your day. There's no reason to get involved with something when you don't have to."

Frank wrinkles his mustache. Eddie used to say he did that when he was uncomfortable with the conversation. That he looked like a rabbit or that damned witch woman.

Frank says, "I can't do that."

"I know," Mitchell says, looking away. "That's why I'm here, but I had to say it at least. Say something to you to get you to see reason. This isn't our fight."

"I know that," Frank says. "But the Lord's speaking to me, and I have to listen. Don't you ever listen? It's what I've done every day while working this job, and it's served me well. Listenin's hard when you don't practice it, but I've learned to listen. It ain't hard anymore."

"The Lord also takes you when it's your time. Sometimes him talking to you doesn't turn out well for you."

"Maybe in this life, but then it's an honor if it works out that way."

Mitchell grimaces. He spits in the dip cup and turns to look at Frank.

"Frank?" he says.

"Yeah,"

"Be careful."

Without looking fully at Mitchell, Frank hesitates before speaking. "Will do."

Before Frank lets off the brake and pulls away, Mitchell says, "I'll let you know if there's any movement here."

———

FRANKFORT CORBIN STEPS inside Moody's BBQ and American Diner and removes his hat, clasping it low at his side, next to his gun and badge. The place smells of barbecue, dry rub spices, sweet barbecue sauce, warmth, and the cacophony of meats smoking, grilling, cooking, and cooling. A one-armed man, dressed nicely except for the apron with the grease spot dark on his left side, greets Frank at the door.

"What can I do for you?" the man says, introducing himself as the name on the sign.

Samuel Moody juts his left hand out between them. Frank shakes the man's left hand with his left. It's awkward but effective. "I'm looking for someone," he tells Samuel.

Samuel studies Frank with narrowed eyes and one raised eyebrow. "You the law?"

Frank says, "That obvious?"

Samuel nods, grinning. "Yup, stink of it. What type of law are you?"

Frank confirms Samuel's suspicion, saying, "The law— in a manner of speaking." Then he says, "I'm with the state."

Samuel's grin breaks into a disarming smile, but there's no kindness behind his eyes. "Interesting," he says, "usually those state boys wear suits and are so damn happy to tell you they're with OSBI—you ain't wearing a suit and you didn't say that. You don't strike me as one of those polished boys, but please don't take offense. That's not me saying you don't clean up. It's me saying you're the type of man who cares more about the work than you do than how you look doing the work."

Frank pats his hat against his leg. "I'm with the Department of Ag. Guess you could say I'm what they call a cattle cop."

Samuel holds up his hand. "I bought all this meat legally. Always do. No need not to."

Frank gestures toward Samuel with the hat. "I'm not here for that."

"Then what are you here for?"

Frank glances around the room. There are no waitresses. It's just Samuel and a cook in the window. Sounds like others in the kitchen. But no one up front except for Samuel which is why he greeted Frank. Turning only his head, Frank glances behind him at the sign, reading it through the back of the paper, configuring the bold black numbers in his head to check the open times. Then he says, "I'm looking for someone."

"Well, let's not just stand here in suspense. Would you like to sit down?"

Samuel shows Frank over to a small two-top table.

Samuel sits first. "Who are you looking for? How can I help?"

Frank takes his seat, setting his hat on the table in front of him. "I'm looking for a waitress that's supposed to work here, goes by the name Jerilyn Kissee."

"J-Lynn?" Samuel says, leaning back in his seat. "She ain't here."

Frank figured that since the place is empty. "Do you know where she is?"

Samuel shakes his head. "She's supposed to be here by now. After dismissing her last night, I told her to be here, but she's not here yet. I told my normal girl to sleep in and have the day off, now I got no one." Samuel glances at the clock on the wall. "Figure I'll give her one more hour before I call my normal girl and ruin her much deserved day off. Whatcha need J-Lynn for?"

"Something I'm working on, well, helping out with."

Samuel digests Frank's answer. "Did you try her mother's?"

"The salon?" Frank says. "I went there first. Her mom said she didn't know where she was. She didn't know where her brother was either or her husband."

Samuel rubs his chin. "That brother's no good. Nothing but trouble. What you wanting to talk to J-Lynn for?"

"I'm looking for her brother ... and her husband."

"And you figured she would help?"

"I thought I'd ask."

"Good 'cause she's not going to tell you nothing. She's like that: stubborn. She does the right thing, but that's not always what we would—you—consider the right thing."

"What's the right thing?"

"Keeping your mouth shut when the law comes around."

"You don't like me, do you?"

"I don't know you."

"But still, because I'm who I am, you don't like me."

"I don't, but that's not for me to say. You come in; you ask questions. I'm supposed to answer your questions. You, personally, I got no problem with. You've treated me with respect. You haven't tried to big dick me with the suit and the holier than thou attitude, so I'll play nice and try my best to answer your questions. But that badge, what you stand for, regardless of what you are, who you work for, that's not what I like. Growing up, sometimes, I learned doing the right thing wasn't having anything to do with your kind."

"Doing the right thing?" Frank asks, "Is that how you got those injuries?"

Samuel snaps his mouth shut tight, clenching his jaw. "Yeah, I got them doing what I thought was right. Some dipshit redneck, country boy, just like you, fucked up in training. I tried my best, grabbed the grenade, and threw it, it went off like those fireworks on the fourth of July. I lost my hand, and they had to take half the arm. That dumb shit was a reserve deputy back in the real world. Gone on to be the real thing in life. Nothing happened to him. He dropped to the ground. Got some scratches, that's it."

"No one ever said doing the right thing didn't cost. It's just what you're willing to pay."

"The price was too high. I should have let that fool die and saved myself."

"But you couldn't do that."

"No sir, I couldn't."

"Where's Jerilyn?"

Samuel is silent for a long moment. "If she's not here or at her momma's salon, then try her trailer. There should be a Toyota Camry in the driveway."

"Do you have the address?"

Samuel glances at the door leading to the back. "Somewhere back there, I'm sure, but if you're going there thinking you're going to get something from her, you're mistaken."

"All I'm trying to do is save some fools from getting themselves killed over nothing."

"Jerilyn don't have anything to do with any of that."

"Still, her brother, her husband, they do."

"Her brother's a dipshit. He's no good. He's an anchor to her, to her mother. He thinks he's going to be something—hell, he thinks he's hot shit as it is—but he's nothing. Her husband's not much different, but his problem isn't the same. He's from two different worlds: mine and yours if you know what I mean. 'Cept, you add in being poor, and he's what you get. He's angry at the world, angry at never having a chance. He has no place in either world and no chance of belonging to either. And with her, she's just as strong as he is. They're like oil and water—but I think they're more like magnesium and water, explosive. It's not that they can't get along, it's that they can't keep from blowing up at the other. Deep down, honestly, if you're asking me—which you ain't—I think they love each other, but neither wants to admit it to the other."

"Either way, I need to find her brother," Frank says, touching the brim of his hat. "Her husband, too."

Samuel mashes his lips together and jerks his head over his shoulder. "Fine, I'll get you what you need, but I want you to do something for me."

Frank lifts the hat and motions for Samuel to continue.

"Favor for a favor, you know. If you go over there, and you find some weed, or your brethren find some, it's mine, not hers. She'll tell you the truth. She don't know no better. She made a boneheaded decision, and I don't want it costing her or her girls. Her brother may have given it to her, but I don't want her having it. I have a license to sell, so I'll take it off her hands. I don't want you or your kind holding it to her, no matter what her dipshit husband and no-good brother have done."

Frank slips his hat on his head and nods.

CHAPTER 20:

JERILYN KISSEE

JERILYN KISSEE SMOKES HER CIGARETTE, waiting for the deputy to wake up, studying the deputy's slumbering body. She traces his body with her eyes, not only seeing the work he's put into it to stay in shape but also seeing where time is winning—wrinkles in his face, sun damage to his skin., prominent scars. These are things she hasn't noticed before. She catches a glimpse of the wound from his story where he said it was. At least that much wasn't bullshit.

Brogdon looks the same as he had when she walked in her trailer and found him pointing a gun at her—that's the last time a man will point a gun at her—he looks the same except for the bandages. She's changed then. What were paper towels and duct tape has now been replaced with sutures, gauze, and medical tape, and maybe a strand or two of duct tape still. Before he passed plum out, he explained that after Wayne and Jeremy dumped him on the side of the road, he robbed a liquor store at gunpoint and forced the guy to patch him up. His shotgun rests at her feet, barrel down, cradled between her legs and well within her reach.

Brogdon stirs as his eyes start to open.

From where she's sitting, in the darkened corner of the trailer in her recliner turned toward him, wearing a tank top under a gray zipped hooded sweatshirt with black yoga pants, no bra, Jerilyn blows smoke out her mouth and says, "Welcome back to the land of the living" to get his attention and get him looking her way.

Brogdon opens his eyes, jumping fully awake, coming back to the moment where he dropped off. His good hand on his good arm jerks toward where the shotgun had been resting across his lap, but he finds nothing but air. He sees it in its new location between her legs. The folder with the pictures is gone too. So is the weed.

She watches Brogdon process the scene. He's not dumb, and she knows he wouldn't be a cop as long as he has if he couldn't work things out quickly. What do cops call it? An evolving situation? Yes, that's what this is.

Jerilyn watches as he forces calm throughout his body. He doesn't need to be told how the situation's changed. He adapts as well as he can. He made a mistake coming here, putting her in this position. He thought he could intimidate her.

Well, he can't.

She'll correct his misunderstanding in a short time.

Jerilyn says, "You aren't the first man to point a gun at me." Then she pauses to see if he will argue or say anything back.

Brogdon knows enough to stay quiet.

Jerilyn lights a new cigarette, holding the lighter to the tip, illuminating her face for him to see her, while saying, "Wayne did it this one time."

She stops as her mind returns to the moment she woke up and found Wayne sitting next to the bed in a chair. Jerilyn fights going there. Not that the memory was more traumatic than any of the others, it's that it brings up all the other times, too, threatening to overwhelm her emotionally.

Jerilyn says, "We had a fight. He slapped me. I kneed him in the nuts. He put my head in that wall over there." She points to the spot in the fake dark brown paneling. Brogdon won't be able to see the hole her head caused because Wayne replaced the paneling during his apology phase. Also, he hung some family portraits to cover up his shoddy handiwork.

"I threatened to stab him," she continues. "We called a truce. Then I locked myself in our room. After a while, he started drinking, licking his wounds the way he does. It always kinda reminded me of an opossum when he did that, playing dead when I knew he's just regrouping. He can't let anything go. I took a bath to calm down and went to bed. Next thing I know, I wake up, it's dark, and he's sitting inches from my face in one of the kitchen chairs. I don't know how he got it in the room and next to the bed without waking me up. Seeing him was surprising, so I wake up more, open my eyes. I see he has this little gun, a seven-shot thing. I think it's called a Shield or something. He had a thumb safety. Wayne's just sitting there staring at me. I ask him what's up, but he doesn't say anything. I asked him again, and he points the gun at me, thumbs the safety down, and says, 'I could kill you.' I was like, what?

Unsure if I heard him right. He says, 'I could kill you … if I wanted to.' I asked if he wanted to…"

Jerilyn's voice fades off as her mind tugs at her to return to that moment, leaving the two of them sitting in silence.

After a while, Brogdon grows tired of the silence and asks, "What happened?"

Jerilyn says, "He never answered if he wanted to. I figured he did. Otherwise, why would he be sitting there with a gun pointed at me?"

She thinks about explaining how Wayne had that gun with the safety on in case the girls got a hold of it thinking that maybe the thumb safety would slow things down long enough to prevent something bad from happening if the girls played with it. Maybe one of them, Jerilyn or Wayne, would get to them before anything happened. She thinks about explaining how Wayne hates that gun, calling it a "noisy cricket" like the little piece in *Men in Black* because he got it in a .40 caliber instead of a nine, and how the damn thing jumps in your hand.

Brogdon clarifies, saying, "No, what happened? I don't feel like I've moved. But everything's different."

"You didn't. I took care of you right there. I just leaned you forward to clean you up."

"So what happened?" he asks for the third time.

"You passed out."

"I did?"

Jerilyn wraps her lips around the filter of her third cigarette and inhales deeply. "You did."

Brogdon assesses the new bandages. His finger picks at the edge of the gauze wrapped around the shoulder wound. Jerilyn's friend Ralph had a hell of a time stopping the bleeding. Compression and padding were about all he could do for Brogdon with what he brought over to her trailer.

Jerilyn adds, "Your plan's a bit fucked now, but I thought saving your life was better than letting you die."

"What did you do?"

"I called a friend of mine and had him come over to patch you up a bit. Ralph's a good guy, but he's not a doctor. He was a vet."

"Was?"

"Meth's a hell of a drug."

Brogdon gives her a look that says he doesn't understand, but Jerilyn doesn't explain it. "Like he was a medic?"

"No, like with animals, a veterinarian."

Brogdon stays quiet.

"After calling Ralph, I called the neighbor and asked her to watch the girls all night, which I've done before. I told her I worked late and had to be back first thing in the morning. I asked if the girls could hang out over there with her girls until my mother could come pick them up. The neighbor agreed, but I didn't give her much of a choice. So you don't have to worry about anyone coming in and interruptin' us."

There are spent butts littering the floor around her. The discarded butts on her floor are the least of her worries.

"Whatever happens next, I control. That's what I want to make clear to you," she says before adding, "We need to talk."

Brogdon struggles in the seat but manages to sit up straighter, wincing in pain as he moves the injured shoulder. Once he's settled again, he tells her, "I'm listening."

"Are you?" she questions. "Because from where I'm sitting, you haven't listened to me at all. Not at all. Not from the beginning. Not ever. You haven't heard me. And you sure as hell don't care about me."

Brogdon jerks his head once and looks wounded like she denied his request to go to the dance. "That's not true."

"It isn't? You didn't put me in this situation? No... I guess I did. I listened to your bullshit plan, and I knew it was bullshit, and I went along with it anyways. Now, why did I do that? No, don't answer. I know why. I spent the last few hours thinking about it, and now I know. I'm not dumb. Slow maybe, but not dumb."

"I don't understand. What are you saying?"

"Before you passed out, I asked you about the skillet, told you you're full of shit or you exaggerated, which is the same thing either way."

"Yeah?"

"So, which is it?"

Brogdon motions with his good hand, touching his chest and flicking his wrist toward her. "You're going to have to help me here. I don't understand what you're talking about."

Jerilyn compresses her lips. "It wasn't cast iron; it wasn't a cast-iron skillet. What kind of skillet was it? Let's start there."

Brogdon's eyes narrow as he tries to read her intention, to see the truth to what she's getting at. His eyes ask what her game is. He shifts in the seat again, which causes him pain. Jerilyn figures he's trying to test his limitations. See if he can clear the couch and distance between them before she can act. He can't. She practiced a few times, getting the shotgun up and pointed his way, between now and when Ralph left.

Finally, he admits, "I think it was a frying pan, but I don't know what kind of skillet it was."

Jerilyn inhales smoke deeply and then snorts it out through her nose. "See, was that so hard?"

"No," he says, shaking his head slowly. "I don't know what kind it was, but the story was true."

"I'm sure there's truth in all your stories," she says. "But then again, you're a cop, so I figure you don't lie like normal people. No, you dress up your lies, the ones you actually utter; you dress them up in pretty little words and phrases, using acronyms and jargon, trying to get the listener all confused or so bored out of their mind they stop listening. You count on your peers being dumb. You count on them being under you. I'm not under you, and I'm not dumb. No matter how much you want it, try, desire, I'll never be under you."

Brogdon fumbles for a response. "That's not what I do... that's not what I... I'm not going to say I don't find you attractive. I do."

"You don't have a chance, never did," Jerilyn says. "I couldn't ever be with someone like you. I don't see you as a strong man. It's quite the opposite, actually. You're weak. You think you're strong. But you aren't."

Brogdon does better this time and keeps his mouth shut. He takes a long time to respond. Maybe he's processing. Or maybe he's still trying to figure out how to get out of a trap of his own making. He doesn't strike Jerilyn as the type that trusts others. "I do think you're attractive."

"No, you don't," she snaps back, surprising him. "You want to fuck me. Thinking I'm good-looking is like thinking a picture of the cow has any bearing on the steak you're about to eat. You want to fuck me. Just like every other guy I meet. You lust for me. And you know what, Wayne's right. You're a racist piece of shit, but also, I remember you now. That night, you couldn't stop staring at my tits. I remember the look on your face. Sure it was dark. Sure the flashlights were blinding. But I remember now. I didn't think it was you. But then I had a realization. You looked like a kid then, shocked at what you saw 'cause you liked it. Afterward, you looked at me like a man, not shocked 'cause you liked what you saw, but ravenous for what you wanted."

"That's not..." but he doesn't finish whatever excuse he was about to say.

"Here's how I figure it," Jerilyn says. "I got set up."

"What?"

"You got used," she says, trying to explain it to him. "We both did. And whatever happens next, we need to think about that first before we go forward."

Brogdon protests. "I didn't get used."

Jerilyn shakes her head. "Yes, you did. We both did. My brother used you. I don't know how or why. I haven't figured out his motivation, but he used you. Maybe he's trying to help me be rid of Wayne, but he's not man enough to do it. Maybe he thought you and I should get together. Maybe he knew you were doing your little side thing with all these poor defenseless domestic violence victims. Maybe you weren't, and he put you up to it. I don't know. I don't know if I believe you actually do anything you claim."

"I told you the truth."

"That you exaggerated or lied about ... some truth."

"That story, it's true. I thought she was dead."

"The one with the skillet. Yeah, I got that. You thought she was dead."

"It's true," he claims again.

"Doesn't matter," Jerilyn says, leaning forward in the chair. "Doesn't matter if it was or isn't. You were used. I was used. Jeremy told you to contact me, to get me on the hook, so I'd finally sell some weed for him."

"Why would he do that?"

"Because he needs me to get to people that he can't get to."

"That doesn't make any sense."

"That's what I thought, but then I looked at your file, and I thought about why you're here—Wayne."

Brogdon's eyes widen, giving her all the confirmation she needs.

"You wanted Wayne. This whole thing's been about Wayne. You knew, my brother knew if I'm on the hook for something, Wayne's on the hook. He'll do whatever he has to do to protect me, protect the girls. Well, so will I."

"You think this is about your dirtbag husband?"

"What—you don't?"

Brogdon indicates he doesn't.

"You don't get it. He loves me. Jeremy knows this. Jeremy's playing cards. I didn't see it at first, but I see it now. Whatever Jeremy's doing, he needed Wayne on board. So he gets me on the hook. He uses you to do it. That's what this is all about."

"No."

"Yes, it is. It makes sense if you look at it that way. I've had men using me my whole life. I know what it looks like. I didn't see it until you showed up here. Probably because whatever you needed Wayne for happened, so now, I'm on my own."

"He's got the truck. They both do. I need it to get out from under a guy—that's why I'm here."

"No, that's only *part* of why you are here. What's this guy got on you?"

"Addiction's a hell of a thing. And once you're in with this guy, he never lets you go."

Jerilyn thinks about that answer and how it's probably true.

"You came here to use me."

"No—"

"You came here to use me to get to them. You came because you have been using me, and you want to use me some more for your own thing. I see that. I see it, and I don't like it. You pointed a gun at me, and that's not going to ever happen again."

"I wasn't going to use it."

Jerilyn smokes as she talks. The cigarette never leaves her lips as she blows smoke out the side of her mouth. "It was loaded. I checked while Ralph was working on you. He took the weed, and we destroyed the photographs. That was to get Wayne on board, control him better."

"I don't care about Wayne."

"You set me up, so I'd do whatever it is you all want."

"No," he says again.

"You searched my house."

"Yeah, but I told you about that already."

Jerilyn removes the cigarette from her lips, wedging it between two fingers. "You know what I didn't find when I went poking around to see what was missing—what should have been in that drawer you mentioned?"

Brogdon knows: the Shield. It was in the drawer. He was bragging before, telling her that he had it. And like always, his eyes give him away, and she spots the slight shift in his body weight. The slide of his good hand off his lap to the seat cushion next to him.

Damn!

Jerilyn didn't check between the cushions. She knew he took it. She knew it was missing. She figured he stashed it somewhere, so she couldn't get to it. So she couldn't use it. She thought he'd keep it on his person, but when Ralph was working on him, she didn't see it.

"I'll do whatever I have to protect my kids, and my kids need me," Jerilyn, in a very calm voice, states. "No one's ever going to point a gun at me again—no one."

They sit in that moment for a few heartbeats, eyeing each other. It could have been two seconds or two hours, Jerilyn doesn't know, but if … and when he reaches for the Shield, she'll be ready for him.

Then Brogdon makes his move.

He shoves his hand down between the cushions. The movement is so sudden it catches Jerilyn off guard. By the time she can bring the shotgun up like she's practiced, Brogdon's brought the small black semi-automatic up, extending it out in the space between them, pointing the gun at her, finger tightening on the trigger—squeezing, knuckles turning white from the pressure—but Jerilyn doesn't hesitate or slow. She brings the shotgun up as Brogdon pulls the trigger and nothing happens. Jerilyn catches the dipping of the barrel and the realization and confusion flashes across his face as he realizes he forgot to thumb the safety. But it's too late for him, she fires. The blast sends lead from twenty feet or so straight into

Brogdon's torso just as he manages to thumb the safety and let off a round. His round buries itself harmlessly into the floor.

The Shield drops to the couch, still clutched in his hand. Brogdon's head slumps forward and to the side.

Jerilyn places the cigarette back between her lips, sucking in deep, and watches Brogdon's life leave his body faster than his blood.

CHAPTER 21:

JEREMY HALL

JEREMY HALL PACES IN FRONT OF SHELIA, who sits on her couch watching him walk back and forth. While she works on her nails, she sits with her legs resting on the the seat in front of her, crossed and feet together, ashtray resting in her crotch. Before Jeremy gave up on sitting and drinking some coffee to wake up, she had been painting her toes. Now she's moved on to her fingers. Shelia wears a tank top and short shorts: both black and both covered in ash. Jeremy, on the other hand, is still in the coveralls, but they are tied around his waist, wearing a Rolling Stones shirt, a Target special with the red lips and tongue. Jeremy tugs at his ear and runs his hand through his hair, over and over, struggling to understand what's happening, while saying for the third time, "What do you mean you haven't been to work?"

Shelia blasts air over her lips, up toward her nose to show her frustration. He sees it but ignores it. Whatever she's feeling, Jeremy feels tenfold. What does he care?

With a cigarette in hand, smoke drifting inches from her face, and mid nail polish brushstroke, Shelia says, "The bar's closed," before returning to puffing on her cigarette, planting it between her lips, and working on her nails.

"The bar's closed? What's that mean? It's never closed."

Without looking up from what she's doing, Shelia says, "It's what he said. He didn't explain it. He just said, 'Don't come in.' So I didn't go in."

Jeremy says, "I don't understand. I don't get it. Kevin never closes the bar. It's almost always open even when it isn't open."

Shelia inspects and blows on her nails. Then she dips the brush back in the nail polish and starts on touch-ups. She doesn't respond.

Jeremy, watching her indifference and growing tired of it, says, "Well, what's he been doing?"

Shelia pauses what she's doing to glance up at him. "I don't know, and I don't care what he's doing. He does what he does to who he does it. He's always been that way. It's me that needs to be doing something, making some money or something. If I'm not working, then I'm not making any money. I need to make some money, Jere."

"I get it. I get it," Jeremy says. He pauses to turn and look at her, then waves her off before returning to pacing. "We did have an agreement. You did what I asked."

"I did."

"Yeah, well, I told you I'll get you your money."

Satisfied with the polish, Shelia places the brush in the bottle and stubs out the cigarette in the ashtray in her lap. She blows on her nails some. Hand fanned in front of her. "I did what you asked. I passed the info along to your sister and then to that deputy."

Jeremy mutters, voice fizzling, "I know. I know," trying to avoid the conversation.

"I know *you* know," she says. "I don't want to know about how you know. I want you to know so you know the job is done. I did my part. It's time for you to do your part and fulfill our agreement."

"This isn't the best time."

It really isn't. The box truck is parked at the airport in a paid lot.

Without missing a beat, Shelia says, "Why not? What time is it?"

Jeremy wants to say it is time to get out of town, but he doesn't. He marches over to the window and splits the blinds with his thumb and middle finger. Through the slit in the blinds, he peers out into the parking lot, wondering if they know he's here? Did someone find him?

Staring at him, Shelia says, "There's no one out there."

"I know that."

"Yeah, but you keep looking like you think there's going to be someone out there, and there ain't. And that's like the tenth time you've done that. So stop. If you damage the blinds, my mom's going to have your ass, and the apartments are going to charge me for it."

Jeremy lets the blinds go. They snap back in place.

"Why was I doing that?" Shelia leans forward and digs another cigarette out of the pack sitting on her coffee table, careful not to ruin the polish on her off-hand. "The thing with your sister, why did I do that? Do you not feel bad about setting your sister up like that?"

Jeremy wants to pull his hair out. "Of course I do … but it needed to be done … and I wasn't setting her up, not like you think. That's not what was happening."

"Oh, so you know how I think."

"That's not what I mean."

"You mean you're telling me what I'm thinking. That's not such a great move."

"Jesus, that's not it. I'm just saying it's not how it looks. You not heard that before? No one's said, 'It's not what you think,' when it's very obviously what you think?"

"But you just said—"

"I know what I said!" Jeremy slaps his leg and starts pacing again. "I had to do it to her."

"Why?"

"Kevin wanted it done."

"Why would he want it done?"

Jeremy stops pacing and stretches his neck. He looks up at the ceiling and feels his vertebrae pop in place down his neck to mid-back.

"He wanted us to shoot Wayne," he finally says. "I talked him out of it."

Shelia stops what she's doing. She likes Wayne, so she asks to clarify, "Wayne, he said that? Kill Wayne?"

Jeremy slaps his thigh. "Not *Wayne* actually, but the driver of that truck. It just so happened to be Wayne. The word was when the big load went. We were to send a message: shoot the driver, kill him if we had to. We needed to make it a statement."

"But you knew it was going to be Wayne?"

Jeremy nods. "I did. I told them we didn't have to do it, but they wanted it done. Kevin wanted it done. He said it would set stuff into motion that I didn't need to know about. I don't know what stuff, so don't ask. Do you know anything about that? What he's talking about?"

Shelia says she doesn't.

Jeremy says, "So what I did—he's my friend, you know—so what I did is say, 'Hey, give me a chance to bring him on board.' And Kevin agreed, but he didn't like it. Told me to work fast."

"But he got arrested," she says, "before you could get to him."

"That wasn't supposed to happen ... at least not at that moment."

"You were going to set up Wayne."

"Not just that, he wasn't supposed to get hurt. I was trying to protect him. I sent that deputy to Jerilyn and told him to charge her money to put the pressure on Wayne."

"And, in turn, put pressure on Jerilyn."

"Which would put more pressure on Wayne." Jeremy frowns. "No matter what happened. Wayne would feel it. That was the idea. I don't feel good about it, using them both that way, but it was a way to keep Wayne from getting hurt and get Jerilyn some money. If things went right, then Wayne would be out of her life for some time, which would be best for everyone. And he'd be protected."

Shelia frowns, disgusted at Jeremy. "That's why you had me give Jerilyn that call about the frat."

Jeremy shakes his head. "That was the deputy's idea. He said if Wayne wasn't on board with the robbery, then we could use Jerilyn to keep him under control. He thought we should turn up the heat."

"Sounds complicated."

"I got it handled. It's like when I'm working on a script."

Shelia cuts in. "You actually write something?" Not believing him. No one ever does. "I've never seen it."

"Yes, I *actually* write," Jeremy asserts. "When I was in Vegas, I wrote a lot. Like a lot, a lot. I played poker at night and then spent the morning writing. I usually sat at a diner with coffee and some pie. Then I slept and did it all over again until I landed my ass back here. I actually sold a couple of things, scripts, but nothing ever happened to them because I wasn't able to make meetings."

Shelia asks, "So what happened?"

"Your boss happened." Jeremy sits down next to her on the couch. "I owed some people money. He came along, and he made me an offer that kept me from the hospital. What was I supposed to do? I was already coming back here. I was broke."

"What was the offer?"

"It was more a business opportunity—I sell his weed and don't ask questions. I don't tell people who I really work for, but I give them a name, one that's not his."

"Sounds simple enough. You've always sold weed."

"No, no, you don't get it. I run this branch of things for him, sell for him. I kick up his profits, his cut, plus what I owe. In turn, he gave me free rein and didn't put any pressure on me. It was... it was a good deal. It gave me just enough money to stay afloat."

"So, what's the problem?"

"He kept asking for more. He always asks for more."

"Tell me about it," Shelia says, face dropping to the ashtray. Maybe thinking on his words. Then she asks, "Like what?"

"He wanted more money," Jeremy says. "He wanted to put our competitors out of business. It's like he's poking the dragon." Jeremy pokes her shoulder. "Sneaking in, pretending to be something he's not, jabbing the thing with a broom. He can't help himself. He's got to push things."

Shelia ignores Jeremy's point and asks, "Why a broom?" But Jeremy says, "What's it matter?" and all she says is, "Like I said, it sounds complicated. I don't like complicated things. They tend to not be good for anyone."

"But it's not complicated," Jeremy says. "It's like when you're working on a story. Logical leaps. Things happen, but they have to happen in certain ways. That's how your boss's mind works."

"I know that. He's my boss. You don't have to tell me that."

"Yeah, but only when you are at the bar, and you don't listen to him half the time."

Shelia gives him a look. "Fair."

"Look, what I've been doing—what he's been doing—it's like working out a story. It's a logic puzzle. It's chess if that works for you. Three-D chess like *Star Trek*. It's one thing happening to another, which influences another, and impacts others. He's like ten moves ahead of everyone else."

"So you have to look at the big picture?"

"Yeah, like take the thousand-foot view."

"How do you do that working for someone else? I guess I don't see the point."

"I do it all in his name, you see. I say all these minor bad things are done in his name. It creates a reputation. One we play on to gain power. He plays."

"So what you are saying is you all just bluff people into thinking you're stronger than you are? That works?"

"It's worked so far," Jeremy says, nodding. "Not every-thing's a bluff, though."

She says, "Like with this truck, these robberies... hijackings or whatever."

"Right," he says. "We still have to show strength at times. It's why I went along with his idea, but I told him no one was going to get hurt. That's the only way I would do it. No one gets hurt."

"Which is why you came up with this plan for Wayne…"

"Right, that's exactly it. I thought I could control things."

"But you can't."

"I know that."

"When did you learn it? When you woke up and Wayne was gone?"

That's what happened. Jeremy woke up from his nap and realized Wayne had left the barn. Jeremy looked around for him, thinking Wayne was getting some air, but he wasn't. Jeremy noticed one of the stashed trucks was gone. "Yeah, kinda. I told him I had an idea, but I needed him to go along with it. Be with me on this. I told him we could get ourselves out of this mess, but he had to be with me on it. I know some things. These things would help."

"But then he left, leaving you in a lurch."

"Yeah, and now I have to change the plan, improvise or something, and I don't know if it's enough. I hope it's enough."

Shelia finally screws the lid of the nail polish back on and sets the polish on the table in front of her, leaning forward to do it. "Which is why you are here and want me to take you to the bar. You knew it was closed, and you know I have a key."

Jeremy nods. "Wayne told me that sometimes you all would hook up, and you'd use the office at the bar as a neutral ground during the day so no one caught on."

Shelia doesn't say anything. Wayne told Jeremy that in confidence.

Jeremy attempts to read her face, but he can't tell if this knowledge upsets her or not. He came here looking for Wayne, but he wasn't here, so Jeremy did what he said, improvised. He's doing that now, not thinking everything through. Nothing's planned other than the big idea, and the big idea is to talk to Kevin.

Jeremy says, "I parked the truck somewhere safe for a few hours, got an Uber over here. Well, I went by Gold's first, but it wasn't open, so then I came here after remembering what Wayne said."

"You thought he might be here."

Jeremy admits he did.

"Well, he's not," she says, motioning to the apartment, and then after a moment, she adds, "He's at Lori's."

"Jerilyn's friend?"

Shelia nods. "Yup, they've been a thing for a while now. It's supposed to be secret. She doesn't want to hurt J-Lynn. Wayne told me. He and I are just friends now. It's alright that way."

"Shit," Jeremy says. "Look, whatever, the idea here is—I figured I'd get a hold of Kevin, tell him where the truck is, and let him handle the heat. But he won't pick up his phone, and Gold's was locked. I thought maybe I could do two things at once, hide out at the bar, waiting for him there, and then talk with him about what happened."

Shelia retrieves a pack of cigarettes from the table and taps one out. She lights it. Then looks at him, sticking the thing in her mouth. "Alright, alright, fine." She stands up, picks her shorts out of her crack, and tells him, "I'll get dressed. We'll go in the back door, and you can wait around there until Kevin gets back. But I'm not staying. You can stay. I'm locking the door after I let you in, and then I'm leaving. You can wait for Kevin there, but let me tell you, nothing better be missing when I do inventory. Everything's got to be accounted for, got it?"

That's all Jeremy wanted. He'll go, wait for Kevin, explain what's going on, where the truck is, and then get out. He tells her, "I got it."

CHAPTER 22:

WAYNE KISSEE

WAYNE KISSEE ROTATES IN THE EMPTY barn, searching for the yellow box truck that's obviously not here. His eyes lock on the stranded armchair as he mutters to himself, wondering where the fuck Jeremy went, saying, "It was here. He was here." But his words don't convey any confidence, even in his own statement. Wayne doesn't believe it. Why should the others? But the armchair is proof enough the truck had been here. It's a bright teal, no way Fat Tommy or Short Philly would forget a piece like that. And they saw the vehicles around back, including Earl's truck he showed up at their office driving. That's evidence, evidence enough. "I don't know where he would have gone, but he was here."

Behind Wayne, just inside the open door letting plenty of light into the barn, enough to see the box truck isn't there, stands Fat Tommy, slender and lanky with his hands in his pockets, clearing his throat, making a point the place is empty except for some strands of dried-up straw and

313

the field equipment—and the armchair, of course—with Short Philly ahead of him, steam nearly coming from his ears, red-faced, shouldering the baseball bat as he does. It's the bat he carries with him everywhere.

Short Philly is wearing a dark, shiny shirt with crisp slacks and freshly polished shoes and is uncomfortable with the film of dust on the floor as if he's worried he's stepped on something, scuffing his shoes and looking every bit the gangster he is. Short Philly says, "Well, there ain't nothing here." He nudges a fallen shingle from a pack of extra shingles near the pillar at the center of the barn.

Dismissing them, Wayne turns once more before bringing it back around to them. "But he was here. I left him here. He was here. You got to believe me."

Tommy, in a long-sleeve work shirt and blue jeans, resembles a farmhand. He says, "I believe you." He folds his hands together in front of him, fingers building a steeple. "But you got to see how this looks. Do you know where he would have gone?" he askes while motioning to the space to highlight the emptiness before jamming his hand in his pocket. "He's not here. The truck's not here."

Wayne shakes his head and, in a quiet voice, repeats, "He was here," barely believing the turn of events. Jeremy was supposed to stay put. But then again, Wayne did run out on him in the middle of the night; what'd Wayne expect to happen? He'd do the same thing. Get lost, go to ground. There is no telling where Jeremy went.

Short Philly steps forward. "Yeah, well, shit stain, he's not here now. Not that I believe that he ever was. I think you made it all up. You're a shithead who's trying to say he wasn't involved." Philly points the tip of the bat at him, leaving it extended in the space between them, inches from Wayne. "But you're involved."

Philly lifts the bat toward Wayne's face as if he were fencing.

"I did what you wanted," Wayne says, knocking the bat out of his face. "I shot back. I didn't want to do that. So I'm in it whether I want to be or not."

Wayne takes the gun out of his pocket to show them it's empty, but Short Philly lunges forward and snatches the gun out of Wayne's hand and tosses it to the side.

Wayne watches it skid into the darkness.

Then he turns his attention back to the two men and watches as Short Philly sneers, his face contorting as if he is about to say something more, but Tommy steps forward, coming even with Philly. He removes his hand from his pocket and motions to Wayne, saying, "And we appreciate that, but you have to see it from our point of view." Tommy touches his chest. "We don't got a truck. We don't got any marijuana. We don't got a lot. What we got is cops. Cops are up our ass. Cops watching our tapes. Cops looking for you. State cops. Local cops. All sorts of cops. And you got nothing to show for it. It's not here, Wayne. That's a problem. That's *your* problem, which makes it *my* problem."

"I'll get you the truck," Wayne says, stepping back. "Have I ever let you down?"

Tommy shakes his head. "We can't just ignore some of these things. What do you want me to tell these cops? Hey, we got furniture on the truck only, don't know why three armed men would want to try to hijack—"

"Two," Wayne says, cutting him off. "There were only two."

"Two what?" Short Philly says, their eyes locking. The bat at his side, ready.

Out of the corner of his eye, Wayne glimpses the tightening and loosening of Philly's sausage fingers on the taped handle.

Wayne stares at Short Philly for half a minute before answering the question. "Only two were armed."

Short Philly crosses the space between them, which is only a few steps, and jabs the bat into Wayne's left pec, nudging him back a few feet. Wayne gives ground, begrudgingly, to keep the peace. Short Philly says, "See, it's things like that that piss me off. You defending these shit sticks. We already know your butt buddy Jeremy was the wheelman."

Wayne is tired of the bat against his chest, but he leaves it alone and says, "I don't know what to tell you."

Tommy says, "How about telling us the whole story."

"I am telling you the whole story," Wayne says. "They came at me. I shot one of them. We loaded up and got the fuck out of there."

"Why'd you save one of them?" Philly says. "See, that's the problem I'm having with this bullshit story you're telling. Why save the other guy, the one Earl plugged... Only reason I can think of is if you were in on it."

Wayne holds up his hands to protest his innocence. "Look around you. I wouldn't have called you if I were in on it. We wouldn't be here."

Tommy spits on the ground. The spit soaks into the dirt. "That's the thing, Wayne. We're here because you said our truck was here. We're here because you said that would prove your innocence. But the thing is, there's no truck, Wayne."

"Where's our truck, Wayne?" Short Philly asks

"The truck, Wayne?" Tommy says. "Where is it?"

Wayne says, "Jeremy has it."

"No shit, dumb fuck," Short Philly says. He glances at Tommy.

"Wait," Wayne says.

Tommy nods once, giving his silent permission. Not that Short Philly would have waited for it. In milliseconds, the bat's up behind him and swinging through, smacking into Wayne's midsection.

Knowing it's too late to deflect it or step out of the way, Wayne tenses and doubles with the blow, absorbing most of it. Then Short Philly rears back to deliver a second blow, but Wayne's ready for him this time.

Short Philly swings again, and Wayne steps to the side, wrapping his arm around the bat, ripping it from Philly's grasp, flipping the bat, catching the handle, and delivering a short-stroke backhand across Short Philly's face, who is trying to avoid the blow rears back, but he's too stunned from the sudden change in circumstances to react fast enough, and the bat catches him. The blow knocks Short Philly back a few steps, making him stumble.

Wayne adjusts his grip on the bat. He says, "You're not used to people fighting back, are you?" Wayne swings through this time, closing the distance. Short Philly absorbs the blow in the stomach. He collapses to his knees. Wayne comes at him again. "Just like fucking T-ball." And he whacks Philly across the head. The big man falls to the ground and doesn't move. Doesn't attempt to get up.

Wayne turns to Tommy. Bat at the ready, says, "I wasn't in on this."

Tommy assesses his partner lying on the ground. "Alright."

"I didn't have nothing to do with this. I want you to understand that. I wasn't in on it."

Tommy, with his hands up, concedes, "You weren't in on it."

Wayne motions like he's going to swing on Tommy to show how serious he is. Tommy flinches, stepping back a few paces. Wayne says, "I wasn't involved."

Tommy twists his face. "You were involved, but I get what you mean. You didn't hijack my truck."

"I need you to believe it."

"I do believe it."

"No, I need you to *really* believe it. I need you to know it. Just as I know, I need his people to know it." Wayne points the bat at Short Philly, who groans coming to, blinking a few times between heavy breaths.

"What the fuck?" Short Philly exclaims as he begins to collect himself. He starts to push his large body off the ground.

Wayne kicks him in the side and tells him to "Stay down."

Short Philly stops trying to push his large body up, settles on the ground, and lays his hands flat on the ground. "Alright, you fuck."

Wayne steps on Short Philly's back. Philly squirms under his weight.

Wayne says, "You explain it to his people... I'm not involved."

Tommy says, "Alright. You're not involved..." his voice fading as if to ask what the unstated *but* is.

So Wayne tells him, "But they came to me, wanted me on board. I didn't know what they meant."

"Who's they?"

"Jeremy, for one."

"What about for two?"

"Some fucking limp dick deputy and obviously the guy I killed, name Daniel, musta still been upset for me kicking his ass couple of weeks ago. But it was Jeremy who came to me."

Tommy waits for a beat. "In whose name? The German?"

"In a manner of speaking. You think that's who's been hitting your trucks?"

Tommy lifts a finger. "It's who I think but can't prove."

Wayne says, "Jeremy works for the German."

"I'm aware."

"And although you're a shipper. This German has to be a competitor to your people."

"That's outside of my concerns," Tommy says. "I care about delivering product. Obviously, that's been an issue lately. Thomas' people are upset about the supply chain issues. They'd like it corrected asap. That's the word. So you weren't involved. That's fine. Don't worry about me. I won't come after you. You did a job as asked, well done, too, but that's not going to stop his people. They don't play by these rules. They won't see a distinction between you and me. So sure, I'll leave you alone, but that won't help you, and it won't help with them."

Wayne considers Tommy's words. "Lori had a plan for this. She's my girl. Well, not my girl. I mean, she's my girlfriend. Even if Jere were here, she figured you would say something like that because problems aren't good for business."

"Smart girl."

Wayne flips the bat around and digs the handle into the side of Short Philly's face, smashing his cheek. "Smarter than me for sure. So what do I have to do to prevent his people from reacting?"

Tommy's eyes, sharp and lizard-like, study Philly, who stays still under Wayne's weight. "I think you know the answer to that question."

Wayne thinks it over and offers the only real piece of valuable information he holds, but he has to be careful about how he delivers it. "I can take you to the German."

Tommy raises an eyebrow and hums to himself. "You know who he is?"

"I do." Wayne lifts the bat from Philly's face and steps off him. "But I need assurances."

"Why—so you can't deliver?" Short Philly says, crawling to his feet. "What are you going to do? Take us to an empty bedroom so you can fuck us. Fuck us in the ass like you did here with this empty fucking barn? Tom, you going to go along with this fuck?"

Tommy says, "I don't see how we have a choice."

Wayne watches them turn on each other.

Standing, Short Philly brushes dirt off his chest and the front of his slacks. "We always have a choice."

"I do not," Tommy stresses. "Your people are not my people. Maybe they will forgive you, but they won't forgive me."

"My people don't forgive shit."

"Which is why we need to deliver them something they can't turn down or ignore."

Short Philly gestures to Wayne. "You think this tit really knows who the German is? You think he's legit? He's full of crap."

Tommy nods. "I do."

"Whatever," Short Philly says, giving up.

Wayne grips the bat with both hands, one on either side of the bat, and brings it down on his knee with enough force to break it in half. The bat fractures with a thundering crack. Wayne lobs the shattered pieces to the side.

He says, "We need to get back to town. I think I know where Jeremy went."

"Yeah, where's that?" Short Philly asks, clearly unhappy with the loss of his bat.

"Back to the one guy who can fix this and get him out of it," Wayne says.

Tommy says, "To the German."

Wayne confirms, "The German."

"And you know who he is?"

"Not only that," Wayne says, stepping to Tommy, holding his hand out, "I know where he is."

Tommy sticks his hand out and connects with Wayne's to shake his hand. But in a flash, Wayne pulls Tommy in close, his open hand finding Tommy's throat, squeezing, cutting off Tommy's airway, until Tommy's eyes bug. Short Philly steps forward, but he comes at Wayne from the wrong angle for him. Wayne kicks Philly back, yelling, "Don't!"

Short Philly stays back.

Wayne turns his attention to Tommy, whose free hand tries to pry Wayne's hand off his throat. Wayne's eyes are fierce and wild, making sure Tommy knows he's serious. "Whatever you fucks think you are going to do or think about doing... know one thing: you come after me, fine. But if you or his people come after my daughters, after my wife—ex-wife, whatever the hell she is—her mother, anyone in my circle, I'll find you and end you. I'll make you fucking disappear, and you'll never see me coming. Do I make myself clear?"

Tommy tries to speak but can't. Wayne squeezes harder, forcing the man to nod.

Wayne growls, "Give me your assurances," and then releases Tommy, throwing the lanky man back.

Staggering, Tommy halts his momentum and massages his throat. "You have my assurances."

Wayne tosses a look at Short Philly.

Short Philly scowls back at Wayne but then reluctantly says, "Fine, what the fuck ever."

"Assurances," Wayne repeats.

"Yeah ... you got whatever the fuck you want," Philly says, stepping between Tommy and Wayne and patting Wayne on the shoulder as he passes as if he were a buddy. "We done in this fucking barn? I want a cuppa coffee."

CHAPTER 23:

KEVIN ALEXANDER

KEVIN ALEXANDER ARRIVES AT GOLD'S and enters through the back door. He finds Jeremy sitting at the bar on the middle stool, an open bottle of Woodford Reserve in front of him, with three shot glasses laid out. One glass is full, one is half full, and the other is empty. Kevin plays it cool and remains calm, acting like finding Jeremy here is neither surprising nor upsetting; it is, however, fortuitous. Kevin says, "I've been looking for you."

Jeremy glances up at Kevin in the mirrored backstop. His eyes are bloodshot. He's still wearing the coveralls, a T-shirt underneath. Jeremy picks up the half-full shot glass and finishes it off in one gulp. He casts his eyes down at the bottle. "I like this one. It's always been my favorite. I did sample a few others."

Kevin circles behind Jeremy, checking the rest of the place out, making sure they are alone. There are only a few ways Jeremy could have gotten in, and both of them mean trouble. Either he broke in, or he was let in. And both

325

make Kevin wonder where Jeremy's friend Wayne is or the deputy.

"How long have you been here?"

Jeremy glances at the bottle on the bar next to him. A third of it is missing. "It was full when I started."

"And you are drinking. Why?"

Jeremy turns in the seat. "I was waiting for you. Waiting. And waiting. And waiting. I figured I might as well start drinking while I wait."

A quick inspection of the front reveals nothing out of place, no broken glass, no shattered window. Everything looks as it did when he left. "Who let you in?" Kevin asks, but he knows who would have done it. The only other person who has a key.

"Shelia," Jeremy says. "She told me not to touch the inventory, but I figured I might as well dig in, considering how things have gone."

"And how's that?"

Jeremy is quiet for a full thirty seconds, giving Kevin time to try to read the young man's face in the mirror, but Kevin sees nothing but hopelessness behind the eyes. Jeremy picks up the full shot glass and drinks it, his whole body leaning back on the stool with the throw of the glass.

Jeremy says, "I unlocked the front door, thinking you might come in that way."

"I see." Kevin walks to the front of the bar. He opens the front door a crack to test the validity of Jeremy's statement. Then he glances out the windows. The deputy's truck and the dead man's motorcycle sit out front. That's going to be a problem. Kevin was so concerned with covering himself within Iris's organization, ensuring Flavia sat things out, and finding Jeremy that he forgot about the vehicles. Eventually, someone will notice. He will have to do something about them. Turning from the windows, Kevin asks, "What happened to the deputy? I haven't heard from him either."

"I didn't shoot him," Jeremy says, chuckling. "That's how the song goes, right? It's not the deputy that gets shot."

Kevin crosses the space between them while Jeremy is talking and positions himself behind the bar. "No, it's the sheriff."

"The man."

"The establishment."

"The one in charge."

"Are you saying I'm the sheriff?"

Jeremy shakes his head. "I'm saying, I'm the deputy."

Kevin ponders the young man's words while thinking that if he were in a different light, Jeremy might be attractive to him. But now he's drunk ... and bitter, and the two don't make for a preferred portrait. Add in desperate, scared, and wanted, and the man becomes quite ugly. "You understand we have problems."

"I do." Jeremy picks up the bottle and uncorks it. He pours the liquid into all three shot glasses and then corks the bottle. He places it on the bar with care. He picks up the first of the three glasses. He holds it under his chin as he speaks. "I think I'm fucked."

"Oh?"

Jeremy sips the liquor. When he's done, he adds, "That's what I've been thinking about the whole time I've been here ... which, to answer your earlier question, hasn't been that long. But just like I'm sure you've been looking for me, you said as much, I've been looking for you." He finishes the glass and slams the shot glass on the bar.

"You have? Why is that?" Kevin selects a bottle of vodka off the shelf. He reads the label carefully, avoiding looking at the sad, desperate man sitting in front of him.

Jeremy doesn't say.

Kevin adds, "I remember the last time I had this vodka. It was at Renaldo Luna's apartment. You don't know him, but he was a local boy."

"I know who he is."

"What?" Stopping Kevin cold.

"I know him. His mom and my mom, I guess they're friends. I don't know if they still are, but she was at the salon the other day. So I guess they still talk. She seems sad now. I guess... I guess I didn't really know him. We didn't hang out or anything, but I know who he is, heard a lot about him... no one's seen him around for a while."

Kevin can't suppress the smile, and he doesn't try. "I see ... well, I was waiting for him to come back from his tryst with Iris King. They were a thing. This was the day the Siriano organization truly started to fall apart. At the time, I didn't realize what had happened, what I was a part of. I didn't put two and two together until long after the event, but that didn't make the event any less memorable."

Jeremy asks, "What?"

"No reason you would understand."

"Try me."

"Even in prison, Russell ... Rosario ... Siriano was still a powerful man. Still is, if rumors are true. Even then, his organization, this *kingdom* was 'contained within these streets' as he liked to say—although he called it an empire, but I just don't see it that way. Empires are vast in scale. This is Tulsa..." Kevin motions outward with both hands, one holding the vodka bottle. "So, a *kingdom* will do.

Those were as small as a city or as large as a nation. Siriano ruled, even from prison. But then, ambition is cancer."

"What?"

Kevin speaks up as if Jeremy hadn't heard him. "Ambition, it infects others. It spreads through everything. Advancement breeds ambition. That's the lesson."

"No, I heard you; I just don't get it. What do you mean about ambition?"

"Yes, you have ambition, ambitions. Or had. I don't know which it is. Supposedly, you tell people you're a writer, but I haven't seen you write since I drove you back from Vegas to make sure you paid Wilson back. All I see is you playing poker and selling marijuana. Both endeavors you are quite good at, to be honest. All I've seen is you working for me."

"I've done a good job."

Kevin sets the vodka on the bar and turns to retrieve a glass from the rack behind him, next to the shelf Daniel and Wayne destroyed a few weeks ago—it seems like days. Turning back to Jeremy, Kevin says, "I don't disagree." He unscrews the lid of the vodka and pours two fingers into the glass. He continues his story. "Renaldo was the de facto ruler on the outside while Siriano was locked up, carrying out all of Siriano's orders. Wilson, Siriano's son, hated that his father overlooked him. I think it had something to do with illegitimacy and the fact that Siriano didn't want Wilson in prison, but you couldn't tell Wilson that. Wilson knew what Renaldo was doing. He knew what ambition was doing, and he used it to his advantage. Only Iris was using Renaldo. All the while, I was nothing but a servant." He sips the vodka. "But being that gave me access because servants are ignored—oh, we see all. And what I saw was

an opportunity. Renaldo had ambition. And I witnessed what a little ambition did to a kingdom. It destroyed it. Remember, Camelot didn't stay golden when King Arthur died. No, a woman destroyed it—actually two, but that's beside the point. The woman, in this case, is Iris King."

"The one you work for?"

"Work with, not for," Kevin spits.

"But she's your boss."

"She's something," Kevin says. He sips more of the vodka. "We were supposed to be partners. That's how it was supposed to be after Wilson's death, but she won't ever see it that way. She's on top. Figuratively and literally. She's been betrayed by men, so she betrays men. Kind of poetic if you stop to think about it."

"I won't."

"No, I don't think you will." Kevin drinks more vodka. "She tore Siriano's organization apart. In doing so, she killed the only man I respected. Oh, she didn't pull the trigger, but her actions, her plans, took Wilson away from me. It was because of him that I betrayed my best friend, set him up, and used an ex-lover to accomplish what Wilson wanted, and what's funny is he was doing it for her. So now I find myself in a unique position. I could toe the line and be her man, or not."

"Which is why you've had me sell marijuana for you."

"You aren't as dumb as I thought."

"I didn't want anyone to get hurt." Jeremy pulls a gun from under the bar and places it on the bar top.

Kevin pauses and glances at the gun. "Yes, your little predilection against violence." He sips the vodka.

Jeremy repeats, "I never wanted anyone to get hurt."

"But someone did," Kevin says. "Lots of people did. What did you think was going to happen?"

Jeremy doesn't answer.

"I hate Iris," Kevin says. "So I sowed chaos, and now it's time for the harvest. Siriano's criminal organization is dead. He is in prison. Iris has run what's left into the ground. What you, and those other fools, have done is widen the cracks, reveal her weaknesses. She can't protect her product. She can't ensure delivery. But I can."

Jeremy's eyes darken. He finishes the last shot glass and asks, "Where does that leave me?"

"You... you're a loose end," Kevin says.

His free hand shoots under the bar top and reaches for the revolver underneath. He yanks the revolver out from under the bar. Jeremy sees this happening, and he snatches up his gun. They both shoot at each other at the same time, Kevin dropping the vodka and diving to the side, firing three shots at Jeremy, who is laying his arm across the bar, firing back. Jeremy takes a round in the shoulder that knocks him off the stool.

In a heap, Kevin lands behind the bar, liquor bottles explode behind him, liquor drains to the floor, and he realizes, with a burning sensation in his side, that he's been shot. He waits for a moment on the floor, collecting himself. The explosion of gunfire only accentuated the now fallen silence. Then Kevin hears the scuffle of feet on the wooden floor, the scrambling of a body, the knocking of stools as Jeremy struggles to his feet, heading for the door.

Kevin crawls to his feet, a hand at his side, blood pouring out between his fingers. Gun up, he extends his arm out and fires. The round catches Jeremy in the back as he pushes through the front door, letting in a flash of light.

Kevin untangles himself from the bar and staggers forward toward the door. He pushes it open with his gun hand and steps into the bright light of the day. Jeremy lies in the parking space closest to the building, next to the deputy's truck.

Two men, both cowboy-looking motherfuckers, both with badges pinned to their belts, round the backside of the pickup, talking, one saying, "I told you I'd call as soon as something happened." The other, the one with the mustache, saying, "I got over here as quick as I…"

In that moment, both sets of eyes land on Kevin with his hand at his side in the bar's doorway, the revolver down by his leg, and then shift to Jeremy lying face down in the parking lot, blood pooling around him.

The man with the mustache says, "Now wait just a minute—"

Kevin doesn't wait. He chances it. He moves to lift the revolver. Both men react and do so faster than Kevin could have predicted. Their hands shoot down to their holsters and come back up with guns, firing from the hip, in the time it takes Kevin to lift the revolver, which seems so damn heavy.

Then Kevin's on the ground, unsure of how he got here, lying on his back. The gun is still in his hand, much heavier now than it's ever been. The sky—a blue and white blur above him. His head lolls to the side where he catches sight of a truck with three occupants slowing to enter the parking lot, blinker glowing. Then tires screech as it accelerates, speeding off.

Still not understanding and struggling to speak, Kevin blinks once—

CHAPTER 24:

GABRIELLA LUNA

GABRIELLA LUNA WATCHES THE POLICE assemble outside the front door. Several of them have rifles, some carry handguns, one has a shield, and the guy behind him has a black metal ram, requiring two hands to hold it. All of them have body armor, but they don't all look like police officers. The jeans, T-shirts, and beards aren't what she thought police officers would look like. She was told they were DEA agents with some OSBI agents thrown in as well. There's a line of them—or a stack, that's what Frank tells her it's called as he explains to her what's going on. He provides a play-by-play, saying, "The stack, that's them officers there, they're goin' to go up to the front door, knock, break it open if they have to. There's some folks in the back, too. Don't worry. She's not goin' anywhere. The place is surrounded."

Gabby sits in Frank's Bronco's passenger seat, watching the whole scene outside his windshield. They are parked down the street. Frank's cowboy hat sits up on the dash.

335

She has to look around it to see what's happening. Frank drinks black coffee from a gas station cup, doing it in a manner where she doesn't know if he's sipping the coffee or spitting dip. She didn't think Frank dipped like his partner Mitchell, who she met the other day, and she was with Frank when he *bought* the coffee. Although that's not the right word 'cause the station attendant gave it to him for free... Gabby's coffee too. Frank still tried to pay. He even said she wasn't an officer. But the attendant just smiled, like this is a game between the two of them, and gave it to him for free anyway.

Gabby grips a rosary in her lap, going through each of the beads, one at a time, fingers squeezing the bead before moving on to the next, half muttering the prayers, half remembering to breathe. Finally, as the stack crosses in front of the driveway of Iris King's house, she asks, "Do you think I did the right thing?"

Frank glances at her. "Tellin' the truth?"

Gabby nods. "Your friend Raley didn't seem too happy when I called him."

"He'll get over it."

Gabby isn't sure. Her face says as much.

Frank says, "We're here, aren't we."

As if that's all that matters, the final destination. And maybe it is. Gabby doesn't have murder in her heart. She can't kill anyone. If what happened taught her anything, it's that she can't kill. Frank saw that—knew that—and he helped her see it.

"I was going to kill her."

"This is better."

But Gabby isn't sure. "I don't know about that. I thought a lot about how I would do it. I thought maybe... I guess what I had decided to do was go up to her front door, knock, and just shoot her when she answered. I thought maybe I'd just sit on her front step and wait for the police so people would know what she's done and why she died. But it wasn't in me, murder. I couldn't do it."

"None of that would have brought your boy back—killin' her. This is better. What this does is it stops her. And everyone knows why."

Gabby grows silent. "I wanted to kill them both: her and Kevin Alexander."

"I know," Frank says. "I had a feeling."

"But then you showed up. You told me what was happening, but you didn't try to stop me."

"No sense in taking justice from you. If you wanted to make the wrong move, that was on you. But I didn't think you had it in you, and I'm glad I was right. It's better this way."

"But you killed him. You shot him. You and Mitchell. I saw the news that night and couldn't believe it. It was supposed to be me."

Frank pauses before he speaks again. "It wasn't though… and I wonder if him bein' dead does… did that make you feel any better?"

Gabby wants to lie and tell him it did, but they both know the truth. "No," she reluctantly admits. "It didn't. I thought it would, but it didn't."

"But what you saw, your truth, telling it, that made a difference, and I bet it made you feel better, too."

Gabby shrugs. "I don't like lying."

"Which is what I saw when I asked you to tell the truth," Frank says. "You still have that gun?"

Gabby shakes her head. Her fingers move to the next decade on the rosary. "Your friend took it."

Frank falls silent, seemingly lost in thought, thinking about all that's happened as he massages his chin like he does when he thinks. His eyes transition from her back to the windshield, where, beyond the glass, he watches the stack move into position. Frank twists the keys in the ignition to bring the battery to life and rolls the windows down, letting in some fresh cool air.

Outside, Gabby hears the agents for the first time, knocking loudly and then shouting, "Law Enforcement!" and "Search Warrant!"

Gabby says, "I miss him."

Frank glances at her. "Your boy?"

Gabby nods. "I miss him every day. I feel like we won't ever find out what happened to him."

Franks says, "We know what happened to him. Whether or not we ever find him, that's a different matter altogether."

His words aren't as abrasive as she once found them. They've spent a lot of time over the last few days talking. "Still, if only someone would say."

"The man that most likely knew is dead. And for that, I'm sorry, but I feel it's better this way. He didn't give us much of a choice. You didn't need to go shooting anyone, and I doubt very much if you would have been able to do it. He was a son of a bitch, but he was crafty and knew how to work his way out of things. I'm glad you listened to me."

"It wasn't easy."

Her mind flashes to her driving from the strip club to when she picked up the phone after leaving Frank behind at the club. She went home, sat the gun in the drawer by her bed, fished out Raley Freeman's card, and called him before she could really think about what she was going to say. Later that night, Raley came over and listened to what she had to say. He took the gun with him.

Frank says, "Doing the right thing seldom is. That's why it's the right thing. If everyone did it, it wouldn't be right. It would just be. But doing what's right is always challenging because I've found most people like to do what's easy. What's easy isn't always right, and what's right isn't ever easy."

At the front of Iris King's house, the stack surges forward. There are shouts of direction, but Gabby doesn't understand anything anyone is saying. She's too far away.

"Why do you care?"

"About your boy?"

"Yes."

"Everyone matters," Frank says. He grows quiet for a long spell. Then he says, "You see, this here is an accumulation of events. Most people think the evil and wicked get found out by good police work—like we just know what them criminals are thinkin'. Now, it is by good police work, but it doesn't work like what people think. You get reformers asking why we need to look into smaller crimes, drug crimes, traffic stops, those types of piddly things most people find annoying when they think of police. Hell, most people only contact the police during those types of things. But we don't know when something major and big is happenin' and burst onto the scene at the last minute to stop the mayhem. No, what happens is someone, someone like you, says something, usually tells us a story about something that seemed both small and insignificant. Something strange stood out—bugged you. It tugged at the back of your mind. Then, what happens is we investigate the small and strange, and what doesn't seem related to you, 'cause you don't have all the pieces, suddenly becomes part of a larger tapestry for us. That is how we get here." Frank gestures to the happenings outside the Bronco.

Gabby doesn't understand.

Frank continues to talk with his hands. "Think about this here," he says. "You were told some information by a woman who heard the information from another and had some of it first-hand. You told all of that to Raley, who in turn mentioned it to a friend of his at the DEA. Now, that friend, he had some information, a different piece but part of the same puzzle. Both men didn't know the pieces went together until they started talkin'. You said this woman told you your son died and how. And that these people were responsible. Add in what I know, and that's how you get here."

Gabby turns to him and raises an eyebrow. "What you know? What do you know?"

Frank, turning away from her, says, "Before all this started, I went to see a man in prison. He told me some things. Some things about your boy. He asked me to look into his death."

"That's why you looked at me the way you did when we met."

Frank nods. "This man, he was concerned about his legacy." He shifts his attention to the events unfolding in front of the house. Two agents lead Iris King into the front grass, handcuffed, hands behind her back, the two officers gripping her arms. She's wearing a robe that has come undone, showing off her pale nude body to the entire neighborhood. She's screaming and thrashing. "He lost his son. That was his legacy. He didn't want her to have what was his. He asked me to find out what happened to your boy, as a kinda test. In exchange, he'd tell us what we needed to know—we being the government—to bring that woman down. He wanted to destroy her."

Two other agents lead a handcuffed man out of the house. He is wearing thick, dark glasses.

Gabby asks, "Is he naked?"

Frank examines the scene unfolding. "I believe he is."

Gabby spots a car that's backed into a driveway two houses down from them come to life, the engine noise catching her attention. She didn't notice it before, but now she sees the woman in the driver's seat and recognizes her—Flavia Sanchez. The car pulls out of the driveway and passes them. The driver stares straight ahead. Frank glances at the car but pays it no mind. Gabby thinks she sees Flavia crying.

"That man got me thinking about legacy," Frank goes on. "Thinkin' about how it doesn't matter what we do on this Earth—the people I arrest, the crime I stop, the buildings you clean or manage, the stories we tell, the art we make, none of it lasts. It all will fade. How many times have you heard a singer one year and then barely can remember their name the next? Legacy isn't in our actions in what we leave behind. It's in the relationships we have. *What we leave behind is who we leave behind.*"

Frank reaches into his vest pocket and withdraws a folded piece of paper.

He says, "Your son is dead. He died trusting the wrong people. Those people are both dead themselves." He points out the window with the paper. "Or going to prison. Whatever anger you feel, you'll eventually have to let it go.

Maybe not today. Maybe not tomorrow ... but sometime soon, or it will eat you up."

Frank passes Gabby the paper. She unfolds it and reads the words.

He says, "The woman who gave me that, I loved her, and she loved me. She liked to work on that art where you paint letters. She was pretty good at it. But you don't want to hear that. What I'm sayin' is, she was dying, and she mailed me that, so I'd get it after she was gone. She put her time into it. And she left it for me in that manner because she wanted me to understand somethin' and come to terms with it."

The paper reads *Frankfort*.

Frank says, "Whatever happens next—*Gabriella*—you need to remember: a new day starts here. Whatever happens, yesterday won't matter, and tomorrow will be brand new... it isn't here. But right now, right here, that's all that matters. You'll just have to go on livin'. Don't do it alone. Go and try to find people to do the livin' with and learn to love again. Be happy... let the dead be dead."

BOOK CLUB QUESTIONS:

1. The author uses motivations to put the story into motion. What are the motivations at the beginning of the novel for each character? How do they change as the story progresses?

2. Although the author uses multiple points of view to tell the story, who would you consider to be the main character or characters?

3. How do life choices affect the trajectory of the novel?

4. Does the revelation of Renaldo Luna's father alter the way the reader sees the first novel, Too Late to Say Goodbye?

5. The Tulsa Underworld series starts with a trilogy focusing on the Siriano Crime Organization. What other threads do the three novels focus on and examine?

6. The title of the novel is linked to the final emotional point. Does using this impact the story in any way? Does the revelation change how the reader interprets the events?

7. What are the major themes of this novel?

8. Do these themes differ from the themes of the previous two in the series? How are they similar, and how do they differ?

9. How do all the major threads come to an end in A New Day Starts Here? What threads were left open? Does that bother the reader?

10. The author promises to entertain the reader. Were you entertained?

11. The author uses dialogue to move the story and reveal information. How does this affect the act of reading? Does it reveal character insights better or worse than an interior monologue?

12. Frankfort Corbin is a unique character. Who in popular media could Frank be based upon? Who would you cast as Frank in a screen adaptation?

13. Would the Tulsa Underworld Trilogy work for the screen (movie/TV)? What would be lost if adapted for the screen? What would be enhanced?

14. The author uses present tense to tell the story. How does this affect the reading experience? Did you like this? Did you dislike this? Why?

15. The author focuses on complex, dynamic relationships. What were some of the relationships in this novel?

BIO:

MARK ATLEY IS THE AUTHOR OF THE *Olympian, American Standard, Too Late To Say Goodbye*, and *A Bright Young Man*, as well as a handful of short fiction. Mark works as a detective for a suburb of Tulsa, OK, and has dedicated his life to solving crime. Check out markatley.com for more information or follow him on Twitter: @mark_atley.

More books from 4 Horsemen Publications

Cozy Mysteries

Ann Shepphird
Destination: Maui

Destination: Monterey

Detective and Noir

Joe Davison
Mike Strong Series

Mark Atley
Tulsa Underworld

Horror, Thriller, & Suspense

Amanda Byrd
sdfasd

Maria DeVivo
Witch of the Black Circle
Witch of the Red Thorn

Erika Lance
Jimmy
Illusions of Happiness
No Place for Happiness
I Hunt You

Mark Tarrant
The Death Riders
Howl of the Windigo
Guts and Garter Belts